ALONE IN SAVAGE AFRICA!

The great barrier that confronted Rhonda Terry seemed impassable. She felt very small and tired. All her remaining strength was gone. She closed her eyes wearily, and two tears rolled down her cheeks. Then suddenly she was startled by a voice speaking near her.

"She is alone," the voice said. "We will take her to God—he will be pleased."

It was an English voice, or at least the accent was English; but the tones were gruff and guttural. She opened her eyes and shrank back with a scream of terror. Standing close to her were two gorillas. One of them opened its mouth and spoke.

"Come with us," it said. "We are going to take you to God." Then it reached out a mighty, hairy hand and seized her!

The *Authorized Editions* of
Edgar Rice Burroughs'
TARZAN NOVELS
available in Ballantine Books Editions
at your local bookstore:

COMPLETE AND UNABRIDGED!

TARZAN AND THE LION MAN

Edgar Rice Burroughs

BALLANTINE BOOKS • NEW YORK

Tarzan and the Lion Man was first published serially in *Liberty* magazine, November 11, 1933, to January 6, 1934.

Copyright © 1933, 1934 Liberty Publishing Company

All rights reserved under International and Pan-American Copyright Conventions. Published in the United States by Ballantine Books, a division of Random House, Inc., New York, and simultaneously in Canada by Random House of Canada Limited, Toronto.

ISBN 0-345-28988-9

This authorized edition published by arrangement with Edgar Rice Burroughs, Inc.

Printed in Canada

First U.S. Edition: March 1964
Ninth U.S. Printing: June 1988

First Canadian Printing: June 1964

Cover painting by Neal Adams

CONTENTS

1

In Conference

M R. MILTON SMITH, Executive Vice President in Charge of Production, was in conference. A half dozen men lounged comfortably in deep, soft chairs and divans about his large, well-appointed office in the B.O. studio. Mr. Smith had a chair behind a big desk, but he seldom occupied it. He was an imaginative, dramatic, dynamic person. He required freedom and space in which to express himself. His large chair was too small; so he paced about the office more often than he occupied his chair, and his hands interpreted his thoughts quite as fluently as did his tongue.

"It's bound to be a knock-out," he assured his listeners; "no synthetic jungle, no faked sound effects, no toothless old lions that every picture fan in the U.S. knows by their first names. No, sir! This will be the real thing."

A secretary entered the room and closed the door behind her. "Mr. Orman is here," she said.

"Good! Ask him to come in, please." Mr. Smith rubbed his palms together and turned to the others. "Thinking of Orman was nothing less than an inspiration," he exclaimed. "He's just the man to make this picture."

"Just another one of your inspirations, Chief," remarked one of the men. "They've got to hand it to you."

Another, sitting next to the speaker, leaned closer to him. "I thought you suggested Orman the other day," he whispered.

"I did," said the first man out of the corner of his mouth.

Again the door opened, and the secretary ushered in a stocky, bronzed man who was greeted familiarly by all in the room. Smith advanced and shook hands with him.

"Glad to see you, Tom," he said. "Haven't seen you since you got back from Borneo. Great stuff you got down there. But I've got something bigger still on the fire for you. You know the clean-up Superlative Pictures made with their last jungle picture?"

"How could I help it; it's all I've heard since I got back.

Now I suppose everybody's goin' to make jungle pictures."

"Well, there are jungle pictures and jungle pictures. We're going to make a real one. Every scene in that Superlative picture was shot inside a radius of twenty-five miles from Hollywood except a few African stock shots, and the sound effects—lousy!" Smith grimaced his contempt.

"And where are we goin' to shoot?" inquired Orman; "fifty miles from Hollywood?"

"No, sir! We're goin' to send a company right to the heart of Africa, right to the—ah—er—what's the name of that forest, Joe?"

"The Ituri Forest."

"Yes, right to the Ituri Forest with sound equipment and everything. Think of it, Tom! You get the real stuff, the real natives, the jungle, the animals, the sounds. You 'shoot' a giraffe, and at the same time you record the actual sound of his voice."

"You won't need much sound equipment for that, Milt."

"Why?"

"Giraffes don't make any sounds; they're supposed not to have any vocal organs."

"Well, what of it? That was just an illustration. But take the other animals for instance; lions, elephants, tigers—Joe's written in a great tiger sequence. It's goin' to yank 'em right out of their seats."

"There ain't any tigers in Africa, Milt," explained the director.

"Who says there ain't?"

"I do," replied Orman, grinning.

"How about it, Joe?" Smith turned toward the scenarist.

"Well, Chief, you said you wanted a tiger sequence."

"Oh, what's the difference? We'll make it a crocodile sequence."

"And you want me to direct the picture?" asked Orman.

"Yes, and it will make you famous."

"I don't know about that, but I'm game—I ain't ever been to Africa. Is it feasible to get sound trucks into Central Africa?"

"We're just having a conference to discuss the whole matter," replied Smith. "We've asked Major White to sit in. I guess you men haven't met—Mr. Orman, Major White," and as the two men shook hands Smith continued, "the major's a famous big game hunter, knows Africa like a book. He's to be technical advisor and go along with you."

"What do you think, Major, about our being able to get sound trucks into the Ituri Forest?" asked Orman.

"What'll they weigh? I doubt that you can get anything across Africa that weighs over a ton and a half."

"Ouch!" exclaimed Clarence Noice, the sound director. "Our sound trucks weigh seven tons, and we're planning on taking two of them."

"It just can't be done," said the major.

"And how about the generator truck?" demanded Noice. "It weighs nine tons."

The major threw up his hands. "Really, gentlemen, it's preposterous."

"Can you do it, Tom?" demanded Smith, and without waiting for a reply, "you've got to do it."

"Sure I'll do it—if you want to foot the bills."

"Good!" exclaimed Smith. "Now that's settled let me tell you something about the story. Joe's written a great story—it's goin' to be a knock-out. You see, this fellow's born in the jungle and brought up by a lioness. He pals around with the lions all his life—doesn't know any other friends. The lion is king of beasts; when the boy grows up he's king of the lions; so he bosses the whole menagerie. See? Big shot of the jungle."

"Sounds familiar," commented Orman.

"And then the girl comes in, and here's a great shot! She doesn't know any one's around, and she's bathing in a jungle pool. Along comes the Lion Man. He ain't ever seen a woman before. Can't you see the possibilities, Tom? It's goin' to knock 'em cold." Smith was walking around the room, acting out the scene. He was the girl bathing in the pool in one corner of the room, and then he went to the opposite corner and was the Lion Man. "Great, isn't it?" he demanded. "You've got to hand it to Joe."

"Joe always was an original guy," said Orman. "Say, who you got to play this Lion Man that's goin' to pal around with the lions? I hope he's got the guts."

"Best ever, a regular find. He's got a physique that's goin' to have all the girls goofy."

"Yes, them and their grandmothers," offered another conferee.

"Who is he?"

"He's the world's champion marathoner."

"Marathon dancer?"

"No, marathon runner."

"If I was playin' that part I'd rather be a sprinter than a distance runner. What's his name?"

"Stanley Obroski."

"Stanley Obroski? Never heard of him."

"Well, he's famous nevertheless; and wait till you see him! He's sure got 'It,' and I don't mean maybe."

"Can he act?" asked Orman.

"He don't have to act, but he looks great stripped—I'll run his tests for you."

"Who else is in the cast?"

"The Madison's cast for lead opposite Obroski, and——"

"M-m-m, Naomi's plenty hot at 34 north; she'll probably melt at the Equator."

"And Gordon Z. Marcus goes along as her father; he's a white trader."

"Think Marcus can stand it? He's getting along in years."

"Oh, he's rarin' to go. Major White, here, is taking the part of a white hunter."

"I'm afraid," remarked the major, "that as an actor I'll prove to be an excellent hunter."

"Oh, all you got to do is act natural. Don't worry."

"No, let the director worry," said the scenarist; "that's what he's paid for."

"And rewritin' bum continuity," retorted Orman. "But say, Milt, gettin' back to Naomi. She's great in cabaret scenes and flaming youth pictures, but when it comes to steppin' out with lions and elephants—I don't know."

"We're sendin' Rhonda Terry along to double for her."

"Good! Rhonda'd go up and bite a lion on the wrist if a director told her to; and she does look a lot like the Madison, come to think of it."

"Which is flatterin' the Madison, if any one asks me," commented the scenarist.

"Which no one did," retorted Smith.

"And again, if any one asks me," continued Joe, "Rhonda can act circles all around Madison. How some of these punks get where they are beats me."

"And you hangin' around studios for the last ten years!" scoffed Orman. "You must be dumb."

"He wouldn't be an author if he wasn't," gibed another conferee.

"Well," asked Orman, "who else am I takin'? Who's my chief cameraman?"

"Bill West."

"Fine."

"What with your staff, the cast, and drivers you'll have between thirty-five and forty whites. Besides the generator truck and the two sound trucks, you'll have twenty five-ton trucks and five passenger cars. We're picking technicians and mechanics who can drive trucks so as to cut down the size of the company as much as possible. I'm sorry you weren't in town to pick your own company, but we had to rush things. Every one's signed up but the assistant director. You can take any one along you please."

"When do we leave?"

"In about ten days."

"It's a great life," sighed Orman. "Six months in Borneo, ten days in Hollywood, and then another six months in Africa! You guys give a fellow just about time to get a shave between trips."

"Between drinks, did you say?" inquired Joe.

"Between drinks!" offered another. "There isn't any be-tween drinks in Tom's young life."

2
Mud

SHEYKH AB EL-GHRENNEM and his swarthy followers sat in silence on their ponies and watched the mad *Nasara* sweat-ing and cursing as they urged on two hundred blacks in an effort to drag a nine-ton generator truck through the muddy bottom of a small stream.

Nearby, Jerrold Baine leaned against the door of a muddy touring car in conversation with the two girls who occupied the back seat.

"How you feeling, Naomi?" he inquired.

"Rotten."

"Touch of fever again?"

"Nothing but since we left Jinja. I wish I was back in Hollywood; but I won't ever see Hollywood again. I'm going to die here."

"Aw, shucks! You're just blue. You'll be all right."

"She had a dream last night," said the other girl. "Naomi believes in dreams."

"Shut up," snapped Miss Madison.

"*You* seem to keep pretty fit, Rhonda," remarked Baine.
Rhonda Terry nodded. "I guess I'm just lucky."

"You'd better touch wood," advised the Madison; then she
added, "Rhonda's physical, purely physical. No one knows
what we artistes suffer, with our high-strung, complex, nervous organizations."

"Better be a happy cow than a miserable artiste," laughed
Rhonda.

"Beside that, Rhonda gets all the breaks," complained
Naomi. "Yesterday they shoot the first scene in which I
appear, and where was I? Flat on my back with an attack of
fever, and Rhonda has to double for me—even in the close-
ups."

"It's a good thing you look so much alike," said Baine.
"Why, knowing you both as well as I do, I can scarcely tell
you apart."

"That's the trouble," grumbled Naomi. "People'll see her
and think it's me."

"Well, what of it?" demanded Rhonda. "You'll get the
credit."

"Credit!" exclaimed Naomi. "Why, my dear, it will ruin
my reputation. You are a sweet girl and all that, Rhonda;
but remember, I am Naomi Madison. My public expects
superb acting. They will be disappointed, and they will blame
me."

Rhonda laughed good-naturedly. "I'll do my best not to
entirely ruin your reputation, Naomi," she promised.

"Oh, it isn't your fault," exclaimed the other. "I don't
blame you. One is born with the divine afflatus, or one is not.
That is all there is to it. It is no more your fault that you can't
act than it is the fault of that sheik over there that he was
not born a white man."

"What a disillusionment that sheik was!" exclaimed
Rhonda.

"How so?" asked Baine.

"When I was a little girl I saw Rudolph Valentino on the
screen; and, ah, brothers, sheiks was sheiks in them days!"

"This bird sure doesn't look much like Valentino," agreed
Baine.

"Imagine being carried off into the desert by that bunch
of whiskers and dirt! And here I've just been waiting all
these years to be carried off."

"I'll speak to Bill about it," said Baine.

The girl sniffed. "Bill West's a good cameraman, but he's no sheik. He's just about as romantic as his camera."

"He's a swell guy," insisted Baine.

"Of course he is; I'm crazy about him. He'd make a great brother."

"How much longer we got to sit here?" demanded Naomi, peevishly.

"Until they get the generator truck and twenty-two other trucks through that mud hole."

"I don't see why we can't go on. I don't see why we have to sit here and fight flies and bugs."

"We might as well fight 'em here as somewhere else," said Rhonda.

"Orman's afraid to separate the safari," explained Baine. "This is a bad piece of country. He was warned against bringing the company here. The natives never have been completely subdued, and they've been acting up lately."

They were silent for a while, brushing away insects and watching the heavy truck being dragged slowly up the muddy bank. The ponies of the Arabs stood switching their tails and biting at the stinging pests that constantly annoyed them.

Sheykh Ab el-Ghrennem spoke to one at his side, a swarthy man with evil eyes. "Which of the *benat*, Atewy, is she who holds the secret of the valley of diamonds?"

"*Billah!*" exclaimed Atewy, spitting. "They are as alike as two pieces of *jella*. I cannot be sure which is which."

"But one of them hath the paper? You are sure?"

"Yes. The old *Nasrany*, who is the father of one of them, had it; but she took it from him. The young man leaning against that invention of *Sheytan*, talking to them now, plotted to take the life of the old man that he might steal the paper; but the girl, his daughter, learned of the plot and took the paper herself. The old man and the young man both believe that the paper is lost."

"But the *bint* talks to the young man who would have killed her father," said the sheykh. "She seems friendly with him. I do not understand these Christian dogs."

"Nor I," admitted Atewy. "They are all mad. They quarrel and fight, and then immediately they sit down together, laughing and talking. They do things in great secrecy while every one is looking on. I saw the *bint* take the paper while the young man was looking on, and yet he seems to know nothing of it. He went soon after to her father and asked to see it. It was then the old man searched for it and could not find it. He said that it was lost, and he was heart-broken."

"It is all very strange," murmured Sheykh Ab el-Ghren-nem. "Are you sure that you understand their accursed tongue and know that which they say, Atewy?"

"Did I not work for more than a year with a mad old *Nasrany* who dug in the sands at *Kheybar?* If he found only a piece of a broken pot he would be happy all the rest of the day. From him I learned the language of *el-Engleys.*"

"Wellah!" sighed the sheykh. "It must be a great treasure indeed, greater than those of Howwara and Geryeh combined; or they would not have brought so many carriages to trans-port it." He gazed with brooding eyes at the many trucks parked upon the opposite bank of the stream waiting to cross.

"When shall I take the *bint* who hath the paper?" demanded Atewy after a moment's silence.

"Let us bide our time," replied the sheykh. "There be no hurry, since they be leading us always nearer to the treasure and feeding us well into the bargain. The *Nasrany* are fools. They thought to fool the *Bedauwy* with their picture taking as they fooled *el-Engleys,* but we are brighter than they. We know the picture making is only a blind to hide the real pur-pose of their safari."

Sweating, mud-covered, Mr. Thomas Orman stood near the line of natives straining on the ropes attached to a heavy truck. In one hand he carried a long whip. At his elbow stood a bearer, but in lieu of a rifle he carried a bottle of Scotch.

By nature Orman was neither a harsh nor cruel taskmaster. Ordinarily, both his inclinations and his judgment would have warned him against using the lash. The sullen silence of the natives which should have counselled him to forbearance only irritated him still further.

He was three months out of Hollywood and already almost two months behind schedule, with the probability staring him in the face that it would be another month before they could reach the location where the major part of the picture could be shot. His leading woman had a touch of fever that might easily develop into something that would keep her out of the picture entirely. He had already been down twice with fever, and that had had its effects upon his disposition. It seemed to him that everything had gone wrong, that everything had conspired against him. And now these damn savages, as he thought of them, were lying down on the job.

"Lay into it, you lazy bums!" he yelled, and the long lash reached out and wrapped around the shoulders of a native.

A young man in khaki shirt and shorts turned away in disgust and walked toward the car where Baine was talking to the two girls. He paused in the shade of a tree, and, removing his sun helmet, wiped the perspiration from his forehead and the inside of the hat band; then he moved on again and joined them.

Baine moved over to make room for him by the rear door of the car. "You look sore, Bill," he remarked.

West swore softly. "Orman's gone nuts. If he doesn't throw that whip away and leave the booze alone we're headed for a lot of grief."

"It's in the air," said Rhonda. "The men don't laugh and sing the way they used to."

"I saw Kwamudi looking at him a few minutes ago," continued West. "There was hate in his eyes all right, and there was something worse."

"Oh, well," said Baine, "you got to treat those workmen rough; and as for Kwamudi, Tom can tie a can to him and appoint some one else headman."

"Those slave driving days are over, Baine; and the natives know it. Orman'll get in plenty of trouble for this if the men report it, and don't fool yourself about Kwamudi. He's no ordinary headman; he's a big chief in his own country, and most of our gang are from his own tribe. If he says quit, they'll quit; and don't you forget it. We'd be in a pretty mess if those fellows quit on us."

"Well, what are we goin' to do about it? Tom ain't asking our advice that I've ever noticed."

"You could do something, Naomi," said West, turning to the girl.

"Who, me? What could I do?"

"Well, Tom likes you a lot. He'd listen to you."

"Oh, nerts! It's his own funeral. I got troubles of my own."

"It may be your funeral, too," said West.

"Blah!" said the girl. "All I want to do is get out of here. How much longer I got to sit here and fight flies? Say, where's Stanley? I haven't seen him all day."

"The Lion Man is probably asleep in the back of his car," suggested Baine. "Say, have you heard what Old Man Marcus calls him?"

"What does he call him?" demanded Naomi.

"Sleeping Sickness."

"Aw, you're all sore at him," snapped Naomi, "because he steps right into a starring part while you poor dubs have been working all your lives and are still doin' bits. Mr. Obroski is a real artiste."

"Say, we're going to start!" cried Rhonda. "There's the signal."

At last the long motorcade was under way. In the leading cars was a portion of the armed guards, the askaris; and another detachment brought up the rear. To the running boards of a number of the trucks clung some of the workgang, but most of them followed the last truck afoot. Pat O'Grady, the assistant director, was in charge of these.

O'Grady carried no long whip. He whistled a great deal, always the same tune; and he joshed his charges unmercifully, wholly ignoring the fact that they understood nothing that he said. But they reacted to his manner and his smile, and slowly their tenseness relaxed. Their sullen silence broke a little, and they talked among themselves. But still they did not sing, and there was no laughter.

"It would be better," remarked Major White, walking at O'Grady's side, "if you were in full charge of these men at all times. Mr. Orman is temperamentally unsuited to handle them."

O'Grady shrugged. "Well, what is there to do about it?"

"He won't listen to me," said the major. "He resents every suggestion that I make. I might as well have remained in Hollywood."

"I don't know what's got into Tom. He's a mighty good sort. I never saw him like this before." O'Grady shook his head.

"Well, for one thing there's too much Scotch got into him," observed White.

"I think it's the fever and the worry." The assistant director was loyal to his chief.

"Whatever it is we're in for a bad mess if there isn't a change," the Englishman prophesied. His manner was serious, and it was evident that he was worried.

"Perhaps you're—" O'Grady started to reply, but his words were interrupted by a sudden rattle of rifle fire coming, apparently, from the direction of the head of the column.

"My lord! What now?" exclaimed White, as, leaving O'Grady, he hurried toward the sound of the firing.

3
Poisoned Arrows

THE ears of man are dull. Even on the open veldt they do not record the sound of a shot at any great distance. But the ears of hunting beasts are not as the ears of man; so hunting beasts at great distances paused when they heard the rifle fire that had startled O'Grady and White. Most of them slunk farther away from the dread sound.

Not so two lying in the shade of a tree. One was a great black-maned golden lion; the other was a man. He lay upon his back, and the lion lay beside him with one huge paw upon his chest.

"Tarmangani!" murmured the man.

A low growl rumbled in the cavernous chest of the carnivore.

"I shall have to look into this matter," said the man, "perhaps tonight, perhaps tomorrow." He closed his eyes and fell asleep again, the sleep from which the shots had aroused him.

The lion blinked his yellow-green eyes and yawned; then he lowered his great head, and he too slept.

Near them lay the partially devoured carcass of a zebra, the kill that they had made at dawn. Neither Ungo, the jackal, nor Dango, the hyena, had as yet scented the feast; so quiet prevailed, broken only by the buzzing of insects and the occasional call of a bird.

Before Major White reached the head of the column the firing had ceased, and when he arrived he found the askaris and the white men crouching behind trees gazing into the dark forest before them, their rifles ready. Two black soldiers lay upon the ground, their bodies pierced by arrows. Already their forms were convulsed by the last throes of death. Naomi Madison crouched upon the floor of her car. Rhonda Terry stood with one foot on the running board, a pistol in her hand.

White ran to Orman who stood with rifle in hand peering

into the forest. "What happened, Mr. Orman?" he asked.

"An ambush," replied Orman. "The devils just fired a volley of arrows at us and then beat it. We scarcely caught a glimpse of them."

"The Bansutos," said White.

Orman nodded. "I suppose so. They think they can frighten me with a few arrows, but I'll show the dirty rats."

"This was just a warning, Orman. They don't want us in their country."

"I don't care what they want; I'm going in. They can't bluff me."

"Don't forget, Mr. Orman, that you have a lot of people here for whose lives you are responsible, including two white women, and that you were warned not to come through the Bansuto country."

"I'll get my people through all right; the responsibility is mine, not yours." Orman's tone was sullen, his manner that of a man who knows that he is wrong but is constrained by stubbornness from admitting it.

"I cannot but feel a certain responsibility myself," replied White. "You know I was sent with you in an advisory capacity."

"I'll ask for your advice when I want it."

"You need it now. You know nothing about these people or what to expect from them."

"The fact that we were ready and sent a volley into them the moment that they attacked has taught 'em a good lesson," blustered Orman. "You can be sure they won't bother us again."

"I wish that I could be sure of that, but I can't. We haven't seen the last of those beggars. What you have seen is just a sample of their regular strategy of warfare. They'll never attack in force or in the open—just pick us off two or three at a time; and perhaps we'll never see one of them."

"Well, if you're afraid, go back," snapped Orman. "I'll give you porters and a guard."

White smiled. "I'll remain with the company, of course." Then he turned back to where Rhonda Terry still stood, a trifle pale, her pistol ready in her hand.

"You'd best remain in the car, Miss Terry," he said. "It will afford you some protection from arrows. You shouldn't expose yourself as you have."

"I couldn't help but overhear what you said to Mr. Orman,"

said the girl. "Do you really think they will keep on picking us off like this?"

"I am afraid so; it is the way they fight. I don't wish to frighten you unnecessarily, but you must be careful."

She glanced at the two bodies that lay quiet now in the grotesque and horrible postures of death. "I had no idea that arrows could kill so quickly." A little shudder accompanied her words.

"They were poisoned," explained the major.

"Poisoned!" There was a world of horror in the single word.

White glanced into the tonneau of the car. "I think Miss Madison has fainted," he said.

"She would!" exclaimed Rhonda, turning toward the unconscious girl.

Together they lifted her to the seat, and Rhonda applied restoratives; and, as they worked, Orman was organizing a stronger advance guard and giving orders to the white men clustered about him.

"Keep your rifles ready beside you all the time. I'll try to put an extra armed man on every truck. Keep your eyes open, and at the first sight of anything suspicious, shoot.

"Bill, you and Baine ride with the girls; I'll put an askari on each running board of their car. Clarence, you go to the rear of the column and tell Pat what has happened. Tell him to strengthen the rear guard, and you stay back there and help him.

"And Major White!" The Englishman came forward. "I wish you'd see old el-Ghrennem and ask him to send half his force to the rear and the other half up with us. We can use 'em to send messages up and down the column, if necessary.

"Mr. Marcus," he turned to the old character man, "you and Obroski ride near the middle of the column." He looked about him suddenly. "Where is Obroski?"

No one had seen him since the attack. "He was in the car when I left it," said Marcus. "Perchance he has fallen asleep again." There was a sly twinkle in the old eyes.

"Here he comes now," said Clarence Noice.

A tall, handsome youth with a shock of black hair was approaching from down the line of cars. He wore a six-shooter strapped about his hips and carried a rifle. When he saw them looking toward him he commenced to run in their direction.

"Where are they?" he called. "Where did they go?"

"Where you been?" demanded Orman.

"I been looking for them. I thought they were back there."

Bill West turned toward Gordon Z. Marcus and winked a slow wink.

Presently the column moved forward again. Orman was with the advance guard, the most dangerous post; and White remained with him.

Like a great snake the safari wound its way into the forest, the creaking of springs, the sound of the tires, the muffled exhausts its only accompaniment. There was no conversation—only tense, fearful expectancy.

There were many stops while a crew of natives with knives and axes hewed a passage for the great trucks. Then on again into the shadows of the primitive wilderness. Their progress was slow, monotonous, heartbreaking.

At last they came to a river. "We'll camp here," said Orman.

White nodded. To him had been delegated the duty of making and breaking camp. In a quiet voice he directed the parking of the cars and trucks as they moved slowly into the little clearing along the river bank.

As he was thus engaged, those who had been passengers climbed to the ground and stretched their legs. Orman sat on the running board of a car and took a drink of Scotch. Naomi Madison sat down beside him and lighted a cigarette. She darted fearful glances into the forest around them and across the river into the still more mysterious wood beyond.

"I wish we were out of here, Tom," she said. "Let's go back before we're all killed."

"That ain't what I was sent out here for. I was sent to make a picture, and I'm goin' to make it in spite of hell and high water."

She moved closer and leaned her lithe body against him. "Aw, Tom, if you loved me you'd take me out of here. I'm scared. I know I'm going to die. If it isn't fever it'll be those poisoned arrows."

"Go tell your troubles to your Lion Man," growled Orman, taking another drink.

"Don't be an old meany, Tom. You know I don't care anything about him. There isn't any one but you."

"Yes, I know it—except when you think I'm not looking. You don't think I'm blind, do you?"

"You may not be blind, but you're all wet," she snapped angrily. "I——"

A shot from the rear of the column halted her in mid-speech. Then came another and another in quick succession, followed by a fusillade.

Orman leaped to his feet. Men started to run toward the rear. He called them back. "Stay here!" he cried. "They may attack here, too—if that's who it is back again. Major White! Tell the sheik to send a horseman back there *pronto* to see what's happened."

Naomi Madison fainted. No one paid any attention to her. They left her lying where she had fallen. The black askaris and the white men of the company stood with rifles in tense fingers, straining their eyes into the woods about them.

The firing at the rear ceased as suddenly as it had begun. The ensuing silence seemed a thing of substance. It was broken by a weird, blood-curdling scream from the dark wood on the opposite bank of the river.

"Gad!" exclaimed Baine. "What was that?"

"I think the bounders are just trying to frighten us," said White.

"Insofar as I am concerned they have succeeded admirably," admitted Marcus. "If one could be scared out of seven years growth retroactively, I would soon be a child again."

Bill West threw a protective arm about Rhonda Terry. "Lie down and roll under the car," he said. "You'll be safe from arrows there."

"And get grease in my eyes? No, thanks."

"Here comes the sheik's man now," said Baine. "There's somebody behind him on the horse—a white man."

"It's Clarence," said West.

As the Arab reined his pony in near Orman, Noice slipped to the ground.

"Well, what was it?" demanded the director.

"Same thing that happened up in front back there," replied Noice. "There was a volley of arrows without any warning, two men killed; then we turned and fired; but we didn't see any one, not a soul. It's uncanny. Say, those porters of ours are all shot. Can't see anything but the whites of their eyes, and they're shaking so their teeth rattle."

"Is Pat hurryin' the rest of the safari into camp?" asked Orman.

Noice grinned. "They don't need any hurryin'. They're comin' so fast that they'll probably go right through without seein' it."

A scream burst in their midst, so close to them that even the stolid Major White jumped. All wheeled about with rifles ready.

Naomi Madison had raised herself to a sitting position. Her hair was dishevelled, her eyes wild. She screamed a second time and then fainted again.

"Shut up!" yelled Orman, frantically, his nerves on edge; but she did not hear him.

"If you'll have our tent set up, I'll get her to bed," suggested Rhonda.

Cars, horsemen, black men afoot were crowding into the clearing. No one wished to be left back there in the forest. All was confusion.

Major White, with the assistance of Bill West, tried to restore order from chaos; and when Pat O'Grady came in, he helped.

At last camp was made. Blacks, whites, and horses were crowded close together, the blacks on one side, the whites on the other.

"If the wind changes," remarked Rhonda Terry, "we're sunk."

"What a mess," groaned Baine, "and I thought this was going to be a lovely outing. I was so afraid I wasn't going to get the part that I was almost sick."

"Now you're sick because you did get it."

"I'll tell the world I am."

"You're goin' to be a whole lot sicker before we get out of this Bansuto country," remarked Bill West.

"You're telling me!"

"How's the Madison, Rhonda?" inquired West.

The girl shrugged. "If she wasn't so darned scared she wouldn't be in such a bad way. That last touch of fever's about passed, but she just lies there and shakes—scared stiff."

"You're a wonder, Rhonda. You don't seem to be afraid of anything."

"Well, I'll be seein' yuh," remarked Baine as he walked toward his own tent.

"Afraid!" exclaimed the girl. "Bill, I never knew what it was to be afraid before. Why, I've got goose-pimples inside."

West shook his head. "You're sure a game kid. No one would ever know you were afraid—you don't show it."

"Perhaps I've just enough brains to know that it wouldn't

get me anything. It doesn't even get her sympathy." She nodded her head toward the tent.

West grimaced. "She's a—" he hesitated, searching for adequate invective.

The girl placed her fingers against his lips and shook her head. "Don't say it," she admonished. "She can't help it. I'm really sorry for her."

"You're a wonder! And she treats you like scum. Gee, kid, but you've got a great disposition. I don't see how you can be decent to her. It's that dog-gone patronizing air of hers toward you that gets my nanny. The great artiste! Why, you can act circles all around her, kid; and as for looks! You got her backed off the boards."

Rhonda laughed. "That's why she's a famous star and I'm a double. Quit your kidding."

"I'm not kidding. The company's all talking about it. You stole the scenes we shot while she was laid up. Even Orman knows it, and he's got a crush on her."

"You're prejudiced—you don't like her."

"She's nothing in my young life, one way or another. But I do like you, Rhonda. I like you a lot. I—oh, pshaw— you know what I mean."

"What are you doing, Bill—making love to me?"

"I'm trying to."

"Well, as a lover you're a great cameraman—and you'd better stick to your camera. This is not exactly the ideal setting for a love scene. I am surprised that a great cameraman like you should have failed to appreciate that. You'd never shoot a love scene against this background."

"I'm shootin' one now, Rhonda. I love you."

"Cut!" laughed the girl.

4

Dissension

KWAMUDI, the black headman, stood before Orman. "My people go back," he said; "not stay in Bansuto country and be killed."

"You can't go back," growled Orman. "You signed up for the whole trip. You tell 'em they got to stay; or, by George, I'll——"

"We not sign up to go Bansuto country; we not sign up be killed. You go back, we come along. You stay, we go back. We go daylight." He turned and walked away.

Orman started up angrily from his camp chair, seizing his ever ready whip. "I'll teach you, you black—— —— —— ————!" he yelled.

White, who had been standing beside him, seized him by the shoulder. "Stop!" His voice was low but his tone peremptory. "You can't do that! I haven't interfered before, but now you've got to listen to me. The lives of all of us are at stake."

"Don't you interfere, you meddlin' old fool," snapped Orman. "This is my show, and I'll run it my way."

"You'd better go soak your head, Tom," said O'Grady; "you're full of hootch. The major's right. We're in a tight hole, and we won't ever get out of it on Scotch." He turned to the Englishman. "You handle things, Major. Don't pay any attention to Tom; he's drunk. Tomorrow he'll be sorry—if he sobers up. We're all back of you. Get us out of the mess if you can. How long would it take to get out of this Bansuto country if we kept on in the direction we want to go?"

Orman appeared stunned by this sudden defection of his assistant. It left him speechless.

White considered O'Grady's question. "If we were not too greatly delayed by the trucks, we could make it in two days," he decided finally.

"And how long would it take us to reach the location we're headed for if we have to go back and go around the Bansuto country?" continued O'Grady.

"We couldn't do it under two weeks," replied the major. "We'd be lucky if we made it in that time. We'd have to go way to the south through a beastly rough country."

"The studio's put a lot of money into this already," said O'Grady, "and we haven't got much of anything to show for it. We'd like to get onto location as quick as possible. Don't you suppose you could persuade Kwamudi to go on? If we turn back, we'll have those beggars on our neck for a day at least. If we go ahead, it will only mean one extra day of them. Offer Kwamudi's bunch extra pay if they'll stick— it'll be a whole lot cheaper for us than wastin' another two weeks."

"Will Mr. Orman authorize the bonus?" asked White.

"He'll do whatever I tell him, or I'll punch his fool head," O'Grady assured him.

Orman had sunk back into his camp chair and was staring at the ground. He made no comment.

"Very well," said White. "I'll see what I can do. I'll talk to Kwamudi over at my tent, if you'll send one of the boys after him."

White walked over to his tent, and O'Grady sent a black boy to summon the headman; then he turned to Orman. "Go to bed, Tom," he ordered, "and lay off that hootch."

Without a word, Orman got up and went into his tent.

"You put the kibosh on him all right, Pat," remarked Noice, with a grin. "How do you get away with it?"

O'Grady did not reply. His eyes were wandering over the camp, and there was a troubled expression on his usually smiling face. He noted the air of constraint, the tenseness, as though all were waiting for something to happen, they knew not what.

He saw his messenger overhaul Kwamudi and the headman turn back toward White's tent. He saw the natives silently making their little cooking fires. They did not sing or laugh, and when they spoke they spoke in whispers.

The Arabs were squatting in the *muk'aad* of the sheykh's *beyt*. They were a dour lot at best; and their appearance was little different tonight than ordinarily, yet he sensed a difference.

Even the whites spoke in lower tones than usual and there was less chaffing. And from all the groups constant glances were cast toward the surrounding forest.

Presently he saw Kwamudi leave White and return to his fellows; then O'Grady walked over to where the Englishman was sitting in a camp chair, puffing on a squat briar. "What luck?" he asked.

"The bonus got him," replied White. "They will go on, but on one other condition."

"What is that?"

"His men are not to be whipped."

"That's fair enough," said O'Grady.

"But how are you going to prevent it?"

"For one thing, I'll throw the whip away; for another, I'll tell Orman we'll all quit him if he doesn't lay off. I can't understand him; he never was like this before. I've worked with him a lot during the last five years."

"Too much liquor," said White; "it's finally got him."

"He'll be all right when we get on location and get to work.

He's been worrying too much. Once we get through this Bansuto country everything'll be jake."

"We're not through it yet, Pat. They'll get some more of us tomorrow and some more the next day. I don't know how the natives will stand it. It's a bad business. We really ought to turn around and go back. It would be better to lose two weeks time than to lose everything, as we may easily do if the natives quit us. You know we couldn't move through this country without them."

"We'll pull through somehow," O'Grady assured him. "We always do. Well, I'm goin' to turn in. Good-night, Major."

The brief equatorial twilight had ushered in the night. The moon had not risen. The forest was blotted out by a pall of darkness. The universe had shrunk to a few tiny earth fires surrounded by the huddled forms of men and, far above, a few stars.

Obroski paused in front of the girls' tent and scratched on the flap. "Who is it?" demanded Naomi Madison from within.

"It's me, Stanley."

She bade him enter; and he came in to find her lying on her cot beneath a mosquito bar, a lantern burning on a box beside her.

"Well," she said peevishly, "it's a wonder any one came. I might lie here and die for all any one cares."

"I'd have come sooner, but I thought of course Orman was here."

"He's probably in his tent soused."

"Yes, he is. When I found that out I came right over."

"I shouldn't think you'd be afraid of him. I shouldn't think you'd be afraid of anything." She gazed admiringly on his splendid physique, his handsome face.

"Me afraid of that big stiff!" he scoffed. "I'm not afraid of anything, but you said yourself that we ought not to let Orman know about—about you and me."

"No," she acquiesced thoughtfully, "that wouldn't be so good. He's got a nasty temper, and there's lots of things a director can do if he gets sore."

"In a picture like this he could get a guy killed and make it look like an accident," said Obroski.

She nodded. "Yes. I saw it done once. The director and the leading man were both stuck on the same girl. The director had the wrong command given to a trained elephant."

Obroski looked uncomfortable. "Do you suppose there's any chance of his coming over?"

"Not now. He'll be dead to the world till morning."

"Where's Rhonda?"

"Oh, she's probably playing contract with Bill West and Baine and old man Marcus. She'd play contract and let me lie here and die all alone."

"Is she all right?"

"What do you mean, all right?"

"She wouldn't tell Orman about us—about my being over here—would she?"

"No, she wouldn't do that—she ain't that kind."

Obroski breathed a sigh of relief. "She knows about us, don't she?"

"She ain't very bright; but she ain't a fool, either. The only trouble with Rhonda is, she's got it in her head she can act since she doubled for me while I was down with the fever. Some one handed her some applesauce, and now she thinks she's some pumpkins. She had the nerve to tell me that I'd get credit for what she did. Believe me, she won't get past the cutting room when I get back to Hollywood—not if I know my groceries and Milt Smith."

"There couldn't anybody act like you, Naomi," said Obroski. "Why, before I ever dreamed I'd be in pictures I used to go see everything you were in. I got an album full of your pictures I cut out of movie magazines and newspapers. And now to think that I'm playin' in the same company with you, and that"—he lowered his voice—"you love me! You do love me, don't you?"

"Of course I do."

"Then I don't see why you have to act so sweet on Orman."

"I got to be diplomatic—I got to think of my career."

"Well, sometimes you act like you were in love with him," he said, petulantly.

"That answer to a bootlegger's dream! Say, if he wasn't a big director I couldn't see him with a hundred-inch telescope."

In the far distance a wailing scream echoed through the blackness of the night, a lion rumbled forth a thunderous answer, the hideous, mocking voice of a hyena joined the chorus.

The girl shuddered. "God! I'd give a million dollars to be back in Hollywood."

"They sound like lost souls out there in the night," whispered Obroski.

"And they're calling to us. They're waiting for us. They know that we'll come, and then they'll get us."

The flap of the tent moved, and Obroski jumped to his feet with a nervous start. The girl sat straight up on her cot, wide-eyed. The flap was pulled back, and Rhonda Terry stepped into the light of the lone lantern.

"Hello, there!" she exclaimed cheerily.

"I wish you'd scratch before you come in," snapped Naomi. "You gave me a start."

"If we have to camp this close to the black belt every night we'll all be scratching." She turned to Obroski. "Run along home now; it's time all little Lion Men were in bed."

"I was just going," said Obroski. "I——"

"You'd better. I just saw Tom Orman reeling in this direction."

Obroski paled. "Well, I'll be running along," he said hurriedly, while making a quick exit.

Naomi Madison looked distinctly worried. "Did you really see Tom out there?" she demanded.

"Sure. He was wallowing around like the Avalon in a heavy sea."

"But they said he went to bed."

"If he did, he took his bottle to bed with him."

Orman's voice came to them from outside. "Hey, you! Come back here!"

"Is that you, Mr. Orman?" Obroski's voice quavered noticeably.

"Yes, it's me. What you doin' in the girls' tent? Didn't I give orders that none of you guys was to go into that tent?"

"I was just lookin' for Rhonda. I wanted to ask her something."

"You're a liar. Rhonda wasn't there. I just saw her go in. You been in there with Naomi. I've got a good mind to bust your jaw."

"Honestly, Mr. Orman, I was just in there a minute. When I found Rhonda wasn't there I came right out."

"You came right out after Rhonda went in, you dirty, sneakin' skunk; and now you listen to me. You lay off Naomi. She's my girl. If I ever find you monkeyin' around her again I'll kill you. Do you get that?"

"Yes, sir."

Rhonda looked at Naomi and winked. "Papa cross; papa spank," she said.

"My God! he'll kill me," shuddered Naomi.

The flap of the tent was thrust violently aside, and Orman burst into the tent. Rhonda wheeled and faced him.

"What do you mean by coming into our tent?" she demanded. "Get out of here!"

Orman's jaw dropped. He was not accustomed to being talked to like that, and it took him off his feet. He was as surprised as might be a pit bull slapped in the face by a rabbit. He stood swaying at the entrance for a moment, staring at Rhonda as though he had discovered a new species of animal.

"I just wanted to speak to Naomi," he said. "I didn't know you were here."

"You can speak to Naomi in the morning. And you did know that I was here; I heard you tell Stanley."

At the mention of Obroski's name Orman's anger welled up again. "That's what I'm goin' to talk to her about." He took a step in the direction of Naomi's cot. "Now look here, you dirty little tramp," he yelled, "you can't make a monkey of me. If I ever catch you playin' around with that Polack again I'll beat you into a pulp."

Naomi shrank back, whimpering. "Don't touch me! I didn't do anything. You got it all wrong, Tom. He didn't come here to see me; he came to see Rhonda. Don't let him get me, Rhonda, for God's sake, don't let him get me."

Orman hesitated and looked at Rhonda. "Is that on the level?" he asked.

"Sure," she replied, "he came to see me. I asked him to come."

"Then why didn't he stay after you came in?" Orman thought he had her there.

"I saw you coming, and I told him to beat it."

"Well, you got to cut it out," snapped Orman. "There's to be no more men in this tent—do your visiting outside."

"That suits me," said Rhonda. "Good-night."

As Orman departed, the Madison sank back on her cot trembling. "Phew!" she whispered after she thought the man was out of hearing. "That was a close shave." She did not thank Rhonda. Her selfish egotism accepted any service as her rightful due.

"Listen," said the other girl. "I'm hired to double for you in pictures, not in your love affairs. After this, watch your step."

Orman saw a light in the tent occupied by West and one of the other cameramen. He walked over to it and went in. West was undressing. "Hello, Tom!" he said. "What brings you around? Anything wrong?"

"There ain't now, but there was. I just run that dirty Polack out of the girls' tent. He was over there with Rhonda."

West paled. "I don't believe it."

"You callin' me a liar?" demanded Orman.

"Yes, you and any one else who says that."

Orman shrugged. "Well, she told me so herself—said she asked him over and made him scram when she saw me coming. That stuff's got to stop, and I told her so. I told the Polack too—the damn pansy." "Then he lurched out and headed for his own tent.

Bill West lay awake until almost morning.

5
Death

WHILE the camp slept, a bronzed white giant, naked but for a loin cloth, surveyed it—sometimes from the branches of overhanging trees, again from the ground inside the circle of the sentries. Then, he moved among the tents of the whites and the shelters of the natives as soundlessly as a shadow. He saw everything, he heard much. With the coming of dawn he melted away into the mist that enveloped the forest.

It was long before dawn that the camp commenced to stir. Major White had snatched a few hours sleep after midnight. He was up early routing out the cooks, getting the whites up so that their tents could be struck for an early start, directing the packing and loading by Kwamudi's men. It was then that he learned that fully twenty-five of the porters had deserted during the night.

He questioned the sentries, but none had seen any one leave the camp during the night. He knew that some of them lied. When Orman came out of his tent he told him what had happened.

The director shrugged. "We still got more than we need anyway."

"If we have any more trouble with the Bansutos today, we'll have more desertions tonight," White warned. "They may all leave in spite of Kwamudi, and if we're left in this country without porters I wouldn't give a fig for our chances of ever getting out.

"I still think, Mr. Orman, that the sensible thing would be to turn back and make a detour. Our situation is extremely grave."

"Well, turn back if you want to, and take the rats with you," growled Orman. "I'm going on with the trucks and the company." He turned and walked away.

The whites were gathering at the mess table—a long table that accommodated them all. In the dim light of the coming dawn and the mist rising from the ground, figures at a little distance appeared spectral, and the illusion was accentuated by the silence of the company. Every one was cold and sleepy. They were apprehensive too of what the day held for them. Memory of the black soldiers, pierced by poisoned arrows, writhing on the ground was too starkly present in every mind.

Hot coffee finally thawed them out a bit. It was Pat O'Grady who thawed first. "Good morning, dear teacher, good morning to you," he sang in an attempt to reach a childish treble.

"Ain't we got fun!" exclaimed Rhonda Terry. She glanced down the table and saw Bill West. She wondered a little, because he had always sat beside her before. She tried to catch his eye and smile at him, but he did not look in her direction—he seemed to be trying to avoid her glance.

"Let us eat and drink and be merry; for tomorrow we die," misquoted Gordon Z. Marcus.

"That's not funny," said Baine.

"On second thought I quite agree with you," said Marcus. "I loosed a careless shaft at humor and hit truth——"

"Right between the eyes," said Clarence Noice.

"Some of us may not have to wait until tomorrow," offered Obroski; "some of us may get it today." His voice sounded husky.

"Can that line of chatter!" snapped Orman. "If you're scared, keep it to yourself."

"I'm not scared," said Obroski.

"The Lion Man scared? Don't be foolish." Baine winked at Marcus. "I tell you, Tom, what we ought to do now that we're in this bad country. It's funny no one thought of it before."

"What's that?" asked Orman.

"We ought to send the Lion Man out ahead to clear the way for the rest of us; he'd just grab these Bansutos and break 'em in two if they got funny."

"That's not a bad idea," replied Orman grimly. "How about it, Obroski?"

Obroski grinned weakly. "I'd like to have the author of that story here and send him out," he said.

"Some of those porters had good sense anyway," volunteered a truck driver at the foot of the table.

"How come?" asked a neighbor.

"Hadn't you heard? About twenty-five or thirty of 'em pulled their freight out of here—they beat it back for home."

"Those bimbos must know," said another; "this is their country."

"That's what we ought to do," growled another—"get out of here and go back."

"Shut up!" snapped Orman. "You guys make me sick. Who ever picked this outfit for me must have done it in a pansy bed."

Naomi Madison was sitting next to him. She turned her frightened eyes up to him. "Did some of the blacks really run away last night?" she asked.

"For Pete's sake, don't you start in too!" he exclaimed; then he got up and stamped away from the table.

At the foot of the table some one muttered something that sounded like that epithet which should always be accompanied with a smile; but it was not.

By ones and twos they finished their breakfasts and went about their duties. They went in silence without the customary joking that had marked the earlier days of the expedition.

Rhonda and Naomi gathered up the hand baggage that they always took in the car with them and walked over to the machine. Baine was at the wheel warming up the motor. Gordon Z. Marcus was stowing a make-up case in the front of the car.

"Where's Bill?" asked Rhonda.

"He's going with the camera truck today," explained Baine.

"That's funny," commented Rhonda. It suddenly occurred to her that he was avoiding her, and she wondered why. She tried to recall anything that she had said or done that might have offended him, but she could not. She felt strangely sad.

Some of the trucks had commenced to move toward the

river. The Arabs and a detachment of askaris had already crossed to guard the passage of the trucks.

"They're going to send the generator truck across first," explained Baine. "If they get her across, the rest will be easy. If they don't, we'll have to turn back."

"I hope it gets stuck so fast they never get it out," said the Madison.

The crossing of the river, which Major White had anticipated with many misgivings, was accomplished with ease; for the bottom was rocky and the banks sloping and firm. There was no sign of the Bansutos,. and no attack was made on the column as it wound its way into the forest ahead.

All morning they moved on with comparative ease, retarded only by the ordinary delays consequent upon clearing a road for the big trucks where trees had to be thinned. The underbrush they bore down beneath them, flattening it out into a good road for the lighter cars that followed.

Spirits became lighter as the day progressed without revealing any sign of the Bansutos. There was a noticeable relaxation. Conversation increased and occasionally a laugh was heard. Even the blacks seemed to be returning to normal. Perhaps they had noticed that Orman no longer carried his whip, nor did he take any part in the direction of the march.

He and White were on foot with the advance guard, both men constantly alert for any sign of danger. There was still considerable constraint in their manner, and they spoke to one another only as necessity required.

The noon-day stop for lunch passed and the column took up its snakelike way through the forest once more. The ring of axes against wood ahead was accompanied by song and laughter. Already the primitive minds of the porters had cast off the fears that had assailed them earlier in the day.

Suddenly, without warning, a dozen feathered missiles sped from the apparently deserted forest around them. Two natives fell. Major White, walking beside Orman, clutched at a feathered shaft protruding from his breast and fell at Orman's feet. The askaris and the Arabs fired blindly into the forest. The column came to a sudden halt.

"Again!" whispered Rhonda Terry.

Naomi Madison screamed and slipped to the floor of the car. Rhonda opened the door and stepped out onto the ground.

"Get back in, Rhonda!" cried Baine. "Get under cover."

The girl shook her head as though the suggestion irritated her. "Where is Bill?" she asked. "Is he up in front?"

"Not way up," replied Baine; "only a few cars ahead of us."

The men all along the line of cars slipped to the ground with their rifles and stood searching the forest to right and left for some sign of an enemy.

A man was crawling under a truck.

"What the hell are you doing, Obroski?" demanded Noice.

"I—I'm going to lie in the shade until we start again." Noice made a vulgar sound with his lips and tongue.

In the rear of the column Pat O'Grady stopped whistling. He dropped back with the askaris guarding the rear. They had faced about and were nervously peering into the forest. A man from the last truck joined them and stood beside O'Grady.

"Wish we could get a look at 'em once," he said.

"It's tough tryin' to fight a bunch of guys you don't ever see," said O'Grady.

"It sort of gets a guy's nanny," offered the other. "I wonder who they got up in front this time."

O'Grady shook his head.

"It'll be our turn next; it was yesterday," said the man.

O'Grady looked at him. He saw that he was not afraid—he was merely stating what he believed to be a fact. "Can't ever tell," he said. "If it's a guy's time, he'll get it; if it isn't, he won't."

"Do you believe that? I wish I did."

"Sure—why not? It's pleasanter. I don't like worryin'."

"I don't know," said the other dubiously. "I ain't superstitious." He paused and lighted a cigarette.

"Neither am I," said O'Grady.

"I got one of my socks on wrong side out this morning," the man volunteered thoughtfully.

"You didn't take it off again, did you?" inquired O'Grady.

"No."

"That's right; you shouldn't."

Word was passed back along the line that Major White and two askaris had been killed. O'Grady cursed. "The major was a swell guy," he said. "He was worth all the lousy savages in Africa. I hope I get a chance to get some of 'em for this."

The porters were nervous, frightened, sullen. Kwamudi came up to O'Grady. "My people not go on," he said. "They turn back—go home."

"They better stick with us," O'Grady told him. "If they turn back they'll all be killed; they won't have a lot of us guys with rifles to fight for 'em. Tomorrow we ought to be out of this Bansuto country. You better advise 'em to stick, Kwa-mudi."

Kwamudi grumbled and walked away.

"That was just a bluff," O'Grady confided to the other white. "I don't believe they'd turn back through this Bansuto country alone."

Presently the column got under way again, and Kwamudi and his men marched with it.

Up in front they had laid the bodies of Major White and the two natives on top of one of the loads to give them decent burial at the next camp. Orman marched well in advance with set, haggard face. The askaris were nervous and held back. The party of Negroes clearing the road for the leading truck was on the verge of mutiny. The Arabs lagged behind. They had all had confidence in White, and his death had taken the heart out of them. They remembered Orman's lash and his cursing tongue; they would not have followed him at all had it not been for his courage. That was so evident that it commanded their respect.

He didn't curse them now. He talked to them as he should have from the first. "We've got to go on," he said. "If we turn back we'll be worse off. Tomorrow we ought to be out of this."

He used violence only when persuasion failed. An axe man refused to work and started for the rear. Orman knocked him down and then kicked him back onto the job. That was something they could all understand. It was right because it was just. Orman knew that the lives of two hundred people depended upon every man sticking to his job, and he meant to see that they stuck.

The rear of the column was not attacked that day, but just before they reached a camping place another volley of arrows took its toll from the head of the column. This time three men died, and an arrow knocked Orman's sun helmet from his head.

It was a gloomy company that made camp late that after-noon. The death of Major White had brought their own personal danger closer to the white members of the party. Before this they had felt a certain subconscious sense of immunity, as though the poisoned arrows of the Bansutos could deal death only to black men. Now they were quick to the horror of their own situation. Who would be next? How many of them were asking themselves this question!

A TEWY, the Arab, taking advantage of his knowledge
of English, often circulated among the Americans, asking questions, gossiping. They had become so accustomed to him that they thought nothing of his presence
among them; nor did his awkward attempts at joviality suggest to them that he might be playing a part for the purpose
of concealing ulterior motives, though it must have been ap-
parent to the least observing that by nature Atewy was far
from jovial.

He was, however, cunning; so he hid the fact that his
greatest interest lay in the two girl members of the company.
Nor did he ever approach them unless men of their own
race were with them.

This afternoon Rhonda Terry was writing at a little camp
table in front of her tent, for it was not yet dark. Gordon Z.
Marcus had stopped to chat with her. Atewy from the cor-
ners of his eyes noted this and strolled casually closer.

"Turning literary, Rhonda?" inquired Marcus.

The girl looked up and smiled. "Trying to bring my diary
up to date."

"I fear that it will prove a most lugubrious document."

"Whatever that is. Oh, by the way!" She picked up a folded
paper. "I just found this map in my portfolio. In the last
scene we shot they were taking close-ups of me examining it.
I wonder if they want it again—I'd like to swipe it for a sou-
venir."

As she unfolded the paper Atewy moved closer, a new
light burning in his eyes.

"Keep it," suggested Marcus, "until they ask you for it.
Perhaps they're through with it. It's a most authentic looking
thing, isn't it? I wonder if they made it in the studio."

"No. Bill says that Joe found it between the leaves of a
book he bought in a secondhand book store. When he was
commissioned to write this story it occurred to him to write
it around this old map. It *is* intriguing, isn't it? Almost makes
one believe that it would be easy to find a valley of dia-

monds." She folded the map and replaced it in her portfolio.
Hawklike, the swarthy Atewy watched her.

Marcus regarded her with his kindly eyes. "You were
speaking of Bill," he said. "What's wrong with you two
children? He used to be with you so much."

With a gesture Rhonda signified her inability to explain.
"I haven't the remotest idea," she said. "He just avoids me as
though I were some particular variety of pollen to which he
reacted. Do I give you hives or hay fever?"

Marcus laughed. "I can imagine, Rhonda, that you might
induce high temperatures in the male of the species; but to
suggest hives or hay fever—that would be sacrilege."

Naomi Madison came from the tent. Her face was white
and drawn. "My God!" she exclaimed. "How can you people
joke at such a time? Why, any minute any of us may be
killed!"

"We must keep up our courage," said Marcus. "We cannot
do it by brooding over our troubles and giving way to our
sorrows."

"Pulling a long face isn't going to bring back Major White
or those other poor fellows," said Rhonda. "Every one knows
how sorry every one feels about it; we don't have to wear
crêpe to prove that."

"Well, we might be respectful until after the funeral anyway," snapped Naomi.

"Don't be stupid," said Rhonda, a little tartly.

"When are they going to bury them, Mr. Marcus?" asked
Naomi.

"Not until after dark. They don't want the Bansutos to
see where they're buried."

The girl shuddered. "What a horrible country! I feel
that I shall never leave it—alive."

"You certainly won't leave it dead." Rhonda, who seldom
revealed her emotions, evinced a trace of exasperation.

The Madison sniffed. "They would never bury *me* here.
My public would never stand for that. I shall lie in state in
Hollywood."

"Come, come!" exclaimed Marcus. "You girls must not
dwell on such morbid, depressing subjects. We must all keep
our minds from such thoughts. How about a rubber of contract before supper? We'll just about have time."

"I'm for it," agreed Rhonda.

"You would be," sneered the Madison; "you have no
nerves. But no bridge for me at such a time. I am too highly

organized, too temperamental. I think that is the way with all true artistes, don't you, Mr. Marcus? We are like high-strung thoroughbreds."

"Well," laughed Rhonda, running her arm through Marcus's, "I guess we'll have to go and dig up a couple more skates if we want a rubber before supper. Perhaps we could get Bill and Jerrold. Neither of them would ever take any prizes in a horse show."

They found Bill West pottering around his cameras. He declined their invitation glumly. "You might get Obroski," he suggested, "if you can wake him up."

Rhonda shot a quick glance at him through narrowed lids. "Another thoroughbred," she said, as she walked away. And to herself she thought, "That's the second crack he's made about Obroski. All right, I'll show him!"

"Where to now, Rhonda?" inquired Marcus.

"You dig up Jerrold; I'm going to find Obroski. We'll have a game yet."

They did, and it so happened that their table was set where Bill West could not but see them. It seemed to Marcus that Rhonda laughed a little more than was usual and a little more than was necessary.

That night white men and black carried each their own dead into the outer darkness beyond the range of the camp fires and buried them. The graves were smoothed over and sprinkled with leaves and branches, and the excess dirt was carried to the opposite side of camp where it was formed in little mounds that looked like graves.

The true graves lay directly in the line of march of the morrow. The twenty-three trucks and the five passenger cars would obliterate the last trace of the new-made graves.

The silent men working in the dark hoped that they were unseen by prying eyes; but long into the night a figure lay above the edge of the camp, hidden by the concealing foliage of a great tree, and observed all that took place below. Then, when the last of the white men had gone to bed, it melted silently into the somber depths of the forest.

Toward morning Orman lay sleepless on his army cot. He had tried to read to divert his mind from the ghastly procession of thoughts that persisted despite his every effort to sleep or to think of other things. In the light of the lantern that he had placed near his head harsh shadows limned his face as a drawn and haggard mask.

From his cot on the opposite side of the tent Pat O'Grady

opened his eyes and surveyed his chief. "Hell, Tom," he said, "you better get some sleep or you'll go nuts."

"I can't sleep," replied Orman wearily. "I keep seein' White. I killed him. I killed all those blacks."

"Hooey!" scoffed O'Grady. "It wasn't any more your fault than it was the studio's. They sent you out here to make a picture, and you did what you thought was the thing to do. There can't nobody blame you."

"It was my fault all right. White warned me not to come this way. He was right; and I knew he was right, but I was too damn pig-headed to admit it."

"What you need is a drink. It'll brace you up and put you to sleep."

"I've quit."

"It's all right to quit; but don't quit so sudden—taper off."

Orman shook his head. "I ain't blamin' it on the booze," he said; "there's no one nor nothing to blame but me—but if I hadn't been drinkin' this would never have happened, and White and those other poor devils would have been alive now."

"One won't hurt, Tom; you need it."

Orman lay silent in thought for a moment; then he threw aside the mosquito bar and stood up. "Perhaps you're right, Pat," he said.

He stepped to a heavy, well-worn pigskin bag that stood at the foot of his cot and, stooping, took out a fat bottle and a tumbler. He shook a little as he filled the latter to the brim.

O'Grady grinned. "I said one drink, not four."

Slowly Orman raised the tumbler toward his lips. He held it there for a moment looking at it; then his vision seemed to pass beyond it, pass through the canvas wall of the tent out into the night toward the new-made graves.

With an oath, he hurled the full tumbler to the ground; the bottle followed it, breaking into a thousand pieces.

"That's goin' to be hell on bare feet," remarked O'Grady.

"I'm sorry, Pat," said Orman; then he sat down wearily on the edge of his cot and buried his face in his hands.

O'Grady sat up, slipped his bare feet into a pair of shoes, and crossed the tent. He sat down beside his friend and threw an arm about his shoulders. "Buck up, Tom!" That was all he said, but the pressure of the friendly arm was more strengthening than many words or many drinks.

From somewhere out in the night came the roar of a lion

and a moment later a blood-curdling cry that seemed neither that of beast nor man.

"Sufferin' cats!" ejaculated O'Grady. "What was that?"

Orman had raised his head and was listening. "Probably some more grief for us," he replied forebodingly.

They sat silent for a moment then, listening.

"I wonder what could make such a noise." O'Grady spoke in hushed tones.

"Pat," Orman's tone was serious, "do you believe in ghosts?"

O'Grady hesitated before he replied. "I don't know—but I've seen some funny things in my time."

"So have I," said Orman.

But perhaps of all that they could conjure to their minds nothing so strange as the reality; for how could they know that they had heard the victory cry of an English lord and a great lion who had just made their kill together?

7

Disaster

THE cold and gloomy dawn but reflected the spirits of the company as the white men dragged themselves lethargically from their blankets. But the first to view the camp in the swiftly coming daylight were galvanized into instant wakefulness by what it revealed.

Bill West was the first to suspect what had happened. He looked wonderingly about for a moment and then started, almost at a run, for the crude shelters thrown up by the blacks the previous evening.

He called aloud to Kwamudi and several others whose names he knew, but there was no response. He looked into shelter after shelter, and always the results were the same. Then he hurried over to Orman's tent. The director was just coming out as West ran up. O'Grady was directly behind him.

"What's the matter with breakfast?" demanded the latter. "I don't see a sign of the cooks."

"And you won't," said West; "they've gone, ducked, vamoosed. If you want breakfast, you'll cook it yourself."

"What do you mean gone, Bill?" asked Orman.

"The whole kit and kaboodle of 'em have run out on us," explained the cameraman. "There's not a smoke in camp. Even the askaris have beat it. The camp's unguarded, and God only knows how long it has been."

"Gone!" Orman's inflection registered incredulity. "But they couldn't! Where have they gone?"

"Search me," replied West. "They've taken a lot of our supplies with 'em too. From what little I saw I guess they outfitted themselves to the queen's taste. I noticed a couple of trucks that looked like they'd been rifled."

Orman swore softly beneath his breath; but he squared his shoulders, and the haggard, hang-dog expression he had worn vanished from his face. O'Grady had been looking at him with a worried furrow in his brow; now he gave a sigh of relief and grinned—the Chief was himself again.

"Rout every one out," Orman directed. "Have the drivers check their loads. You attend to that, Bill, while Pat posts a guard around the camp. I see old el-Gran'ma'am and his bunch are still with us. You better put them on guard duty, Pat. Then round up every one else at the mess tables for a palaver."

While his orders were being carried out Orman walked about the camp making a hurried survey. His brain was clear. Even the effects of a sleepless night seemed to have been erased by this sudden emergency call upon his resources. He no longer wasted his nervous energy upon vain regrets, though he was still fully conscious of the fact that this serious predicament was of his own making.

When he approached the mess table five minutes later the entire company was assembled there talking excitedly about the defection of the blacks and offering various prophecies as to the future, none of which were particularly roseate.

Orman overheard one remark. "It took a case of Scotch to get us into this mess, but Scotch won't ever get us out of it."

"You all know what has happened," Orman commenced; "and I guess you all know why it happened, but recriminations won't help matters. Our situation really isn't so hopeless. We have men, provisions, arms, and transportation. Because the porters deserted us doesn't mean that we've got to sit down here and kiss ourselves good-bye.

"Nor is there any use in turning around now and going back—the shortest way out of the Bansuto country is straight ahead. When we get out of it we can recruit more blacks from friendly tribes and go ahead with the picture.

"In the meantime every one has got to work and work hard. We have got to do the work the blacks did before—make camp, strike camp, unload and load, cook, cut trail, drag trucks through mud holes, stand guard on the march and in camp. That part and trail cutting will be dangerous, but every one will have to take his turn at it—every one except the girls and the cooks; they're the most important members of the safari." A hint of one of Orman's old smiles touched his lips and eyes.

"Now," he continued, "The first thing to do is eat. Who can cook?"

"I can like nobody's business," said Rhonda Terry.

"I'll vouch for that," said Marcus. "I've eaten a chicken dinner with all the trimmings at Rhonda's apartment."

"I can cook," spoke up a male voice.

Every one turned to see who had spoken; he was the only man that had volunteered for the only safe assignment.

"When did you learn to cook, Obroski?" demanded Noice. "I went camping with you once; and you couldn't even build a fire, let alone cook on one after some one else had built it."

Obroski flushed. "Well, some one's got to help Rhonda," he said lamely, "and no one else offered to."

"Jimmy, here, can cook," offered an electrician. "He used to be assistant chef in a cafeteria in L.A."

"I don't want to cook," said Jimmy. "I don't want no cinch job. I served in the Marines in Nicaragua. Gimme a gun, and let me do guard duty."

"Who else can cook?" demanded Orman. "We need three."

"Shorty can cook," said a voice from the rear. "He used to run a hot-dog stand on Ventura Boulevard."

"O.K.!" said Orman. "Miss Terry is chief cook; Jimmy and Shorty will help her; Pat will detail three more for K.P. every day. Now get busy. While the cooks are rustling some grub the rest of you strike the tents and load the trucks."

"Oh, Tom," said Naomi Madison at his elbow, "my personal boy has run away with the others. I wish you would detail one of the men to take his place."

Orman wheeled and looked at her in astonishment. "I'd forgotten all about you, Naomi. I'm glad you reminded me. If you can't cook, and I don't suppose you can, you'll peel spuds, wait on the tables, and help wash dishes."

For a moment the Madison looked aghast; then she smiled

icily. "I suppose you think you are funny," she said, "but really this is no time for joking."

"I'm not joking, Naomi." His tone was serious, his face unsmiling.

"Do you mean to say that you expect me, Naomi Madison, to peel potatoes, wait on tables, and wash dishes! Don't be ridiculous—I shall do nothing of the kind."

"Be yourself, Naomi! Before Milt Smith discovered you you were slinging hash in a joint on Main Street; and you'll do it again here, or you won't eat." He turned and walked away.

During breakfast Naomi Madison sat in haughty aloofness in the back seat of an automobile. She did not wait on table, nor did she eat.

Americans and Arabs formed the advance and rear guards when the safari finally got under way; but the crew that cut trail was wholly American—the Arabs would fight, but they would not work; that was beneath their dignity.

Not until the last kitchen utensil was washed, packed, and loaded did Rhonda Terry go to the car in which she and Naomi Madison rode. She was flushed and a little tired as she entered the car.

Naomi eyed her with compressed lips. "You're a fool, Rhonda," she snapped. "You shouldn't have lowered yourself by doing that menial work. We were not employed to be scullery maids."

Rhonda nodded toward the head of the column. "There probably isn't anything in those boys' contracts about chopping down trees or fighting cannibals." She took a paper-wrapped parcel from her bag. "I brought you some sandwiches. I thought you might be hungry."

The Madison ate in silence, and for a long time thereafter she seemed to be immersed in thought.

The column moved slowly. The axe men were not accustomed to the sort of work they were doing, and in the heat of the equatorial forest they tired quickly. The trail opened with exasperating slowness as though the forest begrudged every foot of progress that they made.

Orman worked with his men, wielding an axe when trees were to be felled, marching with the advance guard when the trail was opened.

"Tough goin'," remarked Bill West, leaning his axe handle against his hip and wiping the perspiration from his eyes.

"This isn't the toughest part of it," replied Orman.

"How come?"

"Since the guides scrammed we don't know where we're goin'."

West whistled. "I hadn't thought of that."

As they trudged on an opening in the forest appeared ahead of them shortly after noon. It was almost treeless and covered with a thick growth of tall grass higher than a man's head.

"That certainly looks good," remarked Orman. "We ought to make a little time for a few minutes."

The leading truck forged into the open, flattening the grass beneath its great tires.

"Hop aboard the trucks!" Orman shouted to the advance guard and the axe men. "Those beggars won't bother us here; there are no trees to hide them."

Out into the open moved the long column of cars. A sense of relief from the oppressive closeness of the forest animated the entire company.

And then, as the rearmost truck bumped into the clearing, a shower of arrows whirred from the tall grasses all along the line. Savage war cries filled the air; and for the first time the Bansutos showed themselves, as their spearmen rushed forward with screams of hate and blood lust.

A driver near the head of the column toppled from his seat with an arrow through his heart. His truck veered to the left and went careening off into the midst of the savages.

Rifles cracked, men shouted and cursed, the wounded screamed. The column stopped, that every man might use his rifle. Naomi Madison slipped to the floor of the car. Rhonda drew her revolver and fired into the faces of the onrushing blacks. A dozen men hurried to the defense of the car that carried the two girls.

Some one shouted, "Look out! They're on the other side too." Rifles were turned in the direction of the new threat. The fire was continuous and deadly. The Bansutos, almost upon them, wavered and fell back. A fusillade of shots followed them as they disappeared into the dense grass, followed and found many of them.

It was soon over; perhaps the whole affair had not lasted two minutes. But it had wrought havoc with the company. A dozen men were dead or dying, a truck was wrecked, the morale of the little force was shattered.

Orman turned the command of the advance guard over to West and hurried back down the line to check up on casualties. O'Grady was running forward to meet him.

"We'd better get out of here, Tom," he cried; "those devils may fire the grass."

Orman paled. He had not thought of that. "Load the dead and wounded onto the nearest cars, and get going!" he ordered. "We'll have to check up later."

The relief that the party had felt when they entered the grassy clearing was only equalled by that which they experienced when they left it to pull into the dense, soggy forest where the menace of fire, at least, was reduced to a minimum.

Then O'Grady went along the line with his roster of the company checking the living and the dead. The bodies of Noice, Baine, seven other Americans and three Arabs were on the trucks.

"Obroski!" shouted O'Grady. "Obroski! Has any one seen Obroski?"

"Bless my soul!" exclaimed Gordon Z. Marcus. "I saw him. I remember now. When those devils came up on our left, he jumped out of the other side of the car and ran off into that tall grass."

Orman started back toward the rear of the column. "Where you goin', Tom?" demanded West.

"To look for Obroski."

"You can't go alone. I'll go with you."

Half a dozen others accompanied them, but though they searched for the better part of an hour they found no sign of Obroski either dead or alive.

Silent, sad, and gloomy, the company found a poor camping site late in the afternoon. When they spoke, they spoke in subdued tones, and there was no joking or laughing. Glumly they sat at table when supper was announced, and few appeared to notice and none commented upon the fact that the famous Naomi Madison waited on them.

8

The Coward

WE ARE all either the victims or the beneficiaries of heredity and environment. Stanley Obroski was one of the victims. Heredity had given him a mighty physique, a noble bearing, and a handsome face. Environment

had sheltered and protected him throughout his life. Also,
every one with whom he had come in contact had admired his great strength and attributed to him courage com-
mensurate to it.

Never until the past few days had Obroski been confronted
by an emergency that might test his courage, and so all his
life he had been wondering if his courage would measure up
to what was expected of it when the emergency developed.

He had given the matter far more thought than does the
man of ordinary physique because he knew that so much
more was expected of him than of the ordinary man. It had
become an obsession together with the fear that he might
not live up to the expectations of his admirers. And finally he
became afraid—afraid of being afraid.

It is a failing of nearly all large men to be keenly affected
by ridicule. It was the fear of ridicule, should he show fear,
rather than fear of physical suffering, that Obroski shrank
from, though perhaps he did not realize this. It was a psyche
far too complex for easy analysis.

But the results were disastrous. They induced a subconscious urge to avoid danger rather than risk showing fear and
thus inducing ridicule.

And when the first shower of arrows fell among the cars
of the safari Obroski leaped from the opposite side of the
automobile in which he was riding and disappeared among
the tall grasses that hemmed them in on both sides. His re-
action to danger had been entirely spontaneous—a thing beyond his will.

As he pushed blindly forward he was as unthinking as a
terrified animal bent only upon escape. But he had covered
only a few yards when he ran directly into the arms of a giant
black warrior.

Here indeed was an emergency. The black was as surprised
as Obroski. He probably thought that all the whites were
charging to the attack; he was terrified. He wanted to flee,
but the white was too close; so he leaped for him, calling
loudly to his fellows as he did so.

It was too late for Obroski to escape the clutching fingers
of the black. If he didn't do something the man would kill
him! If he could get rid of the fellow he could run back to
the safari. He *must* get rid of him!

The black had seized him by the clothes, and now Obroski
saw a knife in the fellow's free hand. Death stared him in

the face! Heretofore Obroski's dangers had always been more or less imaginary; now he was faced with a stark reality.

Terror galvanized his mind and his giant muscles into instant action. He seized the black and lifted him above his head; then he hurled him heavily to the ground.

The black, fearful of his life, started to rise; and Obroski, equally fearful of his own, lifted him again high overhead and again cast him down. As he did so a half dozen blacks closed upon him from the tall surrounding grasses and bore him to the earth.

His mind half numb with terror, Obroski fought like a cornered rat. The blacks were no match for his great muscles. He seized them and tossed them aside; then he turned to run. But the black he had first hurled to the ground reached out and seized him by an ankle, tripping him; then the others were upon him again and more came to their assistance. They held him by force of numbers and bound his hands behind him.

In all his life Stanley Obroski had never fought before. A good disposition and his strange complex had prevented him from seeking trouble, and his great size and strength had deterred others from picking quarrels with him. He had never realized his own strength; and now, his mental faculties cloyed by terror, he only partly appreciated it. All that he could think of was that they had bound his hands and he was helpless; that they would kill him.

At last they dragged him to his feet. Why they did not kill him he could not guess—then. They seemed a little awed by his great size and strength. They jabbered much among themselves as they led him away toward the forest.

Obroski heard the savage war cries of the main body as it attacked the safari and the crack of rifles that told that his fellows were putting up a spirited defense. A few bullets whirred close, and one of his captors lunged forward with a slug in his heart.

They took him into the forest and along a winding trail where presently they were overtaken by other members of the tribe, and with the arrival of each new contingent he was surrounded by jabbering savages who punched him and poked him, feeling of his great muscles, comparing his height with theirs.

Bloodshot eyes glared from hideous, painted faces—glared in hatred that required no knowledge of their language to interpret. Some threatened him with spears and knives, but the party that had captured him preserved him from these.

Stanley Obroski was so terrified that he walked as one in a trance, giving no outward sign of any emotion; but the blacks thought that his manner was indicative of the indifference of great bravery.

At last a very large warrior overtook them. He was resplendent in paint and feathers, in many necklaces and armlets and anklets. He bore an ornate shield, and his spear and his bow and the quiver for his arrows were more gorgeously decorated than those of his fellows.

But it was his commanding presence and his air of authority more than these that led Obroski to infer that he was a chief. As he listened to the words of those who had made the capture, he examined the prisoner with savage disdain; then he spoke commandingly to those about him and strode on. The others followed, and afterward none threatened to harm the white man.

All afternoon they marched, deeper and deeper into the gloomy forest. The cords about Obroski's wrists cut into the flesh and hurt him; another cord about his neck, by which a savage led him, was far too tight for comfort; and when the savage jerked it, as he occasionally did, Obroski was half choked.

He was very miserable, but he was so numb with terror that he made no outcry nor any complaint. Perhaps he felt that it would be useless, and that the less he caused them annoyance or called attention to himself the better off he would be.

The result of this strategy, if such it were, he could not have guessed; for he could not understand their words when they spoke among themselves of the bravery of the white man who showed no fear.

During the long march his thoughts were often of the members of the company he had deserted. He wondered how they had fared in the fight and if any had been killed. He knew that many of the men had held him in contempt before. What would they think of him now! Marcus must have seen him run away at the first threat of danger. Obroski winced, the old terrifying fear of ridicule swept over him; but it was nothing compared to the acute terror he suffered as he shot quick glances about him at the savage faces of his captors and recalled the stories he had heard of torture and death at the hands of such as these.

He heard shouting ahead, and a moment later the trail debouched onto a clearing in the center of which was a palisaded village of conical, straw-thatched huts. It was late in the afternoon, and Obroski knew that they must have covered considerable distance since his capture. He wondered, in the event that he escaped or they released him, if he could find his way back to the trail of the safari. He had his doubts.

As they entered the village, women and children pressed forward to see him. They shouted at him. From the expressions of the faces of many of the women he judged that they were reviling and cursing him. A few struck or clawed at him. The children threw stones and refuse at him.

The warriors guarding him beat his assailants off, as they conducted him down the single street of the village to a hut near the far end. Here they motioned him to enter; but the doorway was so low that one might only pass through it on hands and knees, and as his hands were fastened behind his back that was out of the question for him. So they threw him down and dragged him in. Then they bound his ankles and left him.

The interior of the hut was dark, but as his eyes became accustomed to the change from daylight he was able to see his surroundings dimly. It was then that he became aware that he was not alone in the hut. Within the range of his vision he saw three figures, evidently men. One was stretched out upon the packed earth floor, the other two sat hunched forward over their updrawn knees. He felt the eyes of the latter upon him. He wondered what they were doing there —if they, too, were prisoners.

Presently one of them spoke. "How the Bansuto get you, Bwana Simba?" It was the name the natives of the safari had given him because of the part that he was to take in the picture, that of the Lion Man.

"Who the devil are you?" demanded Obroski.

"Kwamudi," replied the speaker.

"Kwamudi! Well, it didn't do you much good to run away —" He almost added "either" but stopped himself in time. "They attacked the safari shortly after noon. I was taken prisoner then. How did they get you?"

"Early this morning. I had followed my people, trying to get them to return to the safari." Obroski guessed that Kwamudi was lying. "We ran into a party of warriors coming from a distant village to join the main tribe. They killed many of my people. Some escaped. They took some prisoners. Of these they killed all but Kwamudi and these two. They brought us here."

"What are they going to do with you? Why didn't they kill you when they killed the others?"

"They not kill you, they not kill Kwamudi, they not kill these others—yet—all for same reason. Kill by and by."

"Why? What do they want to kill us for?"

"They eat."

"Eh? You don't mean to say they're cannibals!"

"Not like some. Bansuto not eat men all time; not eat all men. Only chiefs, brave men, strong men. Eat brave men, make them brave; eat strong men, make them strong; eat chiefs, make them wise."

"How horrible!" muttered Obroski. "But they can't eat me—I am not a chief—I am not brave—I am a coward," he mumbled.

"What, Bwana?"

"Oh, nothing. When do you suppose they'll do it? Right away?"

Kwamudi shook his head. "Maybe. Maybe not for long time. Witch doctor make medicine, talk to spirits, talk to moon. They tell him when. Maybe soon, maybe long time."

"And will they keep us tied up this way until they kill us? It's mighty uncomfortable. But then you aren't tied, are you?"

"Yes, Kwamudi tied—hands and feet. That why he lean forward across his knees."

"Can you talk their language, Kwamudi?"

"A little."

"Ask them to free our hands, and our feet too if they will."

"No good. Waste talk."

Listen, Kwamudi! They want us to be strong when they eat us, don't they?"

"Yes, Bwana."

"Very well; then get hold of the chief and tell him that if he keeps us tied up like this we'll get weak. He's certainly got brains enough to know that that's true. He's got plenty of warriors to guard us, and I don't see how we could get out of this village anyhow—not with all those harpies and brats hanging around.'"

Kwamudi understood enough of what the white man had said to get the main idea. "First time I get a chance, I tell him," he said.

Darkness fell. The light from the cooking fires was visible

through the low doorway of the prison hut. Women were screaming and wailing for the warriors who had fallen in battle that day. Many had painted their bodies from head to feet with ashes, rendering them even more hideous than nature had fashioned them. Others laughed and gossiped.

Obroski was thirsty and hungry, but they brought him neither water nor food. The hours dragged on. The warriors commenced to dance in celebration of their victory. Tom-toms boomed dismally through the night. The wails of the mourners, the screams and war cries of the dancers rose and fell in savage consonance with the savage scene, adding to the depression of the prisoners.

"This is no way to treat people you're going to eat," grumbled Obroski. "You ought to get 'em fat, not starve 'em thin."

"Bansuto do not care about our fat," observed Kwamudi. "They eat our hearts, the palms of our hands, the soles of our feet. They eat the muscles from your arms and legs. They eat my brains."

"You're not very cheering and you're not very complimentary," said Obroski with a wry smile. "But at that there isn't much to choose between our brains, for they've ended up by getting us both into the same hole."

9
Treachery

O RMAN and Bill West entered the cook tent after supper. "We're going to do the dishes, Rhonda," said the director. "We're so shorthanded now we got to take the K.P.'s off and give 'em to Pat for guard duty. Jimmy and Shorty will stay on cooking and help with the other work."

Rhonda demurred with a shake of her head. "You boys have had a tough day. All we've done is sit in an automobile. Sit down here and smoke and talk to us—we need cheering up. The four of us can take care of the dishes. Isn't that right?" She turned toward Jimmy, Shorty, and Naomi.

"Sure!" said Jimmy and Shorty in unison.

Naomi nodded. "I've washed dishes till after midnight for a lot of Main Street bums many a time. I guess I can wash 'em for you bums, too," she added with a laugh. "But for the love o' Mike, do as Rhonda said—sit down and talk to us, and *say something funny*. I'm nearly nuts."

There was a moment's awkward silence. They could have been only a little more surprised had they seen Queen Mary turn handsprings across Trafalgar Square.

Then Tom Orman laughed and slapped Naomi on the back. "Atta girl!" he exclaimed.

Here was a new Madison; they were all sure that they were going to like her better than the old.

"I don't mind sitting down," admitted West. "And I don't mind talking, but I'm damned if I can be funny—I can't forget Clarence and Jerrold and the rest of them."

"Poor Stanley," said Rhonda. "He won't even get a decent burial."

"He don't deserve one," growled Jimmy, who had served with the Marines; "he deserted under fire."

"Let's not be too hard on him," begged Rhonda. "No one is a coward because he wants to be. It's something one can't help. We ought to pity him." Jimmy grumbled in dissent.

Bill West grunted. "Perhaps we would, if we were all stuck on him."

Rhonda turned and eyed him coolly. "He may have had his faults," she said, "but at least I never heard him say an unkind thing about any one."

"He was never awake long enough," said Jimmy contemptuously.

"I don't know what I'm goin' to do without him," observed Orman. "There isn't anybody in the company I can double for him."

"You don't think you're going on with the picture after what's happened, do you?" asked Naomi.

"That's what we came over here for, and that's what we're goin' to do if it takes a leg," replied Orman.

"But you've lost your leading man and your heavy and your sound man and a lot more, and you haven't any guides, and you haven't any porters. If you think you can go on with a picture like that, you're just plain cuckoo, Tom."

"I never saw a good director who wasn't cuckoo," said Bill West.

Pat O'Grady stuck his head inside the tent. "The Chief here?" he asked. "Oh, there you are! Say, Tom, Atewy says old Ghrennem will stand all the guard with his men from 12 to 6 if we'll take care of it from now to midnight. He wants to know if that's all right with you. Atewy says the Arabs can do better together than workin' with Americans that they can't understand."

"O.K." replied Orman. "That's sort of decent of 'em takin' that shift. It'll give our boys a chance to rest up before we shove off in the morning, and God knows they need it. Tell 'em we'll call 'em at midnight."

Exhausted by the physical and nervous strains of the day, those members of the company that were not on guard were soon asleep. For the latter it was a long stretch to midnight, a tour of duty rendered still more trying by the deadly monotony of the almost unbroken silence of the jungle. Only faintly from great distances came the usual sounds to which they had become accustomed. It was as though they had been abandoned by even the beasts of the forest. But at last midnight came, and O'Grady awoke the Arabs. Tired men stumbled through the darkness to their blankets, and within fifteen minutes every American in the camp was deep in the sleep of utter exhaustion.

Even the unwonted activity of the Arabs could not arouse them; though, to be sure, the swart sons of the desert moved as silently as the work they were engaged upon permitted—rather unusual work it seemed for those whose sole duty it was to guard the camp.

It was full daylight before an American stirred—several hours later than it was customary for the life of the camp to begin.

Gordon Z. Marcus was the first to be up, for old age is prone to awaken earlier than youth. He had dressed hurriedly, for he had noted the daylight and the silence of the camp. Even before he came into the open he sensed that something was amiss. He looked quickly about. The camp seemed deserted. The fires had died to smoldering embers. No sentry stood on guard.

Marcus hastened to the tent occupied by Orman and O'Grady, and without formality burst into the interior. "Mr. Orman! Mr. Orman!" he shouted.

Orman and O'Grady, startled out of deep sleep by the excited voice of the old character man, threw aside their mosquito bars and leaped from their cots.

"What's wrong?" demanded Orman.

"The Arabs!" exclaimed Marcus. "They've gone! Their tents, their horses, everything!"

Neither of the other men spoke as they quickly slipped

into their clothes and stepped out into the open. Orman looked quickly about the camp.

"They must have been gone for hours," he said; "the fires are out." Then he shrugged. "We'll have to get along without them, but that doesn't mean that we got to stop eating. Where are the cooks? Wake the girls, Marcus, please, and rout out Jimmy and Shorty."

"I thought those fellows were getting mighty considerate all of a sudden when they offered to stand guard after midnight last night," remarked O'Grady.

"I might have known there was something phoney about it," growled Orman. "They played me for a sucker. I'm nothin' but a damn boob."

"Here comes Marcus again," said O'Grady. "I wonder what's eatin' him now—he looks fussed."

And Gordon Z. Marcus was fussed. Before he reached the two men he called aloud to them. "The girls aren't there," he shouted, "and their tent's a mess."

Orman turned and started on a run for the cook tent. "They're probably getting breakfast," he explained. But there was no one in the cook tent.

Every one was astir now; and a thorough search of the camp was made, but there was no sign of either Naomi Madison or Rhonda Terry. Bill West searched the same places again and again, unwilling to believe the abhorrent evidence of his own eyes. Orman was making a small pack of food, blankets, and ammunition.

"Why do you suppose they took them?" asked Marcus.

"For ransom, most likely," suggested O'Grady.

"I wish I was sure of that," said Orman; "but there is still a safe market for girls in Africa and Asia."

"I wonder why they tore everything to pieces so in the tent," mused Marcus. "It looks like a cyclone had struck it."

"There wasn't any fight," said O'Grady. "It would have waked some of us up if there had been."

"The Arabs were probably looking for loot," suggested Jimmy.

Bill West had been watching Orman. Now he too was making a pack. The director noticed it.

"What do you think you're goin' to do?" he asked.

"I'm goin' with you," replied West.

Orman shook his head. "Nothing doing! This is my funeral."

West continued his preparations without reply.

"If you fellows are going out to look for the girls, I'm goin' with you," announced O'Grady.

"Same here," said another.

The whole company volunteered.

"I'm goin' alone," announced Orman. "One man on foot can travel faster than this motorcade and faster than men on horseback who will have to stop and cut trail in places."

"But what in hell can one man do after he catches up with those rats?" demanded O'Grady. "He'll just get himself killed. He can't fight 'em all."

"I don't intend to fight," replied Orman. "I got the girls into this mess by not using my head; I'm going to use it to get them out. Those Arabs will do anything for money, and I can offer them more for the girls than they can hope to get from any one else."

O'Grady scratched his head. "I guess you're right, Tom."

"Sure I'm right. You are in charge of the outfit while I'm away. Get it to the Omwamwi Falls, and wait there for me. You'll be able to hire natives there. Send a runner back to Jinja by the southern route with a message for the studio telling what's happened and asking for orders if I don't show up again in thirty days."

"You're not going without breakfast!" demanded Marcus.

"No, I'll eat first," replied Orman.

"How about grub?" shouted O'Grady.

"Comin' right up!" yelled back Shorty from the cook tent.

Orman ate hurriedly, giving final instructions to O'Grady between mouthfuls. When he had finished he got up, shouldered his pack, and picked up his rifle.

"So long, boys!" he said.

They crowded up to shake his hand and wish him luck. Bill West was adjusting the straps of a pack that he had slung to his back. Orman eyed him.

"You can't come, Bill," he said. "This is my job."

"I'm coming along," replied West.

"I won't let you."

"You and who else?" demanded West, and then added in a voice that he tried hard to control, "Rhonda's out there somewhere."

The hard lines of grim stubbornness on Orman's face softened. "Come on then," he said; "I hadn't thought of it that way, Bill."

The two men crossed the camp and picked up the plain trail of the horsemen moving northward.

STANLEY OBROSKI had never before welcomed a dawn with such enthusiasm. The new day might bring him death, but almost anything would be preferable to the hideous discomforts of the long night that had finally dragged its pain-racked length into the past.

His bonds had hurt him; his joints ached from long inaction and from cold; he was hungry, but he suffered more from thirst; vermin crawled over him at will and bit him; they and the cold and the hideous noises of the mourners and the dancers and the drums had combined to deny him sleep.

All these things had sapped his strength, both physical and nervous, leaving him exhausted. He felt like a little child who was afraid and wanted to cry. The urge to cry was almost irresistible. It seemed to offer relief from the maddening tension.

A vague half-conviction forced its way into the muddy chaos of his numb brain—crying would be a sign of fear, and fear meant cowardice! Obroski did not cry. Instead, he found partial relief in swearing. He had never been given to profanity, but even though he lacked practice he acquitted himself nobly.

His efforts awoke Kwamudi who had slept peacefully in this familiar environment. The two men conversed haltingly —mostly about their hunger and thirst.

"Yell for water and food," suggested Obroski, "and keep on yelling until they bring it."

Kwamudi thought that might be a good plan, and put it into execution. After five minutes it brought results. One of the guards outside the hut was awakened. He came in saying things.

In the meantime both the other prisoners had awakened and were sitting up. One of these was nearer the hut doorway than his fellows. He therefore chanced to be the first in the path of the guard, who commenced to belabor him over the head and shoulders with the haft of his spear.

"If you make any more noise like that," said the guard, "I'll cut out the tongues of all of you." Then he went outside and fell asleep again.

"That idea," observed Obroski, "was not so hot."

"What, Bwana?" inquired Kwamudi.

The morning dragged on until almost noon, and still the village slept. It was sleeping off the effects of the previous night's orgy. But at last the women commenced to move about, making preparations for breakfast.

Fully an hour later warriors came to the hut. They dragged and kicked the prisoners into the open and jerked them to their feet after removing the bonds from their ankles; then they led them to a large hut near the center of the village. It was the hut of Rungula, chief of the Bansutos.

Rungula sat on a low stool before the doorway. Behind him were ranged the more important subchiefs; and on the flanks, forming a wide semicircle, were grouped the remainder of the warriors—a thousand savage fighting men from many a far-flung Bansuto village.

From the doorway of the chief's hut several of his wives watched the proceedings, while a brood of children spewed out between their feet into the open sunshine.

Rungula eyed the white prisoner with scowling brows; then he spoke to him.

"What is he saying, Kwamudi?" asked Obroski.

"He is asking what you were doing in his country."

"Tell him that we were only passing through—that we are friends—that he must let us go."

When Kwamudi interpreted Obroski's speech Rungula laughed. "Tell the white man that only a chief who is greater than Rungula can say *must* to Rungula and that there is no chief greater than Rungula.

"The white man will be killed and so will all his people. He would have been killed yesterday had he not been so big and strong."

"He will not stay strong if he does not have food and water," replied Kwamudi. "None of us will do you any good if you starve us and keep us tied up."

Rungula thought this over and discussed it with some of his lieutenants; then he stood up and approached Obroski. He fingered the white man's shirt, jabbering incessantly. He appeared much impressed also by Obroski's breeches and boots.

"He says for you to take off your clothes, Bwana," said Kwamudi; "he wants them."

"All of them?" inquired Obroski.

"All of them, Bwana."

Exhausted by sleeplessness, discomfort, and terror, Obroski had felt that nothing but torture and death could add to his misery, but now the thought of nakedness awoke him to new horrors. To the civilized man clothing imparts a self-confidence that is stripped away with his garments. But Obroski dared not refuse.

"Tell him I can't take my clothes off with my hands tied behind my back."

When Kwamudi had interpreted this last, Rungula directed that Obroski's hands be released.

The white man removed his shirt and tossed it to Rungula. Then the chief pointed at his boots. Slowly Obroski unlaced and removed them, sitting on the ground to do so. Rungula became intrigued by the white man's socks and jerked these off, himself.

Obroski rose and waited. Rungula felt of his great muscles and jabbered some more with his fellows. Then he called his tallest warrior and stood him beside the prisoner. Obroski towered above the man. The blacks jabbered excitedly.

Rungula touched Obroski's breeches and grunted.

"He want them," said Kwamudi.

"Oh, for Pete's sake, tell him to have a heart," exclaimed Obroski. "Tell him I got to have something to wear."

Kwamudi and the chief spoke together briefly, with many gesticulations.

"Take them off, Bwana," said the former. "There is nothing else you can do. He says he will give you something to wear."

As he unbuttoned his breeches and slipped them off, Obroski was painfully aware of giggling girls and women in the background. But the worst was yet to come—Rungula was greatly delighted by the gay silk shorts that the removal of the breeches revealed.

When these had passed to the ownership of Rungula, Obroski could feel the hot flush beneath the heavy coat of tan he had acquired on the beach at Malibu.

"Tell him to give me something to wear," he begged.

Rungula laughed uproariously when the demand was made known to him; but he turned and called something to the women in his hut, and a moment later a little pickaninny came running out with a very dirty G string which he threw at Obroski's feet.

Shortly after, the prisoners were returned to their hut; but their ankles were not bound again, nor were Obroski's wrists. While he was removing the bonds from the wrists of his fellow prisoners a woman came with food and water for them. Thereafter they were fed with reasonable regularity.

Monotonously the days dragged. Each slow, hideous night seemed an eternity to the white prisoner. He shivered in his nakedness and sought warmth by huddling close between the bodies of two of the natives. All of them were alive with vermin.

A week passed, and then one night some warriors came and took one of the black prisoners away. Obroski and the others watched through the doorway. The man disappeared around the corner of a hut near the chief's. They never saw him again.

The tom-toms commenced their slow thrumming; the voices of men rose in a weird chant; occasionally the watchers caught a glimpse of savage dancers as their steps led them from behind the corner of a hut that hid the remainder of the scene.

Suddenly a horrid scream of agony rose above the voices of the dancers. For a half hour occasional groans punctuated the savage cries of the warriors, but at last even these ceased.

"He is gone, Bwana," whispered Kwamudi.

"Yes, thank God!" muttered the white man. "What agony he must have suffered!"

The following night warriors came and took away the second black prisoner. Obroski tried to stop his ears against the sounds of the man's passing. That night he was very cold, for there was only Kwamudi to warm him on one side.

"Tomorrow night, Bwana," said the black man, "you will sleep alone."

"And the next night——?"

"There will be none, Bwana—for you."

During the cold, sleepless hours Obroski's thoughts wandered back through the past, the near past particularly. He thought of Naomi Madison, and wondered if she were grieving much over his disappearance. Something told him she was not.

Most of the other figures were pale in his thoughts—he neither liked nor disliked them; but there was one who stood out even more clearly than the memory picture of Naomi. It was Orman. His hatred of Orman rose above all his other passions—it was greater than his love for Naomi, greater than his fear of torture and death. He hugged it to his breast now and nursed it and thanked God for it, because it made him forget the lice and the cold and the things that were to happen to him on the next night or the next.

The hours dragged on; day came and went, and night came again. Obroski and Kwamudi, watching, saw warriors approaching the hut.

"They come, Bwana," said the black man. "Good-bye!"

But this time they took them both. They took them to the open space before the hut of Rungula, chief of the Bansutos, and tied them flat against the boles of two trees, facing one another.

Here Obroski watched them work upon Kwamudi. He saw tortures so fiendish, so horrible, so obscene that he feared for his reason, thinking that these visions must be the figments of a mad brain. He tried to look away, but the horror of it fascinated him. And so he saw Kwamudi die.

Afterward he saw even more disgusting sights, sights that nauseated him. He wondered when they would commence on him, and prayed that it would be soon and soon over. He tried to steel himself against fear, but he knew that he was afraid. By every means within the power of his will he sought to bolster a determination not to give them the satisfaction of knowing that he suffered when his turn came; for he had seen that they gloated over the agonies of Kwamudi.

It was almost morning when they removed the thongs that bound him to the tree and led him back to the hut. Then it became evident that they were not going to kill him—this night. It meant that his agony was to be prolonged.

In the cold of the coming dawn he huddled alone on the filthy floor of his prison, sleepless and shivering; and the lice swarmed over his body unmolested. He had plumbed the nadir of misery and hopelessness and found there a dull apathy that preserved his reason.

Finally he slept, nor did he awaken until midafternoon. He was warm then; and new life seemed to course through his veins, bringing new hope. Now he commenced to plan. He would not die as the others had died, like sheep led to the slaughter. The longer he considered his plan the more anxious he became to put it into execution, awaiting impatiently those who were to lead him to torture.

His plan did not include escape; for that he was sure was impossible, but it did include a certain measure of revenge and death without torture. Obroski's reason was tottering.

When he saw the warriors coming to get him he came out of the hut and met them, a smile upon his lips.

Then they led him away as they had led the three natives before him.

11

The Last Victim

TARZAN of the Apes was ranging a district that was new to him, and with the keen alertness of the wild creature he was alive to all that was strange or unusual. Upon the range of his knowledge depended his ability to cope with the emergencies of an unaccustomed environment. Nothing was so trivial that it did not require investigation; and already, in certain matters concerning the haunts and habits of game both large and small, he knew quite as much if not more than many creatures that had been born here.

For three nights he had heard the almost continuous booming of tom-toms, faintly from afar; and during the day following the third night he had drifted slowly in his hunting in the direction from which the sounds had come.

He had seen something of the natives who inhabited this region. He had witnessed their methods of warfare against the whites who had invaded their territory. His sympathies had been neither with one side nor the other. He had seen Orman, drunk, lashing his black porters; and he had felt that whatever misfortunes overtook him he deserved them.

Tarzan did not know these Tarmangani; and so they were even less to him than the other beasts that they would have described as lower orders but which Tarzan, who knew all orders well, considered their superiors in many aspects of heart and mind.

Some passing whim, some slight incitement, might have caused him to befriend them actively, as he had often befriended Numa and Sabor and Sheeta, who were by nature his hereditary enemies. But no such whim had seized him, no such incitement had occurred; and he had seen them go upon their way and had scarcely given them a thought since the last night that he had entered their camp.

He had heard the fusillade of shots that had followed the

attack of the Bansutos upon the safari; but he had been far
away, and as he had already witnessed similar attacks during
the preceding days his curiosity was not aroused; and he had
not investigated.

The doings of the Bansutos interested him far more. The
Tarmangani would soon be gone—either dead or departed—
but the Gomangani would be here always; and he must know
much about them if he were to remain in their country.

Lazily he swung through the trees in the direction of their
village. He was alone now; for the great golden lion, Jad-
bal-ja, was hunting elsewhere, hunting trouble, Tarzan thought
with a half smile as he recalled the sleek young lioness that
the great beast had followed off into the forest fastness.

It was dark before the ape-man reached the village of
Rungula. The rhythm of the tom-toms blended with a low,
mournful chant. A few warriors were dancing listlessly—a
tentative excursion into the borderland of savage ecstacy into
which they would later hurl themselves as their numbers increased with the increasing tempo of the dance.

Tarzan watched from the concealment of the foliage of a
tree at the edge of the clearing that encircled the village. He
was not greatly interested; the savage orgies of the blacks
were an old story to him. Apparently there was nothing
here to hold his attention, and he was about to turn away
when his eyes were attracted to the figure of a man who
contrasted strangely with the savage black warriors of the
village.

He was entering the open space where the dancers were
holding forth—a tall, bronzed, almost naked white man
surrounded by a group of warriors. He was evidently a
prisoner.

The ape-man's curiosity was aroused. Silently he dropped
to the ground, and keeping in the dense shadows of the
forest well out of the moonlight he circled to the back of the
village. Here there was no life, the interest of the villagers
being centered upon the activities near the chief's hut.

Cautiously but quickly Tarzan crossed the strip of moonlit
ground between the forest and the palisade. The latter was
built of poles sunk into the ground close together and lashed
with pliant creepers. It was about ten feet high.

A few quick steps, a running jump, and Tarzan's fingers
closed upon the top of the barrier. Drawing himself cautiously up, he looked over into the village. In silence he
listened, sniffing the air. Satisfied, he threw a leg over the

top of the palisade, and a moment later dropped lightly to the ground inside the village of Rungula, the Bansuto.

When the ground had been cleared for the village a number of trees had been left standing within the palisade to afford shelter from the equatorial sun. One of these overhung Rungula's hut, as Tarzan had noticed from the forest; and it was this tree that he chose from which to examine the white prisoner more closely.

Keeping well in the rear of the chief's hut and moving cautiously from the shadow of one hut to that of the next, the ape-man approached his goal. Had he moved noisily the sound of his coming would have been drowned by the tom-toms and the singing; but he moved without sound, as was second nature to him.

The chance of discovery lay in the possibility that some native might not have yet left his hut to join the throng around the dancers and that such a belated one would see the strange white giant and raise an alarm. But Tarzan came to the rear of Rungula's hut unseen.

Here fortune again favored him; for while the stem of the tree he wished to enter stood in front of the hut in plain view of the entire tribe, another, smaller tree grew at the rear of the hut, and, above it, mingled its branches with its fellow.

As the ape-man moved stealthily into the trees and out upon a great branch that would hold his weight without bending, the savage scene below unfolded itself before him. The tempo of the dance had increased. Painted warriors were leaping and stamping around a small group that surrounded the prisoner, and as Tarzan's gaze fell upon the man he experienced something in the nature of a shock. It was as though his disembodied spirit hovered above and looked down upon himself, so startling was the likeness of this man to the Lord of the Jungle.

In stature, in coloring, even in the molding of his features he was a replica of Tarzan of the Apes; and Tarzan realized it instantly although it is not always that we can see our own likeness in another even when it exists.

Now indeed was the ape-man's interest aroused. He wondered who the man was and where he had come from. By the merest accident of chance he had not seen him when he had visited the camp of the picture company, and so he did not connect him with these people. His failure to do so might have been still further explained by the man's nakedness. The clothing that had been stripped from him might, had he still worn it, have served to place him definitely; but his nakedness gave him only fellowship with the beasts. Perhaps that is why Tarzan was inclined to be favorably impressed with him at first sight.

Obroski, unconscious that other eyes than those of black enemies were upon him, gazed from sullen eyes upon the scene around him. Here, at the hands of these people, his three fellow prisoners had met hideous torture and death; but Obroski was in no mind to follow docilely in their footsteps. He had a plan.

He expected to die. He could find no slenderest hope for any other outcome, but he did not intend to submit supinely to torture. He had a plan.

Rungula squatted upon a stool eyeing the scene from bloodshot eyes beneath scowling brows. Presently he shouted directions to the warriors guarding Obroski, and they led him toward the tree on the opposite side of the open space. With thongs they prepared to bind him to the bole of the tree, and then it was that the prisoner put his plan into action; the plan of a fear-maddened brain.

Seizing the warrior nearest him he raised the man above his head as though he had been but a little child and hurled him into the faces of the others, knocking several of them to the ground. He sprang forward and laid hold upon a dancing buck, and him he flung to earth so heavily that he lay still as though dead.

So sudden, so unexpected had been his attack that it left the Bansutos momentarily stunned; then Rungula leaped to his feet. "Seize him!" he cried. "But do not harm him." Rungula wished the mighty stranger to die after a manner of Rungula's own choosing, not the swift death that Obroski had hoped to win by his single-handed attack upon a thousand armed warriors.

As they closed upon him, Obroski felled them to right and left with mighty blows rendered even more terrific by the fear-maddened brain that directed them. Terror had driven him berserk.

The cries of the warriors, the screams of the women and children formed a horried cacophony in his ears that incited him to madder outbursts of fury. The arms that reached out to seize him he seized and broke like pipe stems.

He wanted to scream and curse, yet he fought in silence. He wanted to cry out against the terror that engulfed him, but he made no sound. And so, in terror, he fought a thousand men.

But this one-sided battle could not go on for long. Slowly, by force of numbers, they closed upon him; they seized his ankles and his legs. With heavy fists he struck men unconscious with a single blow; but at last they dragged him down.

And then——

12
The Map

"WEYLEY!" sighed Eyad, dolorously. "Me-thinks the sheykh hath done wrong to bring these *benat* with us. Now will the *Nasara* follow us with many guns; they will never cease until they have destroyed us and taken the *benat* back for themselves—I know *el-Engleys*."

"*Ullah yelbisak berneta!*" scoffed Atewy.

"Thou foundest the map; was not that enough? They would not have followed and killed us for the map, but when you take away men's women they follow and kill—yes! be they Arab, English, or Negro." Eyad spat a period.

"I will tell thee, fool, why we brought the two girls," said Atewy. "There may be no valley of diamonds, or we may not find it. Should we therefore, after much effort, return to our own country empty-handed? These girls are not ill-favored. They will bring money at several places of which I know, or it may be that the mad *Nasara* will pay a large ransom for their return. But in the end we shall profit if they be not harmed by us; which reminds me, Eyad, that I have seen thee cast evil eyes upon them. *Wellah!* If one harms them the sheykh will kill him; and if the sheykh doth not, I will."

"They will bring us nothing but trouble," insisted Eyad. "I wish that we were rid of them."

"And there is still another reason why we brought them," continued Atewy. "The map is written in the language of *el-Engleys*, which I can speak but cannot read; the *benat* will read it to me. Thus it is well to keep them."

But still Eyad grumbled. He was a dour young *Bedauwy* with sinister eyes and a too full lower lip. Also, he did not speak what was in his thoughts; for the truth was not in him.

Since very early in the morning the horsemen had been pushing northward with the two girls. They had found and followed an open trail, and so had suffered no delays. Near the center of the little column rode the prisoners, often side by side; for much of the way the trail had been wide. It had been a trying day for them, not alone because of the fatigue of the hard ride, but from the nervous shock that the whole misadventure had entailed since Atewy and two others had crept into their tent scarcely more than an hour after midnight, silenced them with threats of death, and, after ransacking the tent, carried them away into the night.

All day long they had waited expectantly for signs of rescue, though realizing that they were awaiting the impossible. Men on foot could not have overtaken the horsemen, and no motor could traverse the trail they had followed without long delays for clearing trail in many places.

"I can't stand much more," said Naomi. "I'm about through."

Rhonda reined closer to her. "If you feel like falling, take hold of me," she said. "It can't last much longer today. They'll be making camp soon. It sure has been a tough ride—not much like following Ernie Vogt up Coldwater Canyon; and I used to come home from one of those rides and think I'd done something. Whew! They must have paved this saddle with bricks."

"I don't see how you can stay so cheerful."

"Cheerful! I'm about as cheerful as a Baby Star whose option hasn't been renewed."

"Do you think they're going to kill us, Rhonda?"

"They wouldn't have bothered to bring us all this way to kill us. They're probably after a ransom."

"I hope you're right. Tom'll pay 'em anything to get us back. But suppose they're going to sell us! I've heard that they sell white girls to black sultans in Africa."

"The black sultan that gets me is goin' to be out of luck."

The sun was low in the west when the Arabs made camp that night. Sheykh Ab el-Ghrennem had no doubt but that angry and determined men were pursuing him, but he felt quite certain that now they could not overtake him.

His first thought had been to put distance between himself and the *Nasara* he had betrayed—now he could look into the matter of the map of which Atewy had told him, possession of which had been the principal incentive of his knavery.

Supper over, he squatted where the light of the fire fell

upon the precious document; and Atewy leaning over his shoulder scanned it with him.

"I can make nothing of it," growled the sheykh. "Fetch the *bint* from whom you took it."

"I shall have to fetch them both," replied Atewy, "since I cannot tell them apart."

"Fetch them both then," commanded el-Ghrennem; and while he waited he puffed meditatively upon his *nargily*, thinking of a valley filled with diamonds and of the many riding camels and mares that they would buy; so that he was in a mellow humor when Atewy returned with the prisoners.

Rhonda walked with her chin up and the glint of battle in her eye, but Naomi revealed her fear in her white face and trembling limbs.

Sheykh Ab el-Ghrennem looked at her and smiled. *"Ma aleyk,"* he said in what were meant to be reassuring tones.

"He says," interpreted Atewy, "that thou hast nothing to fear—that there shall no evil befall thee."

"You tell him," replied Rhonda, "that it will be just too bad for him if any evil does befall us and that if he wants to save his skin he had better return us to our people *pronto*."

"The *Bedauwy* are not afraid of your people," replied Atewy, "but if you do what the sheykh asks no harm will come to you."

"What does he want?" demanded Rhonda.

"He wishes you to help us find the valley of diamonds," replied Atewy.

"What valley of diamonds?"

"It is on this map which we cannot read because we cannot read the language of *el-Engleys*." He pointed at the map the sheykh was holding.

Rhonda glanced at the paper and broke into laughter. "You don't mean to tell me that you dumb bunnies kidnapped us because you believe that there *is* a valley of diamonds! Why, that's just a prop map."

"Dumb bunnies! Prop! I do not understand."

"I am trying to tell you that that map doesn't mean a thing. It was just for use in the picture we are making. You might as well return us to our people, for there isn't any valley of diamonds."

Atewy and the sheykh jabbered excitedly to one another for a few moments, and then the former turned again to the girl. "You cannot make fools of the *Bedauwy*," he said. "We are smarter than you. We knew that you would say that there is no valley of diamonds, because you want to save it all for your father. If you know what is well for you, you will read this map for us and help us find the valley. Otherwise—" he scowled horridly and drew a forefinger across his throat.

Naomi shuddered; but Rhonda was not impressed—she knew that while they had ransom or sale value the Arabs would not destroy them except as a last resort for self-protection.

"You are not going to kill us, Atewy," she said, "even if I do not read the map to you; but there is no reason why I should not read it. I am perfectly willing to; only don't blame us if there is no valley of diamonds."

"Come here and sit beside Ab el-Ghrennem and read the map to us," ordered Atewy.

Rhonda kneeled beside the sheykh and looked over his shoulder at the yellowed, timeworn map. With a slender finger she pointed at the top of the map. "This is north," she said, "and up here—this is the valley of diamonds. You see this little irregular thing directly west of the valley and close to it? It has an arrow pointing to it and a caption that says, *'Monolithic column: Red granite outcropping near only opening into valley.'* And right north of it this arrow points to *'Entrance to valley.'*

"Now here, at the south end of the valley, is the word *'Falls'* and below the falls a river that runs south and then southwest."

"Ask her what this is," the sheykh instructed Atewy, pointing to characters at the eastern edge of the map southeast of the falls.

"That says *'Cannibal village,'*" explained the girl. "And all across the map down there it says, *'Forest!'* See this river that rises at the southeast edge of the valley, flows east, southeast, and then west in a big loop before it enters the *'Big river'* here. Inside this loop it says, *'Open country,'* and near the west end of the loop is a *'Barren, cone-shaped hill —volcanic.'* Then here is another river that rises in the southeast part of the map and flows northwest, emptying into the second river just before the latter joins the big river."

Sheykh Ab el-Ghrennem ran his fingers through his beard as he sat in thoughtful contemplation of the map. At last he placed a finger on the falls.

"*Shuf*, Atewy!" he exclaimed. "This should be the Omwamwi Falls, and over here the village of the Bansuto. We are here." He pointed at a spot near the junction of the second and third rivers. "Tomorrow we should cross this other river and come into open country. There we shall find a barren hill."

"*Billah!*" exclaimed Atewy. "If we do we shall soon be in the valley of diamonds, for the rest of the way is plain."

"What did the sheik say?" asked Rhonda.

Atewy told her, adding, "We shall all be very rich; then I shall buy you from the sheykh and take you back to my *ashirat.*"

"You and who else?" scoffed Rhonda.

"*Billah!* No one else. I shall buy you for myself alone."

"*Caveat emptor,*" advised the girl.

"I do not understand, *bint,*" said Atewy.

"You will if you ever buy *me.* And when you call me *bint,* smile. It doesn't sound like a nice word."

Atewy grinned. He translated what she had said to the sheykh, and they both laughed. "The *Narrawia* would be good to have in the *beyt* of Ab el-Ghrennem," said the sheykh, who had understood nothing of what Atewy had said to Rhonda. "When we are through with this expedition, I think that I shall keep them both; for I shall be so rich that I shall not have to sell them. This one will amuse me; she hath a quick tongue that is like *aud* in tasteless food."

Atewy was not pleased. He wanted Rhonda for himself; and he was determined to have her, sheykh or no sheykh. It was then that plans commenced to formulate in the mind of Atewy that would have caused Sheykh Ab el-Ghrennem's blood pressure to rise had he known of them.

The Arabs spread blankets on the ground near the fire for the two girls; and the sentry who watched the camp was posted near, that they might have no opportunity to escape.

"We've got to get away from these highbinders, Naomi," said Rhonda as the girls lay close together beneath their blankets. "When they find out that the valley of diamonds isn't just around the corner, they're going to be sore. The poor saps really believe that that map is genuine—they expect to find that barren, volcanic hill tomorrow. When they don't find it tomorrow, nor next week nor next, they'll just naturally sell us 'down river'; and by that time we'll be so far from the outfit that we won't have a Chinaman's chance ever to find it."

"You mean to go out alone into this forest at night!" whispered Naomi, aghast. "Think of the lions!"

"I am thinking of them; but I'm thinking of some fat,

greasy, black sultan too. I'd rather take a chance with the lion —he'd be sporting at least."

"It's all so horrible! Oh, why did I ever leave Hollywood!"

"D'you know it's a funny thing, Naomi, that a woman has to fear her own kind more than she does the beasts of the jungle. It sort o' makes one wonder if there isn't something wrong somewhere—it's hard to believe that a divine intelligence would create something in His own image that was more brutal and cruel and corrupt than anything else that He created. It kind of explains why some of the ancients worshipped snakes and bulls and birds. I guess they had more sense than we have."

At the edge of the camp Atewy squatted beside Eyad. "You would like one of the white *benat*, Eyad," whispered Atewy. "I have seen it in your eyes."

Eyad eyed the other through narrowed lids. "Who would not?" he demanded. "Am I not a man?"

"But you will not get one, for the sheykh is going to keep them both. You will not get one—unless——"

"Unless what?" inquired Eyad.

"Unless an accident should befall Ab el-Ghrennem. Nor will you get so many diamonds, for the sheykh's share of the booty is one fourth. If there were no sheykh we should divide more between us."

"Thou art *hatab lil nar*," ejaculated Eyad.

"Perhaps I *am* fuel for hell-fire," admitted Atewy, "but I shall burn hot while I burn."

"What dost *thou* get out of it?" inquired Eyad after a short silence.

Atewy breathed an inaudible sigh of relief. Eyad was coming around! "The same as thou," he replied, "my full share of the diamonds and one of the *benat*."

"Accidents befall sheykhs even as they befall other men," philosophized Eyad as he rolled himself in his blanket and prepared to sleep.

Quiet fell upon the camp of the Arabs. A single sentry squatted by the fire, half dozing. The other Arabs slept.

Not Rhonda Terry. She lay listening to the diminishing sounds of the camp, she heard the breathing of sleeping men, she watched the sentry, whose back was toward her.

She placed her lips close to one of Naomi Madison's beautiful ears. "Listen!" she whispered, "but don't move nor make a sound. When I get up, follow me. That is all you have to do. Don't make any noise."

"What are you going to do?" The Madison's voice was quavering.

"Shut up, and do as I tell you."

Rhonda Terry had been planning ahead. Mentally she had rehearsed every smallest piece of business in the drama that was to be enacted. There were no lines—at least she hoped there would be none. If there were the tag might be very different from that which she hoped for.

She reached out and grasped a short, stout piece of wood that had been gathered for the fire. Slowly, stealthily, catlike, she drew herself from her blankets. Trembling, Naomi Madison followed her.

Rhonda rose, the piece of firewood in her hand. She crept toward the back of the unsuspecting sentry. She lifted the stick above the head of the Arab. She swung it far back, and then——

13
A Ghost

ORMAN and Bill West tramped on through the interminable forest. Day after day they followed the plain trail of the horsemen, but then there came a day that they lost it. Neither was an experienced tracker. The trail had entered a small stream, but it had not emerged again directly upon the opposite bank.

Assuming that the Arabs had ridden in the stream bed for some distance either up or down before coming out on the other side, they had crossed and searched up and down the little river but without success. It did not occur to either of them that their quarry had come out upon the same side that they had entered, and so they did not search upon that side at all. Perhaps it was only natural that they should assume that when one entered a river it was for the purpose of crossing it.

The meager food supply that they had brought from camp was exhausted, and they had had little luck in finding game. A few monkeys and some rodents had fallen to their rifles, temporarily averting starvation; but the future looked none too bright. Eleven days had passed, and they had accomplished nothing.

"And the worst of this mess," said Orman, "is that we're lost. We've wandered so far from that stream where we lost the trail that we can't find our back track."

"I don't want to find any back track," said West. "Until I find Rhonda I'll never turn back."

"I'm afraid we're too late to do 'em much good now, Bill."

"We could take a few pot shots at those lousy Arabs."

"Yes, I'd like to do that; but I got to think of the rest of the company. I got to get 'em out of this country. I thought we'd overtake el-Ghrennem the first day and be back in camp the next. I've sure made a mess of everything. Those two cases of Scotch will have cost close to a million dollars and God knows how many lives before any of the company sees Hollywood again.

"Think of it, Bill—Major White, Noice, Baine, Obroski, and seven others killed, to say nothing of the Arabs and blacks—and the girls gone. Sometimes I think I'll go nuts just thinking about them."

West said nothing. He had been thinking about it a great deal, and thinking too of the day when Orman must face the wives and sweethearts of those men back in Hollywood. No matter what Orman's responsibility, West pitied him.

When Orman spoke again it was as though he had read the other's mind. "If it wasn't so damn yellow," he said, "I'd bump myself off; it would be a lot easier than what I've got before me back home."

As the two men talked they were walking slowly along a game trail that wandered out of one unknown into another. For long they had realized that they were hopelessly lost.

"I don't know why we keep on," remarked West. "We don't know where we're headed."

"We won't find out by sitting down, and maybe we'll find something or some one if we keep going long enough."

West glanced suddenly behind him. "I thought so," he said in a low tone. "I thought I'd been hearing something."

Orman's gaze followed that of his companion. "Anyway we got a good reason now for not sitting down or turning back," he said.

"He's been following us for a long time," observed West. "I heard him quite a way back, now that I think of it."

"I hope we're not detaining him."

"Why do you suppose he's following us?" asked West.

"Perhaps he's lonesome."

"Or hungry."

"Now that you mention it, he does look hungry," agreed Orman.

"This is a nasty place to be caught too. The trail's so narrow and with this thick undergrowth on both sides we couldn't get out of the way of a charge. And right here the trees are all too big to climb."

"We might shoot him," suggested Orman, "but I'm leary of these rifles. White said they were a little too light to stop big game, and if we don't stop him it'll be curtains for one of us."

"I'm a bum shot," admitted West. "I probably wouldn't even hit him."

"Well, he isn't coming any closer. Let's keep on going and see what happens."

The men continued along the trail, continually casting glances rearward. They held their rifles in readiness. Often, turns in the trail hid from their view momentarily the grim stalker following in their tracks.

"They look different out here, don't they?" remarked West. "Fiercer and sort of—inevitable, if you know what I mean— like death and taxes."

"Especially death. And they take all the wind out of a superiority complex. Sometimes when I've been directing I've thought that trainers were a nuisance, but I'd sure like to see Charlie Gay step out of the underbrush and say, 'Down, Slats!' "

"Say, do you know this fellow looks something like Slats —got the same mean eye?"

As they talked, the trail debouched into a small opening where there was little underbrush and the trees grew farther apart. They had advanced only a short distance into it when the stalking beast dogging their footsteps rounded the last turn in the trail and entered the clearing.

He paused a moment in the mouth of the trail, his tail twitching, his great jowls dripping saliva. With lowered head he surveyed them from yellow-green eyes, menacingly. Then he crouched and crept toward them.

"We've got to shoot, Bill," said Orman; "he's going to charge."

The director shot first, his bullet creasing the lion's scalp. West fired and missed. With a roar, the carnivore charged. The empty shell jammed in the breech of West's rifle. Orman fired again when the lion was but a few paces from him; then he clubbed his rifle as the beast rose to seize him. A great paw sent the rifle hurtling aside, spinning Orman dizzily after it.

West stood paralyzed, his useless weapon clutched in his hands. He saw the lion wheel to spring upon Orman; then he saw something that left him stunned, aghast. He saw an almost naked man drop from the tree above them full upon the lion's back.

A great arm encircled the beast's neck as it reared and turned to rend this new assailant. Bronzed legs locked quickly beneath its belly. A knife flashed as great muscles drove the blade into the carnivore's side again and again. The lion hurled itself from side to side as it sought to shake the man from it. Its mighty roars thundered in the quiet glade, shaking the earth.

Orman, uninjured, had scrambled to his feet. Both men, spellbound, were watching this primitive battle of Titans. They heard the roars of the man mingle with those of the lion, and they felt their flesh creep.

Presently the lion leaped high in air, and when he crashed to earth he did not rise again. The man upon him leaped to his feet. For an instant he surveyed the carcass; then he placed a foot upon it, and raising his face toward the sky voiced a weird cry that sent cold shivers down the spines of the two Americans.

As the last notes of that inhuman scream reverberated through the forest, the stranger, without a glance at the two he had saved, leaped for an overhanging branch, drew himself up into the tree, and disappeared amidst the foliage above.

Orman, pale beneath his tan, turned toward West. "Did you see what I saw, Bill?" he asked, his voice shaking.

"I don't know what you saw, but I know what I *thought* I saw—but I *couldn't* have seen it."

"Do you believe in ghosts, Bill?"

"I—I don't know—you don't think?"

"You know as well as I do that that couldn't have been him; so it must have been his ghost."

"But we never knew for sure that Obroski was dead, Tom."

"We know it now."

14

A Madman

As STANLEY OBROSKI was dragged to earth in the village of Rungula, the Bansuto, a white man, naked but for a G string, looked down from the foliage of an overhanging tree upon the scene below and upon the bulk of the giant chieftain standing beneath him.

The pliant strands of a strong rope braided from jungle grasses swung in his powerful hands, the shadow of a grim smile played about his mouth.

Suddenly the rope shot downward; a running noose in its lower end settled about Rungula's body, pinning his arms at his sides. A cry of surprise and terror burst from the chief's lips as he felt himself pinioned; and as those near him turned, attracted by his cry, they saw him raised quickly from the ground to disappear in the foliage of the tree above as though hoisted by some supernatural power.

Rungula felt himself dragged to a sturdy branch, and then a mighty hand seized and steadied him. He was terrified, for he thought his end had come. Below him a terrified silence had fallen upon the village. Even the prisoner was forgotten in the excitement and fright that followed the mysterious disappearance of the chief.

Obroski stood looking about him in amazement. Surrounded by struggling warriors as he had been he had not seen the miracle of Rungula's ascension. Now he saw every eye turned upward at the tree that towered above the chief's hut. He wondered what had happened. He wondered what they were looking at. He could see nothing unusual. All that lingered in his memory to give him a clew was the sudden, affrighted cry of Rungula as the noose had tightened about him.

Rungula heard a voice speaking, speaking his own language. "Look at me!" it commanded.

Rungula turned his eyes toward the thing that held him. The light from the village fires filtered through the foliage to dimly reveal the features of a white man bending above him. Rungula gasped and shrank back. *"Walumbe!"* he muttered in terror.

"I am not the god of death," replied Tarzan; "I am not Walumbe. But I can bring death just as quickly, for I am greater than Walumbe. I am Tarzan of the Apes!"

"What do you want?" asked Rungula through chattering teeth. "What are you going to do to me?"

"I tested you to see if you were a good man and your people good people. I made myself into two men, and one I sent where your warriors could capture him. I wanted to see what you would do to a stranger who had not harmed you. Now I know. For what you have done you should die. What have you to say?"

"You are here," said Rungula, "and you are also down there." He nodded toward the figure of Obroski standing in surprised silence amidst the warriors. "Therefore you must be a demon. What can I say to a demon? I can give you food and drink and weapons. I can give you girls who can cook and draw water and fetch wood and work all day in the fields—girls with broad hips and strong backs. All these things will I give you if you will not kill me—if you just go away and leave us alone."

"I do not want your food nor your weapons nor your women. I want but one thing from you, Rungula, as the price of your life."

"What is that, Master?"

"Your promise that you will never again make war upon white men, and that when they come through your country you will help them instead of killing them."

"I promise, Master."

"Then call down to your people, and tell them to open the gates and let the prisoner go out into the forest."

Rungula spoke in a loud voice to his people, and they fell away from Obroski, leaving him standing alone; then warriors went to the village gates and swung them open.

Obroski heard the voice of the chief coming from high in a tree, and he was mystified. He also wondered at the strange action of the natives and suspected treachery. Why should they fall back and leave him standing alone when a few moments before they were trying to seize him and bind him to a tree? Why should they throw the gates wide open? He did not move. He waited, believing that he was being baited into an attempt at escape for some ulterior purpose.

Presently another voice came from the tree above the chief's hut, addressing him in English. "Go out of the village into the forest," it said. "They will not harm you now. I will join you in the forest."

Obroski was mystified; but the quiet English voice reassured him, and he turned and walked down the village street toward the gateway.

Tarzan removed the rope from about Rungula, ran lightly through the tree to the rear of the hut and dropped to the ground. Keeping the huts between himself and the villagers, he moved swiftly to the opposite end of the village, scaled the palisade, and dropped into the clearing beyond. A moment later he was in the forest and circling back toward the point where Obroski was entering it.

The latter heard no slightest noise of his approach, for there was none. One instant he was entirely alone, and the next a voice spoke close behind him. "Follow me," it said.

Obroski wheeled. In the darkness of the forest night he saw dimly only the figure of a man about his own height. "Who are you?" he asked.

"I am Tarzan of the Apes."

Obroski was silent, astonished. He had heard of Tarzan of the Apes, but he had thought that it was no more than a legendary character—a fiction of the folklore of Africa. He wondered if this were some demented creature who imagined that it was Tarzan of the Apes. He wished that he could see the fellow's face; that might give him a clew to the sanity of the man. He wondered what the stranger's intentions might be.

Tarzan of the Apes was moving away into the forest. He turned once and repeated his command, "Follow me!"

"I haven't thanked you yet for getting me out of that mess," said Obroski as he moved after the retreating figure of the stranger. "It was certainly decent of you. I'd have been dead by now if it hadn't been for you."

The ape-man moved on in silence, and Obroski followed him. The silence preyed a little upon his nerves. It seemed to bear out his deduction that the man was not quite normal, not as other men. A normal man would have been asking and answering innumerable questions had he met a stranger for the first time under such exciting circumstances.

And Obroski's deductions were not wholly inaccurate— Tarzan is not as other men; the training and the instincts of the wild beast have given him standards of behavior and a code of ethics peculiarly his own. For Tarzan there are times for silence and times for speech. The depths of the

night, when hunting beasts are abroad, is no time to go gab-
bling through the jungle; nor did he ever care much for speech
with strangers unless he could watch their eyes and the
changing expressions upon their faces, which often told him
more than their words were intended to convey.

So in silence they moved through the forest, Obroski keeping close behind the ape-man lest he lose sight of him in the
darkness. Ahead of them a lion roared; and the American
wondered if his companion would change his course or take
refuge in a tree, but he did neither. He kept on in the direction they had been going.

Occasionally the voice of the lion sounded ahead of them,
always closer. Obroski, unarmed and practically naked, felt
utterly helpless and, not unaccountably, nervous. Nor was
his nervousness allayed when a cry, half roar and half weird
scream, burst from the throat of his companion.

After that he heard nothing from the lion for some time;
then, seemingly just ahead of them, he heard throaty, coughing grunts. The lion! Obroski could scarcely restrain a violent
urge to scale a tree, but he steeled himself and kept on after
his guide.

Presently they came to an opening in the forest beside a
river. The moon had risen. Its mellow light flooded the scene,
casting deep shadows where tree and shrub dotted the grass
carpeted clearing, dancing on the swirling ripples of the river.

But the beauty of the scene held his eye for but a brief
instant as though through the shutter of a camera; then it
was erased from his consciousness by a figure looming
large ahead of them in the full light of the African moon. A
great lion stood in the open watching them as they approached. Obroski saw the black mane ripple in the night
wind, the sheen of the yellow body in the moonlight. Now,
beyond him, rose a lioness. She growled.

The stranger turned to Obroski. "Stay where you are," he
said. "I do not know this Sabor; she may be vicious."

Obroski stopped, gladly. He was relieved to discover that he
had stopped near a tree. He wished that he had a rifle, so that
he might save the life of the madman walking uncon-
cernedly toward his doom.

Now he heard the voice of the man who called himself
Tarzan of the Apes, but he understood no word that the man
spoke: *"Tarmangani yo. Jad-bal-ja tand bundolo. Savor tand
bundolo."*

The madman was talking to the great lion! Obroski trembled for him as he saw him drawing nearer and nearer to the beast.

The lioness rose and slunk forward. *"Kreeg-ah Sabor!"* exclaimed the man.

The lion turned and rushed upon the lioness, snarling; she crouched and leaped away. He stood over her growling for a moment; then he turned and walked forward to meet the man. Obroski's heart stood still.

He saw the man lay a hand upon the head of the huge carnivore and then turn and look back at him. "You may come up now," he said, "that Jad-bal-ja may get your scent and know that you are a friend. Afterward he will never harm you—unless I tell him to."

Obroski was terrified. He wanted to run, to climb the tree beside which he stood, to do anything that would get him away from the lion and the lioness; but he feared still more to leave the man who had befriended him. Paralyzed by fright, he advanced; and Tarzan of the Apes, believing him courageous, was pleased.

Jad-bal-ja was growling in his throat. Tarzan spoke to him in a low voice, and he stopped. Obroski came and stood close to him, and the lion sniffed at his legs and body. Obroski felt the hot breath of the flesh eater on his skin.

"Put your hand on his head," said Tarzan. "If you are afraid do not show it."

The American did as he was bid. Presently Jad-bal-ja rubbed his head against the body of the man; then Tarzan spoke again, and the lion turned and walked away toward the lioness, lying down beside her.

Now, for the first time, Obroski looked at his strange companion under the light of the full moon. He voiced an exclaimation of amazement—he might have been looking into a mirror.

Tarzan smiled—one of his rare smiles. "Remarkable, isn't it?" he said.

"It's uncanny," replied Obroski.

"I think that is why I saved you from the Bansutos—it was too much like seeing myself killed."

"I'm sure you would have saved me anyway."

The ape-man shrugged. "Why should I have? I did not know you."

Tarzan stretched his body upon the soft grasses. "We shall lie up here for the night," he said.

Obroski shot a quick glance in the direction of the two lions lying a few yards away, and Tarzan interpreted his thoughts.

"Don't worry about them," he said. "Jad-bal-ja will see that nothing harms you, but look out for the lioness when he is not around. He just picked her up the other day. She hasn't made friends with me yet, and she probably never will. Now, if you care to, tell me what you are doing in this country."

Briefly Obroski explained, and Tarzan listened until he had finished.

"If I had known you were one of that safari I probably would have let the Bansutos kill you."

"Why? What have you got against us?"

"I saw your leader whipping his blacks," replied Tarzan.

Obroski was silent for a time. He had come to realize that this man who called himself Tarzan of the Apes was a most remarkable man, and that his power for good or evil in this savage country might easily be considerable. He would be a good friend to have, and his enmity might prove fatal. He could ruin their chances of making a successful picture— he could ruin Orman.

Obroski did not like Orman. He had good reasons not to like him. Naomi Madison was one of these reasons. But there were other things to consider than a personal grudge. There was the money invested by the studio, the careers of his fellow players, and even Orman—Orman was a great director.

He explained all this to Tarzan—all except his hatred of Orman. "Orman," he concluded, "was drunk when he whipped the blacks, he had been down with fever, he was terribly worried. Those who knew him best said it was most unlike him."

Tarzan made no comment, and Obroski said no more. He lay looking up at the great full moon, thinking. He thought of Naomi and wondered. What was there about her that he loved? She was petty, inconsiderate, arrogant, spoiled. Her character could not compare with that of Rhonda Terry, for instance; and Rhonda was fully as beautiful.

At last he decided that it was the glamour of the Madison's name and fame that had attracted him—stripped of these, there was little about her to inspire anything greater than an infatuation such as a man might feel for any beautiful face and perfect body.

He thought of his companions of the safari, and wondered what they would think if they could see him now lying down to sleep with a wild man and two savage African lions. Smiling, he dozed and fell asleep. He did not see the lioness rise and cross the clearing with Jad-bal-ja pacing majestically behind her as they set forth upon the grim business of the hunt.

15

Terror

As RHONDA TERRY stood with her weapon poised above the head of the squatting sentry, the man turned his eyes quickly in her direction. Instantly he realized his danger and started to rise as the stick descended; thus the blow had far more force than it otherwise would have, and he sank senseless to the ground without uttering a sound.

The girl looked quickly about upon the sleeping camp. No one stirred. She beckoned the trembling Naomi to follow her and stepped quickly to where some horse trappings lay upon the ground. She handed a saddle and bridle to the Madison and took others for herself.

Half dragging, half carrying their burdens they crept to the tethered ponies. Here, the Madison was almost helpless; and Rhonda had to saddle and bridle both animals, giving thanks for the curiosity that had prompted her days before to examine the Arab tack and learn the method of its adjustment.

Naomi mounted, and Rhonda passed the bridle reins of her own pony to her companion. "Hold him," she whispered, "and hold him tight."

She went quickly then to the other ponies, turning them loose one after another. Often she glanced toward the sleeping men. If one of them should awaken, they would be recaptured. But if she could carry out her plan they would be safe from pursuit. She felt that it was worth the risk.

Finally the last pony was loose. Already, cognizant of their freedom, some of them had commenced to move about. Herein had lain one of the principal dangers of the girl's plan, for free horses moving about a camp must quickly awaken such horsemen as the Beduins.

She ran quickly to her own pony and mounted. "We are going to try to drive them ahead of us for a little way," she whispered. "If we can do that we shall be safe—as far as Arabs are concerned."

As quietly as they could, the girls reined their ponies behind the loose stock and urged them away from camp. It seemed incredible to Rhonda that the noise did not awaken the Arabs.

The ponies had been tethered upon the north side of the camp, and so it was toward the north that they drove them. This was not the direction in which their own safari lay, but Rhonda planned to circle back around the Arabs after she had succeeded in driving off their mounts.

Slowly the unwilling ponies moved toward the black shadows of the forest beyond the little opening in which the camp had been pitched—a hundred feet, two hundred, three hundred. They were almost at the edge of the forest when a cry arose from behind them. Then the angry voices of many men came to them in a babel of strange words and stranger Arab oaths.

It was a bright, starlit night. Rhonda knew that the Arabs could see them. She turned in her saddle and saw them running swiftly in pursuit. With a cowboy yell and a kick of her heels she urged her pony onto the heels of those ahead. Startled, they broke into a trot.

"Yell, Naomi!" cried the girl. "Do anything to frighten them and make them run."

The Madison did her best, and the yells of the running men approaching added to the nervousness of the ponies. Then one of the Arabs fired his musket; and as the bullet whistled above their heads the ponies broke into a run, and, followed by the two girls, disappeared into the forest.

The leading pony had either seen or stumbled upon a trail, and down this they galloped. Every step was fraught with danger for the two fugitives. A low hanging branch or a misstep by one of their mounts would spell disaster, yet neither sought to slacken the speed. Perhaps they both felt that anything would be preferable to falling again into the hands of old Ab el-Ghrennem.

It was not until the voices of the men behind them were lost in the distance that Rhonda reined her pony to a walk. "Well, we made it!" she cried exultantly. "I'll bet old Apple Gran'ma'am is chewing his whiskers. How do you feel—tired?"

The Madison made no reply; then Rhonda heard her sobbing. "What's the matter?" she demanded. "You haven't been hurt, have you?" Her tone was worried and solicitous.

"I—I'm—so frightened. Oh, I—never was so frightened in all my life," sobbed the Madison.

"Oh, buck up, Naomi; neither was I; but weeping and wailing and gnashing our teeth won't do us any good. We got away from them, and a few hours ago that seemed impossible. Now all we have to do is ride back to the safari, and the chances are we'll meet some of the boys looking for us."

"I'll never see any of them again. I've known all along that I'd die in this awful country," and she commenced to sob again hysterically.

Rhonda reined close to her side and put an arm around her. "It *is* terrible, dear," she said; "but we'll pull through. I'll get you out of this, and some day we'll lie in the sand at Malibu again and laugh about it."

For a time neither of them spoke. The ponies moved on through the dark forest at a walk. Ahead of them the loose animals followed the trail that human eyes could not see. Occasionally one of them would pause, snorting, sensing something that the girls could neither see nor hear; then Rhonda would urge them on again, and so the long hours dragged out toward a new day.

After a long silence, Naomi spoke. "Rhonda," she said, "I don't see how you can be so decent to me. I used to treat you so rotten. I acted like a dirty little cat. I can see it now. The last few days have done something to me—opened my eyes, I guess. Don't say anything—I just want you to know—that's all."

"I understand," said Rhonda softly. "It's Hollywood—we all try to be something we're not, and most of us succeed only in being something we ought not to be."

Ahead of them the trail suddenly widened, and the loose horses came to a stop. Rhonda tried to urge them on, but they only milled about and would not advance.

"I wonder what's wrong," she said and urged her pony forward to find a river barring their path. It was not a very large river; and she decided to drive the ponies into it, but they would not go.

"What are we to do?" asked Naomi.

"We can't stay here," replied Rhonda. "We've got to keep on going for a while. If we turn back now we'll run into the sheiks."

"But we can't cross this river."

"I don't know about that. There must be a ford here—this trail runs right to the river, right into it. You can see how it's worn down the bank right into the water. I'm going to try it."

"Oh, Rhonda, we'll drown!"

"They say it's an easy death. Come on!" She urged her pony down the bank into the water. "I hate to leave these other ponies," she said. "The sheiks'll find them and follow us, but if we can't drive them across there's nothing else to be done."

Her pony balked a little at the edge of the water, but at last he stepped in, snorting. "Keep close to me, Naomi. I have an idea two horses will cross better together than one alone. If we get into deep water try to keep your horse's head pointed toward the opposite bank."

Gingerly the two ponies waded out into the stream. It was neither deep nor swift, and they soon gained confidence. On the bank behind them the other ponies gathered, nickering to their companions.

As they approached the opposite shore Ronda heard a splashing in the water behind her. Turning her head, she saw the loose ponies following them across; and she laughed. "Now I've learned something," she said. "Here we've been driving them all night, and if we'd left 'em alone they'd have followed us."

Dawn broke shortly after they had made the crossing, and the light of the new day revealed an open country dotted with trees and clumps of brush. In the northwest loomed a range of mountains. It was very different country from any they had seen for a long time.

"How lovely!" exclaimed Rhonda.

"Anything would be lovely after that forest," replied Naomi. "I got so that I hated it."

Suddenly Rhonda drew rein and pointed. "Do you see what I see?" she demanded.

"That hill?"

"Do you realize that we have just crossed a river out of a forest and come into open country and that there is a 'barren, cone-shaped hill—volcanic'?"

"You don't mean——!"

"The map! And there, to the northwest, are the mountains. If it's a mere coincidence it's a mighty uncanny one."

Naomi was about to reply when both their ponies halted, trembling. With dilated nostrils and up-pricked ears they

stared at a patch of brush close upon their right and just
ahead. Both girls looked in the same direction.

Suddenly a tawny figure broke from the brush with a terrific
roar. The ponies turned and bolted. Rhonda's was to the
right of Naomi's and half a neck in advance. The lion was
coming from Rhonda's side. Both ponies were uncontroll-
able. The loose horses were bolting like frightened antelopes.

Naomi, fascinated, kept her eyes upon the lion. It moved
with incredible speed. She saw it leap and seize the rump
of Rhonda's pony with fangs and talons. Its hindquarters
swung down under the pony's belly. The frightened creature
kicked and lunged, hurling Rhonda from the saddle; and then
the lion dragged it down before the eyes of the terrified Madison.

Naomi's pony carried her from the frightful scene. Once
she looked back. She saw the lion standing with its forepaws
on the carcass of the pony. Only a few feet away Rhonda's
body lay motionless.

The frightened ponies raced back along the trail they had
come. Naomi was utterly powerless to check or guide the
terrified creature that carried her swiftly in the wake of its
fellows. The distance they had covered in the last hour was
traversed in minutes as the frightened animals drew new
terror from the galloping hoofs of their comrades.

The river that they had feared to cross before did not
check them now. Lunging across, they threw water high in
air, waking the echoes of the forest with their splashing.

Heartsick, terrified, hopeless, the girl clung to her mount;
but for once in her life the thoughts of the Madison were not of
herself. The memory of that still figure lying close to the
dread carnivore crowded thoughts of self from her mind—
her terror and her hopelessness and her heartsickness were
for Rhonda Terry.

16
Eyad

L ONG day had followed long day as Orman and West
   searched vainly through dense forest and jungle for the
   trail they had lost. Nearly two weeks had passed since
they had left camp in search of the girls when their en-

counter with the lion and the "ghost" of Obroski took place.

The encounter left them unnerved, for both were weak from lack of food and their nerves harassed by what they had passed through and by worry over the fate of Naomi and Rhonda.

They stood for some time by the carcass of the lion looking and listening for a return of the apparition.

"Do you suppose," suggested West, "that hunger and worry could have affected us so much that we imagined we saw—what we think we saw?"

Orman pointed at the dead lion. "Are we imagining *that*?" he demanded. "Could we both have the same hallucination at the same instant? No! We saw what we saw. I don't believe in ghosts—or I never did before—but if that wasn't Obroski's ghost it was Obroski; and you know as well as I that Obroski would never have had the guts to tackle a lion even if he could have gotten away with it."

West rubbed his chin meditatively. "You know, another explanation has occurred to me. Obroski was the world's prize coward. He may have escaped the Bansutos and got lost in the jungle. If he did, he would have been scared stiff every minute of the days and nights. Terror might have driven him crazy. He may be a madman now, and you know maniacs are supposed to be ten times as strong as ordinary men."

"I don't know about maniacs being any stronger," said Orman; "that's a popular theory, and popular theories are always wrong; but every one knows that when a man's crazy he does things that he wouldn't do when he's sane. So perhaps you're right—perhaps that was Obroski gone nuts. No one but a nut would jump a lion; and Obroski certainly wouldn't have saved my life if he'd been sane—he didn't have any reason to be very fond of me."

"Well, whatever prompted him, he did us a good turn in more ways than one—he left us something to eat." West nodded toward the carcass of the lion.

"I hope we can keep him down," said Orman; "he looks mangy."

"I don't fancy cat meat myself," admitted West, "but I could eat a pet dog right now."

After they had eaten and cut off pieces of the meat to carry with them they set out again upon their seemingly fruitless search. The food gave them new strength; but it did little to raise their spirits, and they plodded on as dejected as before.

Toward evening West, who was in the lead, stopped suddenly and drew back, cautioning Orman to silence. The latter advanced cautiously to where West stood pointing ahead at a long figure squatting over a small fire near the bank of a stream.

"It's one of el-Ghrennem's men," said West.

"It's Eyad," replied Orman. "Do you see any one with him?"

"No. What do you suppose he is doing here alone?"

"We'll find out. Be ready to shoot if he tries any funny business or if any more of them show up."

Orman advanced upon the lone figure, his rifle ready; and West followed at his elbow. They had covered only a few yards when Eyad looked up and discovered them. Seizing his musket, he leaped to his feet; but Orman covered him.

"Drop that gun!" ordered the director.

Eyad understood no English, but he made a shrewd guess at the meaning of the words, doubtless from the peremptory tone of the American's voice, and lowered the butt of his musket to the ground.

The two approached him. "Where is el-Ghrennem?" demanded Orman. "Where are Miss Madison and Miss Terry?"

Eyad recognized the names and the interrogatory inflection. Pointing toward the north he spoke volubly in Arabic. Neither Orman nor West understood what he said, but they saw that he was much excited. They saw too that he was emaciated, his garments in rags, and his face and body covered with wounds. It was evident that he had been through some rough experiences.

When Eyad realized that the Americans could not understand him he resorted to pantomime, though he continued to jabber in Arabic.

"Can you make out what he's driving at, Tom?" asked West.

"I picked up a few words from Atewy but not many. Something terrible seems to have happened to all the rest of the party—this bird is scared stiff. I get *sheykh* and *el-Bedauwy* and *benat;* he's talking about el-Ghrennem, the other Beduins, and the girls—*benat* is the plural of *bint*, girl. One of the girls has been killed by some animal—from the way he growled and roared when he was explaining it, I guess it must have been a lion. Some other fate befell the rest of the party, and I guess it must have been pretty awful."

West paled. "Does he know which girl was killed?" he asked.
"I can't make out which one—perhaps both are dead."

"We've got to find out. We've got to go after them. Can he tell us where they were when this thing happened?"

"I'm going to make him guide us," replied Orman. "There's no use going on tonight—it's too late. In the morning we'll start."

They made a poor camp and cooked some of their lion meat. Eyad ate ravenously. It was evident that he had been some time without food. Then they lay down and tried to sleep, but futile worry kept the two Americans awake until late into the night.

To the south of them, several miles away, Stanley Obroski crouched in the fork of a tree and shivered from cold and fear. Below him a lion and a lioness fed upon the carcass of a buck. Hyenas, mouthing their uncanny cries, slunk in a wide circle about them. Obroski saw one, spurred by hunger to greater courage, slink in to seize a mouthful of the kill. The great lion, turning his head, saw the thief and charged him, growling savagely. The hyena retreated, but not quickly enough. A mighty, raking paw flung it bleeding and lifeless among its fellows. Obroski shuddered and clung more tightly to the tree. A full moon looked down upon the savage scene.

Presently the figure of a man strode silently into the clearing. The lion looked up and growled and an answering growl came from the throat of the man. Then a hyena charged him, and Obroski gasped in dismay. What would become of him if this man were killed! He feared him, but he feared him least of all the other horrid creatures of the jungle.

He saw the man side-step the charge, then stoop quickly and seize the unclean beast by the scruff of its neck. He shook it once, then hurled it onto the kill where the two lions fed. The lioness closed her great jaws upon it once and then cast it aside. The other hyenas laughed hideously.

Tarzan looked about him. "Obroski!" he called.

"I'm up here," replied the American.

Tarzan swung lightly into the tree beside him. "I saw two of your people today," he said—"Orman and West."

"Where are they? What did they say?"

"I did not talk with them. They are a few miles north of us. I think they are lost."

"Who was with them?"

"They were alone. I looked for their safari, but it was

nowhere near. Farther north I saw an Arab from your safari. He was lost and starving."

"The safari must be broken up and scattered," said Obroski. "What could have happened? What could have become of the girls?"

"Tomorrow we'll start after Orman," said Tarzan. "Perhaps he can answer your questions."

17
Alone

FOR several moments Rhonda Terry lay quietly where she had been hurled by her terrified horse. The lion stood with his forefeet on the carcass of his kill growling angrily after the fleeing animal that was carrying Naomi Madison back toward the forest.

As Rhonda Terry gained consciousness the first thing that she saw as she opened her eyes was the figure of the lion standing with its back toward her, and instantly she recalled all that had transpired. She tried to find Naomi without moving her head, for she did not wish to attract the attention of the lion; but she could see nothing of the Madison.

The lion sniffed at his kill; then he turned and looked about. His eyes fell on the girl, and a low growl rumbled in his throat. Rhonda froze in terror. She wanted to close her eyes to shut out the hideous snarling face, but she feared that even this slight movement would bring the beast upon her. She recalled having heard that if animals thought a person dead they would not molest the body. It also occurred to her that this might not hold true in respect to meat eaters.

So terrified was she that it was with the utmost difficulty that she curbed an urge to leap to her feet and run, although she knew that such an act would prove instantly fatal. The great cat could have overtaken her with a single bound.

The lion wheeled slowly about and approached her, and all the while that low growl rumbled in his throat. He came close and sniffed at her body. She felt his hot breath against her face, and its odor sickened her.

The beast seemed nervous and uncertain. Suddenly he

lowered his face close to hers and growled ferociously, his
eyes blazed into hers. She thought that the end had come.
The brute raised a paw and seized her shoulder. He turned
her over on her face. She heard him sniffing and growling
above her. For what seemed an eternity to the frightened
girl he stood there; then she realized that he had walked
away.

From her one unobscured eye she watched him after a
brief instant that she had become very dizzy and almost
swooned. He returned to the body of the horse and worried
it for a moment; then he seized it and dragged it toward the
bushes from which he had leaped to the attack.

The girl marvelled at the mighty strength of the beast,
as it dragged the carcass without seeming effort and disappeared in the thicket. Now she commenced to wonder if
she had been miraculously spared or if the lion, having hidden the body of the horse, would return for her.

She raised her head a little and looked around. About
twenty feet away grew a small tree. She lay between it and
the thicket where she could hear the lion growling.

Cautiously she commenced to drag her body toward the
tree, glancing constantly behind in the direction of the
thicket. Inch by inch, foot by foot she made her slow way.
Five feet, ten, fifteen! She glanced back and saw the lion's
head and forequarters emerge from the brush.

No longer was there place for stealth. Leaping to her feet
she raced for the tree. Behind, she heard the angry roar of
the lion as it charged.

She sprang for a low branch and scrambled upward. Terror gave her an agility and a strength far beyond her normal
powers. As she climbed frantically upward among the
branches she felt the tree tremble to the impact of the lion's
body as it hurtled against the bole, and the raking talons of
one great paw swept just beneath her foot.

Rhonda Terry did not stop climbing until she had reached
a point beyond which she dared not go; then, clinging to the
now slender stem, she looked down.

The lion stood glaring up at her. For a few minutes he
paced about the tree; and then, with an angry growl, he strode
majestically back to his thicket.

It was not until then that the girl descended to a more
secure and comfortable perch, where she sat trembling for a
long time as she sought to compose herself.

She had escaped the lion, at least temporarily; but what

lay in the future for her? Alone, unarmed, lost in a savage
wilderness, upon what thin thread could she hang even the
slightest vestige of a hope!

She wondered what had become of Naomi. She almost
wished that they had never attempted to escape from the
Arabs. If Tom Orman and Bill West and the others were
looking for them they might have had a chance to find them
had they remained the captives of old Sheykh Ab el-Ghrennem, but now how could any one ever find them?

From her tree sanctuary she could see quite a distance
in all directions. A tree-dotted plain extended northwest
toward a range of mountains. Close to the northeast of her
rose the volcanic, cone-shaped hill that she had been pointing
out to Naomi when the lion charged.

All these landmarks, following so closely the description
on the map, intrigued her curiosity and started her to wondering and dreaming about the valley of diamonds. Suddenly
she recalled something that Atewy had told her—that the
falls at the foot of the valley of diamonds must be the Omwamwi Falls toward which the safari had been moving.

If that were true she would stand a better chance of re-
joining the company were she to make her way to the falls
and await them there than to return to the forest where she
was certain to become lost.

She found it a little amusing that she should suddenly be
pinning her faith to a property map, but her situation was
such that she must grasp at any straw.

The mountains did not seem very far away, but she knew
that distances were usually deceiving. She thought that she
might reach them in a day, and believed that she might hold
out without food or water until she reached the river that she
prayed might be there.

Every minute was precious now, but she could not start
while the lion lay up in the nearby thicket. She could hear him
growling as he tore at the carcass of the horse.

An hour passed, and then she saw the lion emerge from his
lair. He did not even glance toward her, but moved off in
a southerly direction toward the river that she and Naomi
had crossed a few hours before.

The girl watched the beast until it disappeared in the
brush that grew near the river; then she slipped from the tree
and started toward the northwest and the mountains.

The day was still young, the terrain not too difficult, and
Rhonda felt comparatively fresh and strong despite her night

ride and the harrowing experiences of the last few hours—
a combination of circumstances that buoyed her with hope.

The plain was dotted with trees, and the girl directed her
steps so that she might at all times be as near as possible to
one of these. Sometimes this required a zigzag course that
lengthened the distance, but after her experience with the
lion she did not dare be far from sanctuary at any time.

She turned often to look back in the direction she had
come, lest the lion follow and surprise her. As the hours
passed the sun shone down hotter and hotter. Rhonda commenced to suffer from hunger and thirst; her steps were
dragging; her feet seemed weighted with lead. More and more
often she stopped beneath the shade of a tree to rest. The
mountains seemed as far away as ever. Doubts assailed her.

A shadow moved across the ground before her. She looked
up. Circling above was a vulture. She shuddered. "I wonder
if he only hopes," she said aloud, "or if he *knows*."

But she kept doggedly on. She would not give up—not
until she dropped in her tracks. She wondered how long it
would be before that happened.

Once as she was approaching a large black rock that lay
across her path it moved and stood up, and she saw that it was
a rhinoceros. The beast ran around foolishly for a moment,
its nose in the air; then it charged. Rhonda clambered into a
tree, and the great beast tore by like a steam locomotive gone
must.

As it raced off with its silly little tail in air the girl smiled.
She realized that she had forgotten her exhaustion under
the stress of emergency, as bedridden cripples sometimes
forget their affliction when the house catches fire.

The adventure renewed her belief in her ability to reach the
river, and she moved on again in a more hopeful frame of
mind. But as hot and dusty hour followed hot and dusty hour
and the pangs of thirst assailed her with increasing violence,
her courage faltered again in the face of the weariness that
seemed to penetrate to the very marrow of her bones.

For a long time she had been walking in a depression of
the rolling plain, her view circumscribed by the higher ground
around her. The day was drawing to a close. Her lengthening
shadow fell away behind her. The low sun was in her eyes.

She wanted to sit down and rest, but she was afraid that
she would never get up again. More than that, she wanted
to see what lay beyond the next rise in the ground. It is always the next summit that lures the traveller on even

though experience may have taught him that he need expect nothing more than another rise of ground farther on.

The climb ahead of her was steeper than she had anticipated, and it required all her strength and courage to reach the top of what she guessed might have been an ancient river bank or, perhaps, a lateral moraine; but the view that was revealed rewarded her for the great effort.

Below her was a fringe of wood through which she could see a broad river, and to her right the mountains seemed very close now.

Forgetful of lurking beast or savage man, the thirst tortured girl hurried down toward the tempting water of the river. As she neared the bank she saw a dozen great forms floating on the surface of the water. A huge head was raised with wide distended jaws revealing a cavernous maw, but Rhonda did not pause. She rushed to the bank of the river and threw herself face down and drank while the hippopotamuses, snorting and grunting, viewed her with disapproval.

That night she slept in a tree, dozing fitfully and awakening to every sudden jungle noise. From the plain came the roar of the hunting lions. Below her a great herd of hippopotamuses came out of the river to feed on land, their grunting and snorting dispelling all thoughts of sleep. In the distance she heard the yelp of the jackal and the weird cry of the hyena, and there were other strange and terrifying noises that she could not classify. It was not a pleasant night.

Morning found her weak from loss of sleep, fatigue, and hunger. She knew that she must get food, but she did not know how to get it. She thought that perhaps the safari had reached the falls by now, and she determined to go up river in search of the falls in the hope that she might find her people—a vague hope in the realization of which she had little faith.

She discovered a fairly good game trail paralleling the river, and this she followed up stream. As she stumbled on she became conscious of an insistent, muffled roaring in the distance. It grew louder as she advanced, and she guessed that she was approaching the falls.

Toward noon she reached them—an imposing sight much of the grandeur of which was lost on her fatigue-benumbed sensibilities. The great river poured over the rim of a mighty escarpment that towered far above her. A smother of white water and spume filled the gorge at the foot of the falls. The thunderous roar of the falling water was deafening.

Slowly the grandeur and the solitude of the scene gripped her. She felt as might one who stood alone, the sole inhabitant of a world, and looked upon an eternal scene that no human eye had ever scanned before.

But she was not alone. Far up, near the top of the escarpment, on a narrow ledge a shaggy creature looked down upon her from beneath beetling brows. It nudged another like it and pointed.

For a while the two watched the girl; then they started down the escarpment. Like flies they clung to the dizzy cliff, and when the ledge ended they swung to sturdy trees that clung to the rocky face of the great wall.

Down, down they came, two great first-men, shaggy, powerful, menacing. They dropped quickly, and always they sought to hide their approach from the eyes of the girl.

The great falls, the noise, the boiling river left Rhonda Terry stunned and helpless. There was no sign of her people, and if they were camped on the opposite side of the river she felt that they might as well be in another world, so impassable seemed the barrier that confronted her.

She felt very small and alone and tired. With a sigh she sat down on a rounded boulder and leaned against another piled behind it. All her remaining strength seemed to have gone from her. She closed her eyes wearily, and two tears rolled down her cheeks. Perhaps she dozed, but she was startled into wakefulness by a voice speaking near her. At first she thought she was dreaming and did not open her eyes.

"She is alone," the voice said. "We will take her to God— he will be pleased."

It was an English voice, or at least the accent was English; but the tones were gruff and deep and guttural. The strange words convinced her she was dreaming. She opened her eyes, and shrank back with a little scream of terror. Standing close to her were two gorillas, or such she thought them to be until one of them opened its mouth and spoke.

"Come with us," it said; "we are going to take you to God;" then it reached out a mighty, hairy hand and seized her.

18

Gorilla King

RHONDA TERRY fought to escape the clutches of the great beast thing that held her, but she was helpless in the grasp of those giant muscles. The creature lifted her easily and tucked her under one arm.

"Be quiet," it said, "or I'll wring your neck."

"You had better not," cautioned his companion. "God will be angry if you do not bring this one to him alive and unharmed. He has been hoping for such a she as this for a long time."

"What does *he* want of her? He is so old now that he can scarcely chew his food."

"He will probably give her to Henry the Eighth."

"He already has seven wives. I think that I shall hide her and keep her for myself."

"You will take her to God," said the other. "If you don't, I will."

"We'll see about that!" cried the creature that held the girl.

He dropped her and sprang, growling, upon his fellow. As they closed, great fangs snapping, Rhonda leaped to her feet and sought to escape.

The whole thing seemed a hideous and grotesque nightmare, yet it was so real that she could not know whether or not she were dreaming.

As she bolted, the two ceased their quarrelling and pursued her. They easily overtook her, and once again she was a captive.

"You see what will happen," said the beast that had wished to take her to God, "if we waste time quarrelling over her. I will not let you have her unless God gives her to you."

The other grumbled and tucked the girl under his arm again. "Very well," he said, "but Henry the Eighth won't get her. I'm sick of that fellow. He thinks he is greater than God."

With the agility of monkeys the two climbed up the tall trees and precarious ledges they had descended while Rhonda Terry closed her eyes to shut out the terror of the dizzy heights and sought to convince herself that she was dreaming.

But the reality was too poignant. Even the crass absurdity of the situation failed to convince her. She knew that she was not dreaming and that she was really in the power of two huge gorillas who spoke English with a marked insular accent. It was preposterous, but she knew that it was true.

To what fate were they bearing her? From their conversation she had an inkling of what lay in store for her. But who was Henry the Eighth? And who was God?

Up and up the beast bore her until at last they stood upon the summit of the escarpment. Below them, to the south, the river plunged over the edge of the escarpment to form Omwamwi Falls; to the north stretched a valley hemmed in by mountains—the valley of diamonds, perhaps.

The surprise, amounting almost to revulsion, that she had experienced when she first heard the two beasts speak a human language had had a strange effect upon her in that while she understood that they were speaking English it had not occurred to her that she could communicate with them in the same language—the adventure seemed so improbable that perhaps she still doubted her own senses.

The first shock of capture had been neutralized by the harrowing ascent of the escarpment and the relief at gaining the top in safety. Now she had an instant in which to think clearly, and with it came the realization that she had the means of communicating with her captors.

"Who are you?" she demanded. "And why have you made me prisoner?"

The two turned suddenly upon her. She thought that their faces denoted surprise.

"She speaks English!" exclaimed one of them.

"Of course I speak English. But tell me what you want of me. You have no right to take me with you. I have not harmed you. I was only waiting for my own people. Let me go!"

"This will please God," said one of her captors. "He has always said that if he could get hold of an English woman he could do much for the race."

"Who is this thing you call God?" she demanded.

"He is not a thing—he is a man," replied the one who had carried her up the escarpment. "He is very old—he is the oldest creature in the world and the wisest. He created us. But some day he will die, and then we shall have no god."

"Henry the Eighth would like to be God," said the other.

"He never will while Wolsey lives—Wolsey would make a far better god than he."

"Henry the Eighth will see that he doesn't live."

Rhonda Terry closed her eyes and pinched herself. She must be dreaming! Henry the Eighth! Thomas Wolsey! How preposterous seemed these familiar allusions to sixteenth century characters from the mouths of hairy gorillas.

The two brutes had not paused at the summit of the escarpment, but had immediately commenced the descent into the valley. Neither of them, not even the one that had carried her up the steep ascent, showed the slightest sign of fatigue even by accelerated breathing.

The girl was walking now, though one of the brutes held her by an arm and jerked her roughly forward when her steps lagged.

"I cannot walk so fast," she said finally. "I have not eaten for a long time, and I am weak."

Without a word the creature gathered her under one arm and continued on down into the valley. Her position was uncomfortable, she was weak and frightened. Several times she lost consciousness.

How long that journey lasted she did not know. When she was conscious her mind was occupied by futile speculation as to the fate that lay ahead of her. She tried to visualize the *God* of these brutal creatures. What mercy, what pity might she expect at the hands of such a thing?—if, indeed, their god existed other than in their imaginations.

After what seemed a very long time the girl heard voices in the distance, growing louder as they proceeded; and soon after he who carried her set her upon her feet.

As she looked about her she saw that she stood at the bottom of a cliff before a city that was built partially at the foot of the cliff and partially carved from its face.

The approach to the city was bordered by great fields of bamboo, celery, fruits, and berries in which many gorillas were working with crude, handmade implements.

As they caught sight of the captive these workers left their fields and clustered about asking many questions and examining the girl with every indication of intelligent interest, but her captors hurried her along into the city.

Here again they were surrounded by curious crowds; but nowhere was any violence offered the captive, the attitude of the gorillas appearing far more friendly than that which she might have expected from human natives of this untracked wilderness.

That portion of the city that was built upon the level ground at the foot of the cliff consisted of circular huts of bamboo with thatched conical roofs, of rectangular buildings of sun dried bricks, and others of stone.

Near the foot of the cliff was a three-story building with towers and ramparts, roughly suggestive of medieval England; and farther up the cliff, upon a broad ledge, was another, even larger structure of similar architecture.

Rhonda's captors led her directly to the former building, before the door of which squatted two enormous gorillas armed with crude weapons that resembled battle axes; and here they were stopped while the two guards examined Rhonda and questioned her captors.

Again and again the girl tried to convince herself that she was dreaming. All her past experience, all her acquired knowledge stipulated the utter absurdity of the fantastic experiences of the past few hours. There could be no such things as gorillas that spoke English, tilled fields, and lived-in stone castles. And yet here were all these impossibilities before her eyes as concrete evidence of their existence.

She listened as one in a dream while her captors demanded entrance that they might take their prisoner before the king; she heard the guard demur, saying that the king could not be disturbed as he was engaged with the Privy Council.

"Then we'll take her to God," threatened one of her captors, "and when the king finds out what you have done you'll be working in the quarry instead of sitting here in the shade."

Finally a young gorilla was summoned and sent into the palace with a message. When he returned it was with the word that the king wished to have the prisoner brought before him at once.

Rhonda was conducted into a large room the floor of which was covered with dried grass. On a dais at one end of the room an enormous gorilla paced to and fro while a half dozen other gorillas squatted in the grass at the foot of the dais—enormous, shaggy beasts, all.

There were no chairs nor tables nor benches in the room, but from the center of the dais rose the bare trunk and leafless branches of a tree.

As the girl was brought into the room the gorilla on the

dais stopped his restless pacing and scrutinized her. "Where did you find her, Buckingham?" he demanded.

"At the foot of the falls, Sire," replied the beast that had captured her.

"What was she doing there?"

"She said that she was looking for her friends, who were to meet her at the falls."

"She *said!* You mean that she speaks English?" demanded the king.

"Yes, I speak English," said Rhonda; "and if I am not dreaming, and you are king, I demand that you send me back to the falls, so that I may find my people."

"Dreaming? What put that into your head? You are not asleep, are you?"

"I do not know," replied Rhonda. "Sometimes I am sure that I must be."

"Well, you are not," snapped the king. "And who put it into your head that there might be any doubt that I am king? That sounds like Buckingham."

"Your majesty wrongs me," said Buckingham stiffly. "It was I who insisted on bringing her to the king."

"It is well you did; the wench pleases us. We will keep her."

"But, your majesty," exclaimed the other of Rhonda's two captors, "it is our duty to take her to God. We brought her here first that your majesty might see her; but we must take her on to God, who had been hoping for such a woman for years."

"What, Cranmer! Are you turning against me too?"

"Cranmer is right," said one of the great bulls squatting on the floor. "This woman should be taken to God. Do not forget, Sire, that you already have seven wives."

"That is just like you, Wolsey," snapped the king peevishly. "You are always taking the part of God."

"We must all remember," said Wolsey, "that we owe everything to God. It was he who created us. He made us what we are. It is he who can destroy us."

The king was pacing up and down the straw covered dais rapidly. His eyes were blazing, his lips drawn back in a snarl. Suddenly he stopped by the tree and shook it angrily as though he would tear it from the masonry in which it was set. Then he climbed quickly up into a fork and glared down at them. For a moment he perched there, but only for a moment. With the agility of a small monkey he leaped to the

floor of the dais. With his great fists he beat upon his hairy
breast, and from his cavernous lungs rose a terrific roar
that shook the building.

"I am king!" he screamed. "My word is law. Take the
wench to the women's quarters!"

The beast the king had addressed as Wolsey now leaped
to his feet and commenced to beat his breast and scream.
"This is sacrilege," he cried. "He who defies God shall die.
That is the law. Repent, and send the girl to God!"

"Never!" shrieked the king. "She is mine."

Both brutes were now beating their breasts and roaring so
loudly that their words could scarcely be distinguished; and
the other bulls were moving restlessly, their hair bristling,
their fangs bared.

Then Wolsey played his ace. "Send the girl to God," he
bellowed, "or suffer excommunication!"

But the king had now worked himself to such a frenzy
that he was beyond reason. "The guard! The guard!" he
screamed. "Suffolk, call the guard, and take Cardinal Wolsey
to the tower! Buckingham, take the girl to the women's
quarters or off goes your head."

The two bulls were still beating their breasts and screaming
at one another as Rhonda Terry was dragged from the apartment by the shaggy Buckingham.

Up a circular stone stairway the brute dragged her and
along a corridor to a room at the rear of the second floor. It
was a large room in the corner of the building, and about its
grass strewn floor squatted or lay a number of adult gorillas,
while young ones of all ages played about or suckled at their
mothers' breasts.

Many of the beasts were slowly eating celery stalks, tender
bamboo tips, or fruit; but all activity ceased as Buckingham
dragged the American girl into their midst.

"What have you there, Buckingham?" growled an old she.

"A girl we captured at the falls," replied Buckingham. "The
king commanded that she be brought here, your majesty."
Then he turned to his captive. "This is Queen Catherine,"
he said, "Catherine of Aragon."

"What does he want of her?" demanded Catherine peevishly.

Buckingham shrugged his broad shoulders and glanced
about the room at the six adult females. "Your majesties
should well be able to guess."

"Is he thinking of taking that puny, hairless thing for a

wife?" demanded another, sitting at a little distance from Catherine of Aragon.

"Of course that's what he's thinking of, Anne Boleyn," snapped Catherine; "or he wouldn't have sent her here."

"Hasn't he got enough wives already?" demanded another.

"That is for the king to decide," said Buckingham as he quitted the room.

Now the great shes commenced to gather closer to the girl. They sniffed at her and felt of her clothing. The younger ones crowded in, pulling at her skirt. One, larger than the rest, grabbed her by the ankles and pulled her feet from under her; and, as she fell, it danced about the room, grimacing and screaming.

As she tried to rise it rushed toward her; and she struck it in the face, thinking it meant to injure her. Whereupon it ran screaming to Catherine of Aragon, and one of the other shes seized Rhonda by the shoulder and pushed her so violently that she was hurled against the wall.

"How dare you lay hands on the Prince of Wales!" cried the beast that had pushed her.

The Prince of Wales, Catherine of Aragon, Anne Boleyn! If not asleep, Rhonda Terry was by this time positive that she had gone mad. What possible explanation could there be for such a mad burlesque in which gorillas acted the parts and spoke with the tongues of men?—what other than the fantasy of sleep or insanity? None.

She sat huddled against the wall where she had fallen and buried her face in her arms.

19
Despair

THE frightened pony carried Naomi Madison in the wake of its fellows. She could only cling frantically to the saddle, constantly fearful of being brushed to the ground.

Presently, where the trail widened into a natural clearing, the horses in front of her stopped suddenly; and the one she rode ran in among them before it stopped too.

Then she saw the reason—Sheykh Ab el-Ghrennem and his followers. She tried to rein her horse around and escape;

but he was wedged in among the other horses, and a moment later the little herd was surrounded. Once more she was a prisoner.

The sheykh was so glad to get his horses back that he almost forgot to be angry over the trick that had robbed him of them temporarily. He was glad, too, to have one of his prisoners. She could read the map to them and be useful in other ways if he decided not to sell her.

"Where is the other one?" demanded Atewy.

"She was killed by a lion," replied Naomi.

Atewy shrugged. "Well, we still have you; and we have the map. We shall not fare so ill."

Naomi recalled the cone-shaped volcanic hill and the mountains in the distance. "If I lead you to the valley of diamonds will you return me to my people?" she asked.

Atewy translated to el-Ghrennem. The old sheykh nodded. "Tell her we will do that if she leads us to the valley of diamonds," he said. *"Wellah!* yes; tell her that; but after we find the valley of diamonds we may forget what we have promised. But do not tell her *that."*

Atewy grinned. "Lead us to the valley of diamonds," he said to Naomi, "and all that you wish will be done."

Unaccustomed to the strenuous labor of pushing through the jungle on foot that the pursuit of the white girls and their ponies had necessitated, the Arabs made camp as soon as they reached the river.

The following day they crossed to the open plain; and when Naomi called their attention to the volcanic hill and the location of the mountains to the northwest, and they had compared these landmarks with the map, they were greatly elated.

But when they reached the river below the falls the broad and turbulent stream seemed impassable and the cliffs before them unscalable.

They camped that night on the east side of the river, and late into the night discussed plans for crossing to the west side, for the map clearly indicated but a single entrance to the valley of diamonds, and that was several miles northwest of them.

In the morning they started downstream in search of a crossing, but it was two days before they found a place where they dared make the attempt. Even here they had the utmost difficulty in negotiating the river, and consumed most of the day in vain attempts before they finally succeeded in winning to the opposite shore with the loss of two men and their mounts.

The Madison had been almost paralyzed by terror, not alone by the natural hazards of the swift current but by the constant menace of the crocodiles with which the stream seemed alive. Wet to the skin, she huddled close to the fire; and finally, hungry and miserable, dropped into a sleep of exhaustion.

What provisions the Arabs had had with them had been lost or ruined in the crossing, and so much time had been consumed in reaching the west bank that they had been unable to hunt for game before dark. But they were accustomed to a life of privation and hardship, and their spirits were buoyed by the certainty that all felt that within a few days they would be scooping up diamonds by the handfuls from the floor of the fabulous valley that now lay but a short distance to the north.

Coming down the east bank of the river they had consumed much time in unsuccessful attempts to cross the stream, and they had been further retarded by the absence of a good trail. But on the west side of the river they found a wide and well beaten track along which they moved rapidly.

Toward the middle of the afternoon of the first day after crossing the river Naomi called to Atewy who rode near her.

"Look!" she said, pointing ahead. "There is the red granite column shown on the map. Directly east of it is the entrance to the valley."

Atewy, much excited, transmitted the information to el-Ghrennem and the others; and broad grins wreathed their usually saturnine countenances.

"And now," said Naomi, "that I have led you to the valley, keep your promise to me and send me back to my people."

"Wait a bit," replied Atewy. "We are not in the valley yet. We must be sure that this is indeed the valley of diamonds. You must come with us yet a little farther."

"But that was not the agreement," insisted the girl. "I was to lead you to the valley, and that I have done. I am going back to look for my people now whether you send any one with me or not."

She wheeled her pony to turn back along the trail they had come. She did not know where her people were; but she had heard the Arabs say that the falls they had passed were the Omwamwi Falls, and she knew that the safari had been marching for this destination when she had been stolen more than a week before. They must be close to them by this time.

But she was not destined to carry her scheme into execu-tion, for as she wheeled her mount Atewy spurred to her side, grasped her bridle rein, and, with an oath, struck her across the face.

"The next time you try that you'll get something worse," he threatened.

Suffering from the blow, helpless, hopeless, the girl broke into tears. She thought that she had plumbed the uttermost depths of terror and despair, but she did not know what the near future held in store for her.

That night the Arabs camped just east of the red granite monolith that they believed marked the entrance to the valley of diamonds, at the mouth of a narrow canyon.

Early the following morning they started up the canyon on the march that they believed would lead them to a country of fabulous wealth. From far above them savage eyes looked down from scowling black faces, watching their progress.

20

"Come with Me!"

IN THE light of a new day Tarzan of the Apes stood looking down upon the man who resembled him so closely that the ape-man experienced the uncanny sensation of standing apart, like a disembodied spirit, viewing his corporeal self.

It was the morning that they were to have set off in search of Orman and West, but Tarzan saw that it would be some time before Obroski would travel again on his own legs.

With all the suddenness with which it sometimes strikes, fever had seized the American. His delirious ravings had awakened Tarzan, but now he lay in a coma.

The lord of the jungle considered the matter briefly. He neither wished to leave the man alone to the scant mercy of the jungle, nor did he wish to remain with him. His conver-sations with Obroski had convinced him that no matter what his inclinations might be the dictates of simplest humanity re-quired that he do what he might to succor the innocent members of Orman's party. The plight of the two girls appealed especially to his sense of chivalry, and it was with his usual celerity that he reached a decision.

Lifting the unconscious Obroski in his arms he threw him across one of his broad shoulders and swung off through the jungle toward the south.

All day he travelled, stopping briefly once for water, eating no food. Sometimes the American lay unconscious, sometimes he struggled and raved in delirium; or, again, consciousness returning, he begged the ape-man to stop and let him rest. But Tarzan ignored his pleas, and moved on toward the south.

Toward evening the two came to a native village beyond the Bansuto country. It was the village of the chief, Mpugu, whom Tarzan knew to be friendly to whites as well as under obligations to the lord of the jungle who had once saved his life.

Obroski was unconscious when they arrived in the village, and Tarzan placed him in a hut which Mpugu placed at his disposal.

"When he is well, take him to Jinja," Tarzan instructed Mpugu, "and ask the commissioner to send him on to the coast."

The ape-man remained in the village only long enough to fill his empty belly; then he swung off again through the gathering dusk toward the north, while far away, in the city of the gorilla king, Rhonda Terry crouched in the dry grass that littered the floor of the quarters of the king's wives and dreamed of the horrid fate that awaited her.

A week had passed since she had been thrust into this room with its fierce denizens. She had learned much concerning them since then, but not the secret of their origin. Most of them were far from friendly, though none offered her any serious harm. Only one of them paid much attention to her, and from this one and the conversations she had overheard she had gained what meager information she had concerning them.

The six adult females were the wives of the king, Henry the Eighth; and they bore the historic names of the wives of that much married English king. There were Catherine of Aragon, Anne Boleyn, Jane Seymour, Anne of Cleves, Catherine Howard, and Catherine Parr.

It was Catherine Parr, the youngest, who had been the least unfriendly; and that, perhaps, because she had suffered at the hands of the others and hated them.

Rhonda told her that there had been a king in a far

country four hundred years before who had been called Henry the Eighth and who had had six wives of the same names as theirs and that such an exact parallel seemed beyond the realms of possibility—that in this far off valley their king should have found six women that he wished to marry who bore those identical names.

"Those were not our names before we became the wives of the king," explained Catherine Parr. "When we were married to the king we were given these names."

"By the king?"

"No—by God."

"What is your god like?" asked Rhonda.

"He is very old. No one knows how old he is. He has been here in England always. He is the god of England. He knows everything and is very powerful."

"Have you ever seen him?"

"No. He has not come out of his castle for many years. Now, he and the king are quarrelling. That is why the king has not been here since you came. God has threatened to kill him if he takes another wife."

"Why?" asked Rhonda.

"God says Henry the Eighth may have only six wives—there are no names for more."

"There doesn't seem much sense in that," commented the girl.

"We may not question God's reasons. He created us, and he is all-wise. We must have faith; otherwise he will destroy us."

"Where does your god live?"

"In the great castle on the ledge above the city. It is called The Golden Gates. Through it we enter into heaven after we die—if we have believed in God and served him well."

"What is the castle like inside?" asked Rhonda, "this castle of God?"

"I have never been in it. Only the king and a few of his nobles, the cardinal, the archbishop, and the priests have ever entered The Golden Gates and come out again. The spirits of the dead enter, but, of course, they never come back. And occasionally God sends for a young man or a young woman. What happens to them no one knows, but they never come back either. It is said—" she hesitated.

"What is said?" Rhonda found herself becoming intrigued by the mystery surrounding this strange god that guarded the entrance to heaven.

"Oh, terrible things are said; but I dare not even whisper them. I must not think them. God can read our thoughts. Do not ask me any more questions. You have been sent by the devil to lure me to destruction," and that was the last that Rhonda could get out of Catherine Parr.

Early the next day the American girl was awakened by horrid growls and roars that seemed to come not only from outside the palace but from the interior as well.

The she gorillas penned in the quarters with her were restless. They growled as they crowded to the windows and looked down into the courtyard and the streets beyond.

Rhonda came and stood behind them and looked over their shoulders. She saw shaggy beasts struggling and fighting at the gate leading through the outer wall, surging through the courtyard below, and battling before the entrance to the palace. They fought with clubs and battle axes, talons and fangs.

"They have freed Wolsey from the tower," she heard Jane Seymour say, "and he is leading God's party against the king."

Catherine of Aragon squatted in the dry grass and commenced to peel a banana. "Henry and God are always quarrelling," she said wearily—"and nothing ever comes of it. Every time Henry wants a new wife they quarrel."

"But I notice he always gets his wife," said Catherine Howard.

"He has had Wolsey on his side before—this time it may be different. I have heard that God wants this hairless she for himself. If he gets her that will be the last that any one will ever see of her—which will suit me." Catherine of Aragon bared her fangs at the American girl, and then returned her attention to the banana.

The sound of fighting surged upward from the floor below until they heard it plainly in the corridor outside the closed door of their quarters. Suddenly the door was thrown open, and several bulls burst into the room.

"Where is the hairless one?" demanded the leading bull. "Ah, there she is!"

He crossed the room and seized Rhonda roughly by the wrist.

"Come with me!" he ordered. "God has sent for you."

21

Abducted

T HE Arabs made their way up the narrow canyon toward the summit of the pass that led into the valley of diamonds. From above, fierce, cruel eyes looked down. Ab el-Ghrennem gloated exultantly. He had visions of the rich treasure that was soon to give him wealth beyond his previous wildest dreams of avarice. Atewy rode close to Naomi Madison to prevent her from escaping.

At last they came to a precipitous wall that no horse could scale. The perpendicular sides of the rocky canyon had drawn close together.

"The horses can go no farther," announced Ab el-Ghrennem. "Eyad, thou shalt remain with them. The rest of us will continue on foot."

"And the girl?" asked Atewy.

"Bring her with us, lest she escape Eyad while he is guarding the horses," replied the sheykh. "I would not lose her."

They scrambled up the rocky escarpment, dragging Naomi Madison with them, to find more level ground above. The rocky barrier had not been high, but sufficient to bar the progress of a horse.

Sitting in his saddle, Eyad could see above it and watch his fellows continuing on up the canyon, which was now broader with more sloping walls upon which timber grew as it did upon the summit.

They had proceeded but a short distance when Eyad saw a black, shaggy, manlike figure emerge from a bamboo thicket above and behind the sheykh's party. Then another and another followed the first. They carried clubs or axes with long handles.

Eyad shouted a warning to his comrades. It brought them to a sudden halt, but it also brought a swarm of the hairy creatures pouring down the canyon sides upon them.

Roaring and snarling, the beasts closed in upon the men. The matchlocks of the Arabs roared, filling the canyon with thundering reverberations, adding to the bedlam.

A few of the gorillas were hit. Some fell; but the others, goaded to frightful rage by their wounds, charged to close quarters. They tore the weapons from the hands of the Arabs and cast them aside. Seizing the men in their powerful hands, they sank great fangs into the throats of their adversaries. Others wielded club or battle axe.

Screaming and cursing, the Arabs sought now only to escape. Eyad was filled with terror as he saw the bloody havoc being wrought upon his fellows. He saw a great bull gather the girl into his arms and start up the slope of the canyon wall toward the wooded summit. He saw two mighty bulls descending the canyon toward him. Then Eyad wheeled and put spurs to his horse. Clattering down the canyon, he heard the sounds of conflict growing dimmer and dimmer until at last he could hear them no longer.

And as Eyad disappeared in the lower reaches of the canyon, Buckingham carried Naomi Madison into the forest above the strange city of the gorilla king.

Buckingham was mystified. He thought that this hairless she was the same creature he had captured many days before below the great falls that he knew as Victoria Falls. Yet only this very morning he had seen her taken by Wolsey to the castle of God.

He paused beyond the summit at a point where the city of the gorillas could be seen below them. He was in a quandary. He very much wanted this she for himself, but then both God and the king wanted her. He stood scratching his head as he sought to evolve a plan whereby he might possess her without incurring the wrath of two such powerful personages.

Naomi, hanging in the crook of his arm, was frozen with horror. The Arabs had seemed bad enough, but this horrid brute! She wondered when he would kill her and how.

Presently he stood her on her feet and looked at her. "How did you escape from God?" he demanded.

Naomi Madison gasped in astonishment, and her eyes went wide. A great fear crept over her, a fear greater than the physical terror that the brute itself aroused—she feared that she was losing her reason. She stood with wild, staring eyes gazing at the beast. Then, suddenly, she burst into wild laughter.

"What are you laughing at?" growled Buckingham.

"At you," she cried. "You think you can fool me, but you

can't. I know that I am just dreaming. In a moment I'll be awake, and I'll see the sun coming in my bedroom window. I'll see the orange tree and the loquat in my patio. I'll see Hollywood stretching below me with its red roofs and its green trees."

"I don't know what you are talking about," said Buckingham. "You are not asleep. You are awake. Look down there, and you will see London and the Thames."

Naomi looked where he indicated. She saw a strange city on the banks of a small river. She pinched herself; and it hurt, but she did not awake. Slowly she realized that she was not dreaming, that the terrible unrealities she had passed through were real.

"Who are you? What are you?" she asked.

"Answer my question," commanded Buckingham. "How did you escape from God?"

"I don't know what you mean. The Arabs captured me. I escaped from them once, but they got me again."

"Was that before I captured you several days ago?"

"I never saw you before."

Buckingham scratched his head again. "Are there two of you?" he demanded. "I certainly caught you or another just like you at the falls over a week ago."

Suddenly Naomi thought that she comprehended. "You caught a girl like me?" she demanded.

"Yes."

"Did she wear a red handkerchief around her neck?"

"Yes."

"Where is she?"

"If you are not she, she is with God in his castle— down there." He leaned out over the edge of the cliff and pointed to a stone castle on a ledge far below. He turned toward her as a new idea took form in his mind. "If you are not she," he said, "then God has the other one—and I can have you!"

"No! No!" cried the girl. "Let me go! Let me go back to my people."

Buckingham seized her and tucked her under one of his huge arms. "Neither God nor Henry the Eighth shall ever see you," he growled. "I'll take you away where they can't find you—they shan't rob me of you as they robbed me of the other. I'll take you to a place I know where there is food and water. I'll build a shelter among the trees. We'll be safe there from both God and the king."

Naomi struggled and struck at him; but he paid no attention to her, as he swung off to the south toward the lower end of the valley.

22
The Imposter

THE Lord of the Jungle awoke and stretched. A new day was dawning. He had travelled far from Mpugu's village the previous night before he lay up to rest. Now, refreshed, he swung on toward the north. He would make a kill and eat on the way, or he would go hungry—it depended upon the fortunes of the trail. Tarzan could go for long periods without food with little inconvenience. He was no such creature of habit as are the poor slaves of civilization.

He had gone but a short distance when he caught the scent spoor of men—tarmangani—white men. And before he saw them he had recognized them by their scent.

He paused in a tree above them and looked down upon them. There were three of them—two whites and an Arab. They had made a poor camp the night before. Tarzan saw no sign of food. The men looked haggard, almost exhausted. Not far from them was a buck, but the starving men did not know it. Tarzan knew it because Usha, the wind, was carrying the scent of the buck to his keen nostrils.

Seeing their dire need and fearing that they might frighten the animal away before he could kill it, Tarzan passed around them unseen and swung silently on through the trees.

Wappi, the antelope, browsed on the tender grasses of a little clearing. He would take a few mouthfuls; then raise his head, looking and listening—always alert. But he was not sufficiently alert to detect the presence of the noiseless stalker creeping upon him.

Suddenly the antelope started! He had heard, but it was too late. A beast of prey had launched itself upon him from the branches of a tree.

A quarter of a mile away Orman had risen to his feet. "We might as well get going, Bill," he said.

"Can't we make this bird understand that we want him to guide us to the point where he last saw one of the girls?"

"I've tried. You've heard me threaten to kill him if he doesn't, but he either can't or won't understand."

"If we don't get something to eat pretty soon we won't ever find anybody. If—" The incompleted sentence died in a short gasp.

An uncanny cry had come rolling out of the mysterious jungle fastness, freezing the blood in the veins of all three men.

"The ghost!" said Orman in a whisper.

An involuntary shudder ran through West's frame. "You know that's all hooey, Tom," he said.

"Yes, I know it," admitted Orman; "but——"

"That probably wasn't—Obroski at all. It must have been some animal," insisted West.

"Look!" exclaimed Orman, pointing beyond West.

As the cameraman wheeled he saw an almost naked white man walking toward them, the carcass of a buck across one broad shoulder.

"Obroski!" exclaimed West.

Tarzan saw the two men gazing at him in astonishment, he heard West's ejaculation, and he recalled the striking resemblance that he and Obroski bore to one another. If the shadow of a smile was momentarily reflected by his grey eyes it was gone when he stopped before the two men and tossed the carcass of the buck at their feet.

"I thought you might be hungry," he said. "You look hungry."

"Obroski!" muttered Orman. "Is it really you?" He stepped closer to Tarzan and touched his shoulder.

"What did you think I was—a ghost?" asked the ape-man.

Orman laughed—an apologetic, embarrassed laugh. "I—well—we thought you were dead. It was so surprising to see you—and then the way that you killed the lion the other day—you did kill the lion, didn't you?"

"He seemed to be dead," replied the ape-man.

"Yes, of course; but then it didn't seem exactly like you, Obroski—we didn't know that you could do anything like that."

"There are probably a number of things about me that you don't know. But never mind about that. I've come to find out what you know about the girls. Are they safe? And how about the rest of the safari?"

"The girls were stolen by the Arabs almost two weeks

ago. Bill and I have been looking for them. I don't know where the rest of the outfit are. I told Pat to try to get everything to Omwamwi Falls and wait for me there if I didn't show up before. We captured this Arab. It's Eyad—you probably remember him. Of course we can't understand his lingo; but from what we can make out one of the girls has been killed by a wild beast, and something terrible has happened to the other girl and the rest of the Arabs."

Tarzan turned to Eyad; and, much to the Arab's surprise, questioned him in his own tongue while Orman and West looked on in astonishment. The two spoke rapidly for a few minutes; then Tarzan handed Eyad an arrow, and the man, squatting on his haunches, smoothed a little area of ground with the palm of his hand and commenced to draw something with the point of the arrow.

"What's he doing?" asked West. "What did he say?"

"He's drawing a map to show me where this fight took place between the Arabs and the gorillas."

"Gorillas! What did he say about the girls?"

"One of them was killed by a lion a week or more ago, and the last he saw of the other she was being carried off by a big bull gorilla."

"Which one is dead?" asked West. "Did he say?"

Tarzan questioned Eyad, and then turned to the American. "He does not know. He says that he could never tell the two girls apart."

Eyad had finished his map and was pointing out the different landmarks to the ape-man. Orman and West were also scrutinizing the crude tracing.

The director gave a short laugh. "This bird's stringin' you, Obroski." he said. "That's a copy of a fake map we had for use in the picture."

Tarzan questioned Eyad rapidly in Arabic; then he turned again to Orman. "I think he is telling the truth," he said. "Anyway, I'll soon know. I am going up to this valley and look around. You and West follow on up to the falls. Eyad can guide you. This buck will last you until you get there." Then he turned and swung into the trees.

The three men stood staring at the spot for a moment. Finally Orman shook his head. "I never was so fooled in any one before in my life," he said. "I had Obroski all wrong—we all did. By golly, I never saw such a change in a man before in my whole life."

"Even his voice has changed," said West.

"He certainly was a secretive son-of-a-gun," said Orman. "I never had the slightest idea that he could speak Arabic."

"I think he mentioned that there were several things about him that you did not know."

"If I wasn't so familiar with that noble mug of his and that godlike physique I'd swear that this guy isn't Obroski at all."

"Not a chance," said West. "I'd know him in a million."

23

Man and Beast

THE great bull gorilla carried Naomi Madison south along the wooded crest of the mountains toward the southern end of the valley. When they came to open spaces he scurried quickly across them, and he looked behind him often as though fearing pursuit.

The girl's first terror had subsided, to be replaced by a strange apathy that she could not understand. It was as though her nervous system was under the effects of an anesthetic that deadened her susceptibility to fear but left all her other faculties unimpaired. Perhaps she had undergone so much that she no longer cared what befell her.

That she could converse in English with this brutal beast lent an unreality to the adventure that probably played a part in inducing the mental state in which she found herself. After this, anything might be, anything might happen.

The uncomfortable position in which she was being carried and her hunger presently became matters of the most outstanding importance, relegating danger to the background.

"Let me walk," she said.

Buckingham grunted and lowered her to her feet. "Do not try to run away from me," he warned.

They continued on through the woods towards the south, the beast sometimes stopping to look back and listen. He was moving into the wind; so his nose was useless in apprehending danger from the rear.

During one of these stops Naomi saw fruit growing upon a tree. "I am hungry," she said. "Is this fruit good to eat?"

"Yes," he replied and permitted her to gather some; then he pushed on again.

They had come almost to the end of the valley and were crossing a space almost devoid of trees at a point where the mountains fell in a series of precipitous cliffs down to the floor of the valley when the gorilla paused as usual under such circumstances to glance back.

The girl, thinking he feared pursuit by the Arabs, always looked hopefully back at such times. Even the leering countenance of Atewy would have been a welcome sight under the circumstances. Heretofore they had seen no sign of pursuit, but this time a figure emerged from the patch of wood they had just quitted—it was the lumbering figure of a bull gorilla.

With a snarl, Buckingham lifted the girl from her feet and broke into a lumbering run. A short distance within the forest beyond the clearing he turned abruptly toward the cliff; and when he reached the edge he swung the girl to his back, telling her to put her arms about his neck and hang on.

Naomi Madison glanced once into the abyss below; then she shut her eyes and prayed for strength to hang onto the hairy creature making its way down the sheer face of the rocky escarpment.

What he found to cling to she did not know, for she did not open her eyes until he loosed her hands by main strength and let her drop to her feet behind him.

"I'll come back for you when I have thrown Suffolk off the trail," said the beast and was gone.

The Madison found herself in a small natural cave in the face of the cliff. A tiny stream of water trickled from a hidden spring, formed a little pool at the front of the cave, and ran over the edge down the face of the cliff. A part of the floor of the cave was dry; but there was no covering upon it, only the bare rock.

The girl approached the ledge and looked down. The great height of the seemingly bare cliff face made her shrink back, giddy. Then she tried it again and looked up. There seemed scarcely a hand or foothold in any direction. She marvelled that the heavy gorilla had been able to make his way to the cave safely, burdened by her weight.

As she examined her situation, Buckingham clambered quickly to the summit of the cliff and continued on toward the south. He moved slowly, and it was not long before the pursuing beast overtook him.

The creature upon his trail hailed him. "Where is the hairless she?" he demanded.

"I do not know," replied the other. "She has run away from me. I am looking for her."

"Why did you run away from me, Buckingham?"

"I did not know it was you, Suffolk. I thought you were one of Wolsey's men trying to rob me of the she so that I could not take her to the king."

Suffolk grunted. "We had better find her. The king is not in a good humor. How do you suppose she escaped from God?"

"She did not escape from God—this is a different she, though they look much alike." The two passed on through the forest, searching for the Madison.

For two nights and two days the girl lay alone in the rocky cave. She could neither ascend nor descend the vertical cliff. If the beast did not return for her, she must starve. This she knew, yet she hoped that it would not return.

The third night fell. Naomi was suffering from hunger. Fortunately the little trickle of water through the cave saved her from suffering from thirst also. She heard the savage sounds of the night life of the wilderness, but she was not afraid. The cave had at least that advantage. If she had food she could live there in safety indefinitely, but she had no food.

The first pangs of hunger had passed. She did not suffer. She only knew that she was growing weaker. It seemed strange to her that she, Naomi Madison, should be dying of hunger—and alone! Why, in all the world the only creature that could save her from starvation, the only creature that knew where she was was a great, savage gorilla—she who numbered her admirers by the millions, whose whereabouts, whose every act was chronicled in a hundred newspapers and magazines. She felt very small and insignificant now. Here was no room for arrogant egotism.

During the long hours she had had more opportunity for self-scrutiny than ever before, and what she discovered was not very flattering. She realized that she had already changed much during the past two weeks—she had learned much from the attitude of the other members of the safari toward her but most from the example that Rhonda Terry had set her. If she were to have the chance, she knew that she would be a very different woman; but she did not expect the chance. She did not want life at the price she would have to pay. She prayed that she might die before the gorilla returned to claim his prize.

She slept fitfully through the third night—the rocky floor that was her bed was torture to her soft flesh. The morning sun, shining full into the mouth of her cave, gave her renewed hope even though her judgment told her that there was no hope.

She drank, and bathed her hands and face; then she sat and looked out over the valley of diamonds. She should have hated it, for it had aroused the avarice that had brought her to this sorry pass; but she did not—it was too beautiful.

Presently her attention was attracted by a scraping sound outside the cave and above it. She listened intently. What could it be?

A moment later a black, hairy leg appeared below the top of the mouth of the cave; and then the gorilla dropped to the narrow ledge before it. The thing had returned! The girl crouched against the back wall, shuddering.

The brute stopped and peered into the gloomy cavern. "Come here!" it commanded. "I see you. Hurry—we have no time to waste. They may have followed me. Suffolk has had me watched for two days. He did not believe that you had run away. He guessed that I had hidden you. Come! Hurry!"

"Go away and leave me," she begged. "I would rather stay here and die."

He made no answer at once, but stooped and came toward her. Seizing her roughly by the arm he dragged her to the mouth of the cave. "So I'm not good enough for you?" he growled. "Don't you know that I am the Duke of Buckingham? Get on my back, and hold tight."

He swung her up into position, and she clung about his neck. She wanted to hurl herself over the edge of the cliff, but she could not raise her courage to the point. Against her will she clung to the shaggy brute as he climbed the sheer face of the cliff toward the summit. She did not dare even to look down.

At the top he lowered her to her feet and started on southward toward the lower end of the valley, dragging her after him.

She was weak; and she staggered, stumbling often. Then he would jerk her roughly to her feet and growl at her, using strange, medieval oaths.

"I can't go on," she said. "I am weak. I have had nothing to eat for two days."

"You are just trying to delay me so that Suffolk can overtake us. You would rather belong to the king, but you won't. You'll never see the king. He is just waiting for an excuse to have my head, but he won't ever get it. We're never going back to London, you and I. We'll go out of the valley and find a place below the falls."

Again she stumbled and fell. The beast became enraged. He kicked her as she lay on the ground; then he seized her by the hair and dragged her after him.

But he did not go far thus. He had taken but a few steps when he came to a sudden halt. With a savage growl and up-turned lips baring powerful yellow fangs he faced a figure that had dropped from a tree directly in his path.

The girl saw too, and her eyes went wide. "Stanley!" she cried. "Oh, Stanley, save me, save me!"

It was the startled cry of a forlorn hope, but in the instant of voicing it she knew that she could expect no help from Stanley Obroski, the coward. Her heart sank, and the horror of her position seemed suddenly more acute because of this brief instant of false reprieve.

The gorilla released his hold upon her hair and dropped her to the ground, where she lay too weak to rise, watching the great beast at her side and the bronzed white giant facing it.

"Go away, Bolgani!" commanded Tarzan in the language of the great apes. "The she is mine. Go away, or I kill!"

Buckingham did not understand the tongue of this stranger, but he understood the menace of his attitude. "Go away!" he cried in English. "Go away, or I will kill you!" Thus a beast spoke in English to an Englishman who spoke the language of beasts!

Tarzan of the Apes is not easily astonished; but when he heard Bolgani, the gorilla, speak to him in English he at first questioned his hearing and then his sanity. But whatever the condition of either it could not conceal the evident intent of the bull gorilla advancing menacingly toward him as it beat its breast and screamed its threats.

Naomi Madison watched with horror-wide, fascinated eyes. She saw the man she thought to be Stanley Obroski crouch slightly as though waiting to receive the charge. She wondered why he did not turn and run—that was what all who knew him, including herself, would have expected of Stanley Obroski.

Suddenly the gorilla charged, and still the man held his ground. Great hairy paws reached out to seize him; but he eluded them with quick, panther-like movements. Stooping, he sprang beneath a swinging arm; and before the beast could turn leaped upon its back. A bronzed arm encircled the squat neck of the hairy Buckingham. In a frenzy of rage the beast swung around, clawing futilely to rid himself of his antagonist.

He felt the steel thews of the ape-man's arm tightening, and realized that he was coping with muscles far beyond what he had expected. He threw himself to the ground in an effort to crush his foe with his great weight, but Tarzan broke the fall with his feet and slipped partially from beneath the hairy body.

Then Buckingham felt powerful jaws close upon his neck near the jugular, he heard savage growls mingling with his own. Naomi Madison heard too, and a new horror filled her soul. Now she knew why Stanley Obroski had not fled in terror—he had gone mad! Fear and suffering had transformed him into a maniac.

She shuddered at the thought, she shrank within herself as she saw his strong white teeth sink into the black hide of the gorilla and heard the bestial growls rumbling from that handsome mouth.

The two beasts rolled over and over upon the ground, the roars of the gorilla mingling with the growls of the man; and the girl, leaning upon her hands, watched through fascinated, horror-stricken eyes.

She knew that there could be but one outcome—even though the man appeared to have a slight initial advantage, the giant strength of the mighty bull must prevail in the end. Then she saw a knife flash, reflecting the rays of the morning sun. She saw it driven into the great bull's side. She heard his agonized shriek of pain and rage. She saw him redouble his efforts to dislodge the creature clinging to his back.

Again and again the knife was driven home. Suddenly the maddened struggles of the bull grew weaker; then they ceased, and with a convulsive shudder the great form relaxed and lay inert.

The man leaped erect; he paid no attention to the girl; upon his face was the savage snarl of a wild beast. Naomi was terrified; she tried to crawl away and hide from him, but she was too weak. He placed a foot upon the carcass of the dead bull and threw back his head; then from his parted lips burst a cry that made her flesh creep. It was the victory cry of the bull ape, and as its echoes died away in the distance the man turned toward her.

All the savagery had vanished from his face; his gaze was intent and earnest. She looked for a maniacal light in his eyes, but they seemed sane and normal.

"Are you injured?" he asked.

"No," she said and tried to rise, but she had not the strength.

He came and lifted her to her feet. He was so strong! A sense of security swept over her and unnerved her. She threw her arms about his neck and commenced to sob.

"Oh, Stanley! Stanley!" she gasped. She tried to say more, but her sobs choked her.

Obroski had told Tarzan a great deal about the members of the company. He knew the names of all of them, and had identified most of them from having seen them while he had watched the safari in the past. He knew of the budding affair between Obroski and Naomi Madison, and he guessed now from the girl's manner that she must be Naomi. It suited him that these people should think him Stanley Obroski, for the sometimes grim and terrible life that he led required the antidote of occasional humor.

He lifted her in his arms. "Why are you so weak?" he asked. "Is it from hunger?"

She sobbed a scarcely audible "Yes," and buried her face in the hollow of his neck. She was still half afraid of him. It was true that he did not act like a madman, but what else could account for the remarkable accession of courage and strength that had transformed him in the short time since she had last seen him.

She had known that he was muscular; but she had never attributed to him such superhuman strength as that which he had displayed during his duel with the gorilla, and she had known that he was a coward. But this man was no coward.

He carried her for a short distance, and then put her down on a bed of soft grasses. "I will get you something to eat," he said.

She saw him swing lightly into the trees and disappear, and again she was afraid. What a difference it made when he was near her! She puckered her brows to a sudden thought. Why did she feel so safe with Stanley Obroski now? She had never looked upon him as a protector or as able to protect. Every one had considered him a coward. Whatever metamorphosis had occurred had been sufficiently deeprooted to carry its impression to her subconscious mind imparting this new feeling of confidence.

He was gone but a short time, returning with some nuts and fruit. He came and squatted beside her. "Eat a little at a time," he cautioned. "After a while I will get flesh for you; that will bring back your strength."

As she ate she studied him. "You have changed, Stanley," she said.

"Yes?"

"But I like you better. To think that you killed that terrible creature single-handed! It was marvellous."

"What sort of a beast was it?" he asked. "It spoke English."

"It is a mystery to me. It called itself an Englishman and said that it was the Duke of Buckingham. Another one pursued it whom it called Suffolk. A great number of them attacked us at the time that this one took me from the Arabs. They live in a city called London—he pointed it out to me. And Rhonda is a captive there in a castle on a ledge a little above the main part of the city—he said that she was with God in his castle."

"I thought Rhonda had been killed by a lion," said Tarzan.

"So did I until that creature told me differently. Oh, the poor dear! Perhaps it would have been better had the lion killed her. Think of being in the power of those frightful half-men!"

"Where is this city?" asked Tarzan.

"It is back there a way at the foot of the cliff—one can see it plainly from the summit."

The man rose and lifted the girl into his arms again. "Where are you going?" she asked.

"I am going to take you to Orman and West. They should be at the falls before night."

"Oh! They are alive?"

"They were looking for you, and they got lost. They have been hungry, but otherwise they have gotten along all right. They will be glad to see you."

"And then we can get out of this awful country?" she asked.

"First we must find out what became of the others and save Rhonda," he replied.

"Oh, but she can't be saved!" exclaimed the girl. "You should see how those devils fight—the Arabs, even with their guns, were helpless against them. There isn't a chance in the world of saving poor Rhonda, even if she is alive—which I doubt."

"We must try—and, anyway, I wish to see this gorilla city of London."

"You mean you would go there!"

"How else can I see it?"

"Oh, Stanley, please don't go back there!"

"I came here for you."

"Well, then, let Bill West go after Rhonda."

"Do you think he could get her?"

"I don't think any one can get her."

"Perhaps not," he said, "but at least I shall see the city and possibly learn something about these gorillas that talk English. There is a mystery worth solving."

They had reached the south end of the valley where the hills drop down almost to the level of the river. The current here, above the falls, was not swift; and Tarzan waded in with the girl still in his arms.

"Where are you going?" she cried, frightened.

"We have got to cross the river, and it is easier to cross here than below the falls. There the current is much swifter, and there are hippopotamuses and crocodiles. Take hold of my shoulders and hold tight."

He plunged in and struck for the opposite shore, while the terrified girl clung to him in desperation. The farther bank looked far away indeed. Below she could hear the roar of the falls. They seemed to be drifting down toward them.

But presently the strong, even strokes of the swimmer reassured her. He seemed unhurried and unexcited, and gradually she relaxed as though she had absorbed a portion of his confidence. But she sighed in relief as he clambered out on solid ground.

Her terror at the river crossing was nothing to that which she experienced in the descent of the escarpment to the foot of the falls—it froze her to silent horror.

The man descended as nimbly as a monkey; the burden of her weight seemed nothing to him. Where had Stanley Obroski acquired this facility that almost put to shame the mountain goat and the monkey?

Half way down he called her attention to three figures near the foot of the cliff. "There are Orman and West and the Arab," he said, but she did not dare look down.

The three men below them were watching in astonishment —they had just recognized that of the two descending toward them one was Obroski and the other a girl, but whether Naomi or Rhonda they could not be sure.

Orman and West ran forward to meet them as they neared the foot of the cliff. Tears came to Orman's eyes as he took Naomi in his arms; and West was glad to see her too, but he was saddened when he discovered that it was not Rhonda.

"Poor girl!" he muttered as they walked back to their little camp. "Poor Rhonda! What an awful death!"

"But she is not dead," said Naomi.

"Not dead! How do you know?"

"She is worse than dead, Bill," and then Naomi told all that she knew of Rhonda's fate.

When she was through, Tarzan rose. "You have enough of that buck left to last until you can make a kill?" he asked.

"Yes," replied Orman.

"Then I'll be going," said the ape-man.

"Where?" asked the director.

"To find Rhonda."

West leaped to his feet. "I'll go with you, Stanley," he cried.

"But, my God, man! you can't save her now. After what Eyad has told us of those beasts and Naomi's experience with them you must know that you haven't a chance." Orman spoke with great seriousness.

"It is my duty to go anyway," said West, "not Stanley's; and I'm going."

"You'd better stay here," advised Tarzan. "You wouldn't have a chance."

"Why wouldn't I have as good a chance as you?" demanded West.

"Perhaps you would, but you would delay me." Tarzan turned away and walked toward the foot of the escarpment.

Naomi Madison watched him through half closed eyes. "Good bye, Stanley!" she called.

"Oh, good-bye!" replied the ape-man and continued on.

They saw him seize a trailing liana and climb to another handhold; the quick equatorial night engulfed him before he reached the top.

West had stood silently watching him, stunned by his grief. "I'm going with him," he said finally and started for the escarpment.

"Why, you couldn't climb that place in the daytime, let alone after dark," warned Orman.

"Don't be foolish, Bill," counselled Naomi. "We know how you feel, but there's no sense throwing away another life uselessly. Even Stanley'll never come back." She commenced to sob.

"Then I won't either," said West; "but I'm goin'."

24
God

BEYOND the summit of the escarpment the ape-man moved silently through the night. He heard familiar noises, and his nostrils caught familiar scents that told him that the great cats roamed this strange valley of the gorillas.

He crossed the river farther up than he had swum it with Naomi, and he kept to the floor of the valley as he sought the mysterious city. He had no plan, for he knew nothing of what lay ahead of him—his planning must await the result of his reconnaissance.

He moved swiftly, often at a trot that covered much ground; and presently he saw dim lights ahead. That must be the city! He left the river and moved in a straight line toward the lights, cutting across a bend in the river which again swung back into his path just before he reached the shadowy mass of many buildings.

The city was walled, probably, he thought, against lions; but Tarzan was not greatly concerned—he had scaled walls before. When he reached this one he discovered that it was not high—perhaps ten feet—but sharpened stakes, pointing downward, had been set at close intervals just below the capstones, providing an adequate defense against the great cats.

The ape-man followed the wall back toward the cliff, where it joined the rocky, precipitous face of the escarpment. He listened, scenting the air with his delicate nostrils, seeking to assure himself that nothing was near on the opposite side of the wall.

Satisfied, he leaped for the stakes. His hands closed upon two of them; then he drew himself up slowly until his hips were on a level with his hands, his arms straight at his sides. Leaning forward, he let his body drop slowly forward until it rested on the stakes and the top of the wall.

Now he could look down into the narrow alleyway beyond the barrier. There was no sign of life as far as he could see in either direction—just a dark, shadowy, deserted alleyway. It required but a moment now to draw his body to the wall top and drop to the ground inside the city of the gorillas.

From the vantage point of the wall he had seen lights a short distance above the level of the main part of the city and what seemed to be the shadowy outlines of a large building. That, he conjectured, must be the castle of God, of which Naomi Madison had spoken.

If he were right, that would be his goal; for there the other girl was supposed to be imprisoned. He moved along the face of the cliff in a narrow, winding alley that followed generally the contour of the base of the mountain, though sometimes it wound around buildings that had been built against the cliff.

He hoped that he would meet none of the denizens of the city, for the passage was so narrow that he could not avoid detection; and it was so winding that an enemy might be upon him before he could find concealment in a shadowy doorway or upon a rooftop, which latter he had decided would make the safest hiding place and easy of access, since many of the buildings were low.

He heard voices and saw the dim glow of lights in another part of the city, and presently there rose above the strange city the booming of drums.

Shortly thereafter Tarzan came to a flight of steps cut from the living rock of the cliff. They led upward, disappearing in the gloom above; but they pointed in the general direction of the building he wished to reach. Pausing only long enough to reconnoiter with his ears, the ape-man started the ascent.

He had climbed but a short distance when he turned to see the city spread out below him. Not far from the foot of the cliff rose the towers and battlements of what appeared to be a medieval castle. From within its outer walls came the light that he had seen dimly from another part of the city; from here too came the sound of drumming. It was reminiscent of another day, another scene. In retrospection it all came vividly before him now.

He saw the shaggy figures of the great apes of the tribe of Kerchak. He saw an earthen drum. About it the apes were forming a great circle. The females and the young squatted in a thin line at its periphery, while just in front of them ranged the adult males. Before the drum sat three old females,

each armed with a knotted branch fifteen or eighteen inches
in length.

Slowly and softly they began tapping upon the resounding
surface of the drum as the first, faint rays of the ascending
moon silvered the encircling tree-tops. Then, as the light in
the amphitheater increased, the females augmented the fre-
quency and force of their blows until presently a wild, rhyth-
mic din pervaded the great jungle for miles in every direction.

As the din of the drum rose to almost deafening volume
Kerchak sprang into the open space between the squatting
males and the drummers. Standing erect he threw his head
far back and looking full into the eye of the rising moon he
beat upon his breast with his great hairy paws and emitted
a fearful, roaring shriek.

Then, crouching, Kerchak slunk noiselessly around the
open circle, veering away from a dead body that lay before
the altar-drum; but, as he passed, keeping his fierce, wicked
eyes upon the corpse.

Another male then sprang into the arena and, repeating the
horrid cries of his king, followed stealthily in his wake.
Another and another followed in quick succession until the
jungle reverberated with the now almost ceaseless notes of
their bloodthirsty screams. It was the challenge and the hunt.

How plainly it all came back to the ape-man now as he
heard the familiar beating of the drums in this far-off city!

As he ascended the steps farther he could see over
the top of the castle wall below into the courtyard beyond.
He saw a number of gorillas dancing to the booming of the
drums. The scene was lit by torches, and as he watched, a fire
was lighted near the dancers. The dry material of which it was
built ignited quickly and blazed high, revealing the scene in
the courtyard like daylight and illuminating the face of the
cliff and the stairway that Tarzan was ascending; then it died
down as quickly as it had arisen.

The ape-man hastened up the stone stairway that wound
and zigzagged up the cliff face, hoping that no eye had discerned him during the brief illumination of the cliff. There
was no indication that he had been discovered as he approached the grim pile now towering close above him, because
the strange figure gazing down upon him from the ramparts of
the castle gave no sign that might apprise the ape-man of its
presence. Chuckling, it turned away and disappeared through
an embrasure in a turret.

At the top of the stairway Tarzan found himself upon a

broad terrace, the fore part of the great ledge upon which the castle was built. Before him rose the grim edifice without wall or moat looming menacingly in the darkness.

The only opening on the level of the ledge was a large double doorway, one of the doors of which stood slightly ajar. Perhaps the lord of the jungle should have been warned by this easy accessibility. Perhaps it did arouse his suspicions— the natural suspicion of the wild thing for the trap—but he had come here for the purpose of entering this building; and he could not ignore such a God-given opportunity.

Cautiously he approached the doorway. Beyond was only darkness. He pushed against the great door, and it swung silently inward. He was glad that the hinges had not creaked. He paused a moment in the opening, listening. From within came the scent of gorillas and a strange man-like scent that intrigued and troubled him, but he neither heard nor saw signs of life beyond the doorway.

As his eyes became accustomed to the gloom of the interior he saw that he was in a semi-circular foyer in the posterior wall of which were set several doors. Approaching the door farthest to the left he tried it; but it was locked, nor could he open the second. The third, however, swung in as he pushed upon it, revealing a descending staircase.

He listened intently but heard nothing; then he tried the fourth door. It too was locked. So were the fifth and sixth. This was the last door, and he returned to the third. Passing through it he descended the stairway, feeling his way through the darkness.

Still all was silence. Not a sound had come to his ears since he had entered the building to suggest that there was another within it than himself; yet he knew that there were living creatures there. His sensitive nostrils had told him that and the strange, uncanny instinct of the jungle beast.

At the foot of the stairs he groped with his hands, finding a door. He felt for and found a latch. Lifting it, he pushed upon the door; and it opened. Then there came strongly to his nostrils the scent of a woman—a white woman! Had he found her? Had he found the one he sought?

The room was utterly dark. He stepped into it, and as he released the door he heard it close behind him with a gentle click. With the quick intuition of the wild beast, he guessed that he was trapped. He sprang back to the door, seeking to open it; but his fingers found only a smooth surface.

He stood in silence, listening, waiting. He heard rapid

breathing at a little distance from him. Insistent in his nostrils was the scent of the woman. He guessed that the breathing he heard was hers; its tempo connoted fear. Cautiously he approached the sound.

He was quite close when a noise ahead of him brought him to a sudden halt. It sounded like the creaking of rusty hinges. Then a light appeared revealing the whole scene.

Directly before him on a pallet of straw sat a white woman. Beyond her was a door constructed of iron bars through which he saw another chamber. At the far side of this second chamber was a doorway in which stood a strange creature holding a lighted torch in one hand. Tarzan could not tell if it were human or gorilla.

It approached the barred doorway, chuckling softly to itself. The woman had turned her face away from Tarzan and was looking at the thing in horror. Now she turned a quick glance toward the ape-man. He saw that she was quite like the girl, Naomi, and very beautiful.

As her eyes fell upon him, revealed by the flickering light of the torch, she gasped in astonishment. "Stanley Obroski!" she ejaculated. "Are you a prisoner too?"

"I guess I am," replied the ape-man.

"What were you doing here? How did they get you? I thought that you were dead."

"I came here to find you," he replied.

"You!" Her tone was incredulous.

The creature in the next room had approached the bars, and stood there chuckling softly. Tarzan looked up at it. It had the face of a man, but its skin was black like that of a gorilla. Its grinning lips revealed the heavy fangs on the anthropoid. Scant black hair covered those portions of its body that an open shirt and a loin cloth revealed. The skin of the body, arms, and legs was black with large patches of white. The bare feet were the feet of a man; the hands were black and hairy and wrinkled, with long, curved claws; the eyes were the sunken eyes of an old man—a very old man.

"So you are acquainted?" he said. "How interesting! And you came to get her, did you? I thought that you had come to call on me. Of course it is not quite the proper thing for a stranger to come by night without an invitation—and by stealth.

"It was just by the merest chance that I learned of your coming. I have Henry to thank for that. Had he not been staging a dance I should not have known, and thus I should have been denied the pleasure of receiving you as I have.

"You see, I was looking down from my castle into the courtyard of Henry's palace when his bonfire flared up and lighted the Holy Stairs—and there you were!"

The creature's voice was well modulated, its diction that of a cultivated Englishman. The incongruity between its speech and its appearance rendered the latter all the more repulsive and appalling by contrast.

"Yes, I came for this girl," said the ape-man.

"And now you are a prisoner too." The creature chuckled.

"What do you want of us?" demanded Tarzan. "We are not enemies; we have not harmed you."

"What do I want of you! That is a long story. But perhaps you two would understand and appreciate it. The beasts with which I am surrounded hear, but they do not understand. Before you serve my final purpose I shall keep you for a while for the pleasure of conversing with rational human beings.

"I have not seen any for a long time, a long, long time. Of course I hate them none the less, but I must admit that I shall find pleasure in their companionship for a short time. You are both very good-looking too. That will make it all the more pleasant, just as it increases your value for the purpose for which I intend you—the final purpose, you understand. I am particularly pleased that the girl is so beautiful. I always did have a fondness for blonds. Were I not already engaged along other lines of research, and were it possible, I should like nothing better than to conduct a scientific investigation to determine the biological or psychological explanation of the profound attraction that the blond female has for the male of all races."

From the pocket of his shirt he extracted a couple of crudely fashioned cheroots, one of which he proferred through the bars to Tarzan. "Will you not smoke Mr.—ah—er—Obroski I believe the young lady called you. Stanley Obroski! That would be a Polish name, I believe; but you do not resemble a Pole. You look quite English—quite as English as I."

"I do not smoke," said Tarzan, and then added, "than you."

"You do not know what you miss—tobacco is such a boon to tired nerves."

"My nerves are never tired."

"Fortunate man! And fortunate for me too. I could not ask for anything better than a combination of youth with a healthy body and a healthy nervous system—to say nothing of your unquestionable masculine beauty. I shall be wholly regenerated."

"I do not know what you are talking about," said Tarzan.

"No, of course not. How could one expect that you would understand what I alone in all the world know! But some other time I shall be delighted to explain. Right now I must go up and have a look down into the king's courtyard. I find that I must keep an eye on Henry the Eighth. He has been grossly misbehaving himself of late—he and Suffolk and Howard. I shall leave this torch burning for you—it will make it much more pleasant; and I want you to enjoy yourselves as much as possible before the—ah—er—well, *au revoir!* Make yourselves quite at home." He turned and crossed toward a door at the opposite side of the room, chuckling as he went.

Tarzan stepped quickly to the bars separating the two rooms. "Come back here!" he commanded. "Either let us out of this hole or tell us why you are holding us—what you intend doing with us."

The creature wheeled suddenly, its expression transformed by a hideous snarl. "You dare issue orders to me!" it screamed.

"And why not?" demanded the ape-man. "Who are you?"

The creature took a step nearer the bars and tapped its hairy chest with a horny talon. "I am God!" it cried.

25
"Before I Eat You!"

A S THE thing that called itself God departed from the other chamber, closing the door after it, Tarzan turned toward the girl sitting on the straw of their prison cell.

"I have seen many strange things in my life," he said, "but this is by far the strangest. Sometimes I think that I must be dreaming."

"That is what I thought at first," replied the girl; "but this is no dream—it is a terrible, a frightful reality."

"Including God?" he asked.

"Yes; even God is a reality. That thing is the god of these gorillas. They all fear him and most of them worship him.

They say that he created them. I do not understand it—it is all like a hideous chimera."

"What do you suppose he intends to do with us?"

"Oh, I don't know; but it is something horrible," she replied. "Down in the city they venture hideous guesses, but even they do not know. He brings young gorillas here, and they are never seen again."

"How long have you been here?"

"I have been in God's castle since yesterday, but I was in the palace of Henry the Eighth for more than a week. Don't those names sound incongruous when applied to beasts?"

"I thought that nothing more could ever sound strange to me after I met *Buckingham* this morning and heard him speak English—a bull gorilla!"

"You met Buckingham? It was he who captured me and brought me to this city. Did he capture you too?"

Tarzan shook his head. "No. He had captured Naomi Madison."

"Naomi! What became of her?"

"She is with Orman and West and one of the Arabs at the foot of the falls. I came here to find you and take you to them; but it is commencing to look as though I had made a mess of it—getting captured myself."

"But how did Naomi get away from Buckingham?" demanded the girl.

"I killed him."

"*You* killed *Buckingham!*" She looked at him with wide, unbelieving eyes.

From the reactions of the others toward his various exploits Tarzan had already come to understand that Obroski's friends had not held his courage in very high esteem, and so it amused him all the more that they should mistake him for this unquestioned coward.

The girl surveyed him in silence through level eyes for several moments as though she were trying to read his soul and learn the measure of his imposture; then she shook her head.

"You're not a bad kid, Stanley," she said; "but you mustn't tell naughty stories to your Aunt Rhonda."

One of the ape-man's rare smiles bared his strong, white teeth. "No one can fool you, can they?" he asked admiringly.

"Well, I'll admit that they'd have to get up pretty early in the morning to put anything over on Rhonda Terry. But what I can't understand is that make-up of yours—the scenery—where did you get it and why? I should think you'd freeze."

"You will have to ask Rungula, chief of the Bansutos," replied Tarzan.

"What has he to do with it?"

"He appropriated the Obroski wardrobe."

"I commence to see the light. But if you were captured by the Bansutos, how did you escape?"

"If I told you you would not believe me. You do not believe that I killed Buckingham."

"How could I, unless you sneaked up on him while he was asleep? It just isn't in the cards, Stanley, for any man to have killed that big gorilla unless he had a rifle—that's it! You shot him."

"And then threw my rifle away?" inquired the ape-man.

"M-m-m, that doesn't sound reasonable, does it? No, I guess you're just a plain damn liar, Stanley."

"Thank you."

"Don't get sore. I really like you and always have; but I have seen too much of life to believe in miracles, and the idea of you killing Buckingham single-handed would be nothing short of a miracle."

Tarzan turned away and commenced to examine the room in which they were confined. The flickering light of the torch in the adjoining room lighted it dimly. He found a square chamber the walls of which were faced with roughly hewn stone. The ceiling was of planking supported by huge beams. The far end of the room was so dark that he could not see the ceiling at that point; the last beam cast a heavy shadow there upon the ceiling. He thought he detected a steady current of air moving from the barred doorway of the other room to this far corner of their cell, suggesting an opening there; but he could find none, and abandoned the idea.

Having finished his inspection he came and sat down on the straw beside Rhonda. "You say you have been here a week?" he inquired.

"In the city—not right here," she replied. "Why?"

"I was thinking—they must feed you, then?" he inquired.

"Yes; celery, bamboo tips, fruit, and nuts—it gets monotonous."

"I was not thinking of *what* they fed you but of how. How is your food brought to you and when? I mean since you have been in this room."

"When they brought me here yesterday they gave me

enough food for the day; this morning they brought me another day's supply. They bring it into that next room and shove it through the bars—no dishes or anything like that—they just shove it through onto the floor with their dirty, bare hands, or paws. All except the water—they bring water in that gourd there in the corner."

"They don't open the door, then, and come into the room?"

"No."

"That is too bad."

"Why?"

"If they opened the door we might have a chance to escape," explained the ape-man.

"Not a chance—the food is brought by a big bull gorilla. Oh, I forgot!" she exclaimed, laughing. "You'd probably break him in two and throw him in the waste basket like you did Buckingham."

Tarzan laughed with her. "I keep forgetting that I am a coward," he said. "You must be sure to remind me if any danger threatens us."

"I guess you won't have to be reminded, Stanley." She was looking at him again closely. "But you have changed in some way," she ventured finally. "I don't know just how to explain it, but you seem to have more assurance. And you sure put up a good front when you were talking to God. Say! Do you suppose what you've been through the past few weeks has affected your mind?"

Further conversation was interrupted by the return of God. He pulled a chair up in front of the barred door and sat down.

"Henry is a fool," he announced. "He's trying to work his followers up to a pitch that will make it possible for him to induce them to attack heaven and kill God. Henry wants to be God. But he gave them too much to drink; and now most of them are asleep in the palace courtyard, including Henry. They won't bother me tonight; so I thought I'd come down and have a pleasant visit with you. There won't be many more opportunities, for you will have to serve your purpose before something happens to prevent. I can't take any chances."

"What is this strange purpose we are to serve?" asked Rhonda.

"It is purely scientific; but it is a long story and I shall have to start at the beginning," explained God.

"The beginning!" he repeated dreamily. "How long ago it was! It was while I was still an undergraduate at Oxford that I first had a glimmering of the light that finally dawned. Let me see—that must have been about 1855. No, it was before that—I graduated in '55. That's right, I was born in '33 and I was twenty-two when I graduated.

"I had always been intrigued by Lamarck's investigations and later by Darwin's. They were on the right track, but they did not go far enough; then, shortly after my graduation, I was travelling in Austria when I met a priest at Brunn who was working along lines similar to mine. His name was Mendel. We exchanged ideas. He was the only man in the world who could appreciate me, but he could not go all the way with me. I got some help from him; but, doubtless, he got more from me; though I never heard anything more about him before I left England.

"In 1857 I felt that I had practically solved the mystery of heredity, and in that year I published a monograph on the subject. I will explain the essence of my discoveries in as simple language as possible, so that you may understand the purpose you are to serve.

"Briefly, there are two types of cells that we inherit from our parents—body cells and germ cells. These cells are composed of chromosomes containing genes—a separate gene for each mental and physical characteristic. The body cells, dividing, multiplying, changing, growing, determine the sort of individual we are to be; the germ cells, remaining practically unchanged from our conception, determine what characteristics our progeny will inherit, through us, from our progenitors and from us.

"I determined that heredity could be controlled through the transference of these genes from one individual to another. I learned that the genes never die; they are absolutely indestructible—the basis of all life on earth, the promise of immortality throughout all eternity.

"I was certain of all this, but I could carry on no experiments. Scientists scoffed at me, the public laughed at me, the authorities threatened to lock me up in a madhouse. The church wished to crucify me.

"I hid, and carried on my research in secret. I obtained genes from living subjects—young men and women whom I enticed to my laboratory on various pretexts. I drugged them and extracted germ cells from them. I had not discovered at that time, or, I should say, I had not perfected the technic of recovering body cells.

"In 1858 I managed, through bribery, to gain access to a

number of tombs in Westminster Abbey; and from the corpses of former kings and queens of England and many a noble lord and lady I extracted the deathless genes.

"It was the rape of Henry the Eighth that caused my undoing. I was discovered in the act by one who had not been bribed. He did not turn me over to the authorities, but he commenced to blackmail me. Because of him I faced either financial ruin or a long term in prison.

"My fellow scientists had flouted me; the government would punish me; I saw that my only rewards for my labors for mankind were to be ingratitude and persecution. I grew to hate man, with his bigotry, his hypocrisy, and his ignorance. I still hate him.

"I fled England. My plans were already made. I came to Africa and employed a white guide to lead me to gorilla country. He brought me here; then I killed him, so that no one might learn of my whereabouts.

"There were hundreds of gorillas here, yes, thousands. I poisoned their food, I shot them with poisoned arrows; but I used a poison that only anesthetized them. Then I removed their germ cells and substituted human cells that I had brought with me from England in a culture medium that encouraged their multiplication."

The strange creature seemed warmed by some mysterious inner fire as he discoursed on this, his favorite subject. The man and the girl listening to him almost forgot the incongruity of his cultured English diction and his hideous, repulsive appearance—far more hideous and repulsive than that of the gorillas; for he seemed neither beast nor man but rather some horrid hybrid born of an unholy union. Yet the mind within that repellant skull held them fascinated.

"For years I watched then," he continued, "with increasing disappointment. From generation to generation I could note no outward indication that the human germ cells had exerted the slightest influence upon the anthropoids; then I commenced to note indications of greater intelligence among them. Also, they quarrelled more, were more avaricious, more vindictive—they were revealing more and more the traits of man. I felt that I was approaching my goal.

"I captured some of the young and started to train them. Very shortly after this training commenced I heard them repeating English words among themselves—words that they had heard me speak. Of course they did not know the meaning of the words; but that was immaterial—they had revealed the truth to me. My gorillas had inherited the minds and vocal organs of their synthetic human progenitors.

"The exact reason why they inherited these human attributes and not others is still a mystery that I have not solved. But I had proved the correctness of my theory. Now I set to work to educate my wards. It was not difficult. I sent these first out as missionaries and teachers.

"As the gorillas learned and came to me for further instruction, I taught them agriculture, architecture, and building—among other things. Under my direction they built this city, which I named London, upon the river that I have called Thames. We English always take England wherever we go.

"I gave them laws, I became their god, I gave them a royal family and a nobility. They owe everything to me, and now some of them want to turn upon me and destroy me—yes, they have become very human. They have become ambitious, treacherous, cruel—they are almost men."

"But you?" asked the girl. "You are not human. You are part gorilla. How could you have been an Englishman?"

"I am an Englishman, nevertheless," replied the creature. "Once I was a very handsome Englishman. But old age overtook me. I felt my powers failing. I saw the grave beckoning. I did not wish to die, for I felt that I had only commenced to learn the secrets of life.

"I sought some means to prolong my own and to bring back youth. At last I was successful. I discovered how to segregate body cells and transfer them from one individual to another. I used young gorillas of both sexes and transplanted their virile, youthful body cells to my own body.

"I achieved success in so far as staying the ravages of old age is concerned and renewing youth, but as the body cells of the gorillas multiplied within me I began to acquire the physical characteristics of gorillas. My skin turned black, hair grew upon all parts of my body, my hands changed, my teeth; some day I shall be, to all intent and purpose, a gorilla. Or rather I should have been had it not been for the fortunate circumstance that brought you to me."

"I do not understand," said Rhonda.

"You will. With the body cells from you and this young man I shall not only insure my youth, but I shall again take on the semblance of man." His eyes burned with a mad fire.

The girl shuddered. "It is horrible!" she exclaimed.

The creature chuckled. "You will be serving a noble purpose—a far more noble purpose than as though you had merely fulfilled the prosaic biological destiny for which you were born."

"But you will not have to kill us!" she exclaimed. "You take the germ cells from gorillas without killing them. When you have taken some from us, you will let us go?"

The creature rose and came close to the bars. His yellow fangs were bared in a fiendish grin. "You do not know all," he said. A mad light shone in his blazing eyes. "I have not told you all that I have learned about rejuvenation. The new body cells are potent, but they work slowly. I have found that by eating the flesh and the glands of youth the speed of the metamorphosis is accelerated.

"I leave you now to meditate upon the great service that you are to render science!" He backed toward the far door of the other apartment. "But I will return. Later I shall eat you— eat you both. I shall eat the man first; and then, my beauty, I shall eat you! But before I eat you—ah, before I eat you!"

Chuckling, he backed through the doorway and closed the door after him.

26
Trapped

IT LOOKS like curtains," said the girl.

"Curtains?"

"The end of the show."

Tarzan smiled. "I suppose you mean that there is no hope for us—that we are doomed."

"It looks like it, and I am afraid. Aren't you afraid?"

"I presume that I am supposed to be, eh?"

She surveyed him from beneath puckered brows. "I cannot understand you, Stanley," she said. "You do not seem to be afraid now, but you used to be afraid of everything. Aren't you really afraid, or are you just posing—the actor, you know?"

"Perhaps I feel that what is about to happen is about to happen and that being afraid won't help any. Fear will never get us out of here alive, and I certainly don't intend to stay here and die if I can help it."

"I don't see how we are going to get out," said Rhonda.

"We are nine tenths out now."

"What do you mean?"

"We are still alive," he laughed, "and that is fully nine tenths of safety. If we were dead we would be a hundred per cent lost; so alive we should certainly be at least ninety per cent saved."

Rhonda laughed. "I didn't know you were such an optimist," she declared.

"Perhaps I have something to be optimistic about," he replied. "Do you feel that draft on the floor?"

She looked up at him quickly. There was a troubled expression in her eyes as she scrutinized his. "Perhaps you had better lie down and try to sleep," she suggested. "You are overwrought."

It was his turn to eye her. "What do you mean?" he asked. "Do I seem exhausted?"

"No, but—but I just thought the strain might have been too great on you."

"What strain?" he inquired.

"What strain!" she exclaimed. "Stanley Obroski, you come and lie down here and let me rub your head—perhaps it will put you to sleep."

"I'm not sleepy. Don't you want to get out of here?"

"Of course I do, but we can't."

"Perhaps not, but we can try. I asked you if you felt the draft on the floor."

"Of course I feel it, but what has that to do with anything. I'm not cold."

"It may not have anything to do with anything," Tarzan admitted, "but it suggests possibilities."

"What possibilities?" she demanded.

"A way out. The fresh air comes in from that other room through the bars of that door; it has to go out somewhere. The draft is so strong that it suggests a rather large opening. Do you see any large opening in this room through which the air could escape."

The girl rose to her feet. She was commencing to understand the drift of his remarks. "No," she said, "I see no opening."

"Neither do I; but there must be one, and we know that it must be some place that we cannot see." He spoke in a whisper.

"Yes, that is right."

"And the only part of this room that we can't see plainly is among the dark shadows on the ceiling over in that far corner. Also, I have felt the air current moving in that direction."

He walked over to the part of the room he had indicated and looked up into the darkness. The girl came and stood beside him, also peering upward.

"Do you see anything?" she asked, her voice barely audible.

"It is very dark," he replied, "but I think that I do see something—a little patch that appears darker than the rest, as though it had depth."

"Your eyes are better than mine," she said. "I see nothing."

From somewhere apparently directly above them, but at a distance, sounded a hollow chuckle, weird, uncanny.

Rhonda laid her hand impulsively on Tarzan's arm. "You are right," she whispered. "There is an opening above us—that sound came down through it."

"We must be very careful what we say above a whisper," he cautioned.

The opening in the ceiling, if such it were, appeared to be directly in the corner of the room. Tarzan examined the walls carefully, feeling every square foot of them as high as he could reach; but he found nothing that would give him a handhold. Then he sprang upward with outstretched hand—and felt an edge of an opening in the ceiling.

"It is there," he whispered.

"But what good will it do us? We can't reach it."

"We can try," he said; then he stooped down close to the wall in the corner of the room. "Get on my shoulders," he directed—"Stand on them. Support yourself with your hands against the wall."

Rhonda climbed to his broad shoulders. Grasping her legs to steady her, he rose slowly until he stood erect.

"Feel carefully in all directions," he whispered. "Estimate the seize of the opening; search for a handhold."

For some time the girl was silent. He could tell by the shifting of her weight from one foot to the other and by the stretching of her leg muscles that she was examining the opening in every direction as far as she could reach.

Presently she spoke to him. "Let me down," she said.

He lowered her to the floor. "What did you discover?" he asked.

"The opening is about two feet by three. It seems to extend inward over the top of the wall at one side—I could distinctly feel a ledge there. If I could get on it I could explore higher."

"We'll try again," said Tarzan. "Put your hands on my shoulders." They stood facing one another. "Now place your left foot in my right hand. That's it! Straighten up and put your other foot in my left hand. Now keep your legs and body rigid, steady yourself with your hands against the wall; and I'll lift you up again—probably a foot and a half higher than you were before."

"All right," she whispered. "Lift!"

He raised her easily but slowly to the full extent of his arms. For a moment he held her thus; then, first from one hand and then from the other, her weight was lifted from him.

He waited, listening. A long minute of silence ensued; then, from above him, came a surprised "Ouch!"

Tarzan made no sound, he asked no question—he waited. He could hear her breathing, and knew that nothing very serious had surprised that exclamation from her. Presently he caught a low whisper from above.

"Toss me your rope!"

He lifted the grass rope from where it lay coiled across one shoulder and threw a loop upward into the darkness toward the girl above. The first time, she missed it and it fell back; but the next, she caught it. He heard her working with it in the darkness above.

"Try it," she whispered presently.

He seized the rope above his head and raised his feet from the ground so that it supported all his weight. It held without slipping; then, hand over hand, he climbed. He felt the girl reach out and touch his body; then she guided one of his feet to the ledge where she stood—a moment later he was standing by her side.

"What have you found?" he asked, straining his eyes through the darkness.

"I found a wooden beam," she replied. "I bumped my head on it."

He understood now the origin of the exclamation he had heard, and reaching out felt a heavy beam opposite his shoulders. The rope was fastened around it. The ledge they were standing on was evidently the top of the wall of the room below. The shaft that ran upward was, as the girl had said, about two feet by three. The beam bisected its longer axis, leaving a space on each side large enough to permit a man's body to pass.

Tarzan wedged himself through, and clambered to the top of the beam. Above him, the shaft rose as far as he could reach without handhold or foothold.

He leaned down toward the girl. "Give me your hand," he said, and lifted her to the beam. "We've got to do a little more exploring," he whispered. "I'll lift you as I did before."

"I hope you can keep your balance on this beam," she said, but she did not hesitate to step into his cupped hands.

"I hope so," he replied laconically.

For a moment she groped about above her; then she whispered, "Let me down."

He lowered her to his side, holding her so that she would not lose her balance and fall.

"Well?" he asked.

"I found another beam," she said, "but the top of it is just out of my reach. I could feel the bottom and a part of each side, but I was just a few inches too short to reach the top. What are we to do? It is just like a nightmare—straining here in the darkness, with some horrible menace lurking ready to seize one, and not being quite able to reach the sole means of safety."

Tarzan stooped and untied the rope that was still fastened around the beam upon which they stood.

"The tarmangani have a number of foolish sayings," he remarked. "One of them is that there are more ways than one of skinning a cat."

"Who are the tarmangani?" she asked.

Tarzan grinned in the safety of the concealing darkness. For a moment he had forgotten that he was playing a part. "Oh, just a silly tribe," he replied.

"That is an old saying in America. I have heard my grandfather use it. It is strange that an African tribe should have an identical proverb."

He did not tell her that in his mother tongue, the first language that he had learned, the language of the great apes, tarmangani meant any or all white men.

He coiled the rope; and, holding one end, tossed the coils into the darkness of the shaft above him. They fell back on top of them. Again he coiled and threw—again with the same result. Twice more he failed, and then the end of the rope that he held in his hand remained stretching up into the darkness while the opposite end dropped to swing against them. With the free end that he had thrown over the beam he bent a noose around the length that depended from the opposite side of the beam, making it fast with a bowline knot; then he pulled the noose up tight against the beam above.

"Do you think you can climb it?" he asked the girl.

"I don't know," she said, "but I can try."

"You might fall," he warned. "I'll carry you." He swung her lightly to his back before she realized what he purposed. "Hold tight!" he admonished; then he swarmed up the rope like a monkey.

At the top he seized the beam and drew himself and the girl onto it; and here they repeated what they had done before, searching for and finding another beam above the one upon which they stood.

As the ape-man drew himself to the third beam he saw an opening directly before his face, and through the opening a star. Now the darkness was relieved. The faint light of a partially cloudy night revealed a little section of flat roof bounded by a parapet, and when Tarzan reconnoitered further he discovered that they had ascended into one of the small towers that surmounted the castle.

As he was about to step from the tower onto the roof he heard the uncanny chuckle with which they were now so familiar, and drew back into the darkness of the interior. Silent and motionless the two stood there waiting, listening.

The chuckling was repeated, this time nearer; and to the keen ears of Tarzan came the sound of naked feet approaching. His ears told him more than this; they told him that the thing that walked did not walk alone—there was another with it.

Presently they came in sight, walking slowly. One of them, as the ape-man had guessed, was the creature that called itself God; the other was a large bull gorilla.

As they came opposite the two fugitives they stopped and leaned upon the parapet, looking down into the city.

"Henry should not have caroused tonight, Cranmer," remarked the creature called God. "He has a hard day before him tomorrow."

"How is that, My Lord God?" inquired the other.

"Have you forgotten that this is the anniversary of the completion of the Holy Stairway to Heaven?"

"'Sblood! So it is, and Henry has to walk up it on his hands to worship at the feet of his God."

"And Henry is getting old and much too fat. The sun will

be hot too. But—it humbleth the pride of kings and teacheth humility to the common people."

"Let none forget that thou art the Lord our God, O Father!" said Cranmer piously.

"And what a surprise I'll have for Henry when he reaches the top of the stairs! There I'll stand with this English girl I stole from him kneeling at my feet. You sent for her, didn't you, Cranmer?"

"Yes, My Lord, I sent one of the lesser priests to fetch her. They should be here any minute now. But, My Lord, do you think that it will be wise to anger Henry further? You know that many of the nobles are on his side and are plotting against you."

A horrid chuckle broke from the lips of the gorilla-man. "You forget that I am God," he said. "You must never forget that fact, Cranmer. Henry is forgetting it, and his poor memory will prove his undoing." The creature straightened up to its full height. An ugly growl supplanted the chuckle of a moment before. "You all forget," he cried, "that it was I who created you; it is I who can destroy you! First I shall make Henry mad, and then I shall crush him. That is the kind of god that humans like—it is the only kind they can understand. Because they are jealous and cruel and vindictive they have to have a jealous, cruel, vindictive god. I was able to give you only the minds of humans; so I have to be a god that such minds can appreciate. Tomorrow Henry shall appreciate me to the full!"

"What do you mean, My Lord?"

The gorilla god chuckled again. "When he reaches the top of the stairs I am going to blast him; I am going to destroy him."

"You are going to kill the king! But, My Lord, the Prince of Wales is too young to be king."

"He will not be king—I am tired of kings. We shall pass over Edward VI and Mary. That is one of the advantages of having God on your side, Cranmer—we shall skip eleven years and save you from burning at the stake. The next sovereign of England will be Queen Elizabeth."

"Henry has many daughters from which to choose, My Lord," said Cranmer.

"I shall choose none of them. I have just had an inspiration, Cranmer."

"From whence, My Lord God?"

"From myself, of course, you fool! It is perfect. It is

ideal." He chuckled appreciatively. "I am going to make this English girl queen of England—Queen Elizabeth! She will be tractable—she will do as I tell her; and she will serve all my other purposes as well. Or almost all. Of course I cannot eat her, Cranmer. One cannot eat his queen and have her too."

"Here comes the under priest, My Lord," interrupted Cranmer.

"He is alone," exclaimed God. "He has not brought the girl."

An old gorilla lumbered up to the two. He appeared excited.

"Where is the girl?" demanded God.

"She was not there, My Lord. She is gone, and the man too."

"Gone! But that is impossible."

"The room is empty."

"And the doors! Had they been unlocked—either of them?"

"No, My Lord; they were both locked," replied the under priest.

The gorilla god went suddenly silent. For a few moments he remained in thought; then he spoke in very low tones to his two companions.

Tarzan and the girl watched them from their place of concealment in the tower. The ape-man was restless. He wished that they would go away so that he could search for some avenue of escape from the castle. Alone, he might have faced them and relied on his strength and agility to win his freedom; but he could not hope to make good the escape of the girl and himself both in the face of their ignorance of a way out of the castle and the numbers which he was sure the gorilla god could call to his assistance in case of need.

He saw the priest turn and hurry away. The other two walked a short distance from the tower, turned so that they faced it, leaned against the parapet, and continued their conversation; though now Tarzan could no longer overhear their exact words. The position of the two was such that the fugitives could not have left the tower without being seen by them.

The ape-man became apprehensive. The abnormal sensibility of the hunted beast warned him of impending danger; but he did not know where to look for it, nor in what form to expect it.

Presently he saw a bull gorilla roll within the range of

his vision. The beast carried a poke. Behind him came another similarly armed, and another and another and another until twenty of the great anthropoids were gathered on the castle roof.

They clustered about Cranmer and the gorilla god for a minute or two. The latter was talking to them. Tarzan could recognize the tones if not the words. Then the twenty approached the tower and grouped themselves in a semicircle before the low aperture leading into it.

Both Rhonda Terry and the lord of the jungle were assured that their hiding place was guessed if not known, yet they could not be certain. They would wait. That was all that they could do. However, it was an easy place to defend; and they might remain there awaiting some happy circumstance that would give them a better chance of escape than was presented to them at the moment.

The gorillas on the roof seemed only to be waiting. They did not appear to be contemplating an investigation of the interior of the tower. Perhaps, thought Tarzan, they were there for some other purpose than that which he had imagined. They might have been gathered in preparation for the coming of the king to his death in the morning.

By the parapet stood the gorilla god with the bull called Cranmer. The weird chuckle of the former was the only sound that broke the silence of the night. The ape-man wondered why the thing was chuckling.

A sudden upward draft from the shaft below them brought a puff of acrid smoke and a wave of heat. Tarzan felt the girl clutch his arm. Now he knew why the gorillas waited so patiently before the entrance to the tower. Now he knew why the gorilla god chuckled.

27

Holocaust

TARZAN considered the problem that confronted him. It was evident that they could not long endure the stifling, blinding smoke. To make a sudden attack upon the gorillas would be but to jeopardize the life of his companion without offering her any hope of escape. Had he been alone

it would have been different, but now there seemed no alternative to coming quietly out and giving themselves up.

On the other hand he knew that the gorilla god purposed
death for him and either death or a worse fate for the girl.
Whatever course he pursued, then, would evidently prove
disastrous. The ape-man, seldom hesitant in reaching a decision, was frankly in a quandary.

Briefly he explained his doubts to Rhonda. "I think I'll
rush them," he concluded. "At least there will be some satisfaction in that."

"They'd only kill you, Stanley," she said. "Oh, I wish you
hadn't come. It was brave, but you have just thrown away
your life. I can never—" The stifling smoke terminated
her words in a fit of coughing.

"We can't stand this any longer," he muttered. "I'm going
out. Follow me, and watch for a chance to escape."

Stooping low, the ape-man sprang from the tower. A
savage growl rumbled from his deep chest. The girl, following directly behind him, heard and was horrified. She thought
only of the man with her as Stanley Obroski, the coward; and
she believed that his mind must have been deranged by the
hopelessness of his situation.

The gorillas leaped forward to seize him. "Capture him!"
cried the gorilla god. "But do not kill him."

Tarzan leaped at the nearest beast. His knife flashed in the
light of the torches that some of the creatures carried. It
sank deep into the chest of the victim that chance had placed
in the path of the lord of the jungle. The brute screamed,
clutched at the ape-man only to collapse at his feet.

But others closed upon the bronzed giant; then another
and another tasted the steel of that swift blade. The gorilla
god was beside himself with rage and excitement. "Seize
him! Seize him!" he screamed. "Do not kill him! He is mine!"

During the excitement Rhonda sought an avenue of escape. She slunk behind the battling beasts to search for a
stairway leading from the roof. Every eye, every thought
was on the battle being waged before the tower. No one
noticed the girl. She came to a doorway in another tower.
Before her she saw the top of a flight of stairs. They were
illuminated by the flickering light of torches.

At a run she started down. Below her, smoke was billowing, shutting off her view. It was evident, she guessed, that
the smoke from the fire that had been lighted to dislodge

Obroski and herself from the tower had drifted to other parts of the castle.

At a turn in the stairs she ran directly into the arms of a gorilla leaping upward. Behind him were two others. The first seized her and whirled her back to the others. "She must be trying to escape," said her captor. "Bring her along to God." Then he leaped swiftly on up the stairs.

Three gorillas had fallen before Tarzan's knife, but the fourth seized his wrist and struck at him with the haft of his pike. The ape-man closed; his teeth sought the jugular of his antagonist and fastened there. The brute screamed and sought to tear himself free; then one of his companions stepped in and struck Tarzan heavily across one temple with the butt of a battle axe.

The lord of the jungle sank senseless to the roof amid the victorious shouts of his foemen. The gorilla god pushed forward.

"Do not kill him!" he screamed again.

"He is already dead, My Lord," said one of the gorillas.

The god trembled with disappointment and rage, and was about to speak when the gorilla that had recaptured Rhonda forced its way through the crowd.

"The castle is afire, My Lord!" he cried. "The smudge that was built to smoke out the prisoners spread to the dry grass on the floor of their cell, and now the beams and floor above are all ablaze—the first floor of the castle is a roaring furnace. If you are not to be trapped, My Lord, you must escape at once."

Those who heard him looked quickly about. A dense volume of smoke was pouring from the tower from which Tarzan and Rhonda had come; smoke was coming from other towers nearby; it was rising from beyond the parapet, evidently coming from the windows of the lower floors.

There was instant uneasiness. The gorillas rushed uncertainly this way and that. All beasts are terrified by fire, and the instincts of beasts dominated these aberrant creatures. Presently, realizing that they might be cut off from all escape, panic seized them.

Screaming and roaring, they bolted for safety, deserting their prisoners and their god. Some rushed headlong down blazing stairways to death, others leaped the parapet to an end less horrible, perhaps, but equally certain.

Their piercing shrieks, their terrified roars rose above the crackling and the roaring of the flames, above the

screamed commands of their gorilla god, who, seeing himself deserted by his creatures, completely lost his head and
joined in the mad rush for safety.

Fortunately for Rhonda, the two who had her in charge
ignored the instructions of their fellow to bring her before
their god; but, instead, turned and fled down the stairway
before retreat was cut off by the hungry flames licking their
upward way from the pits beneath the castle.

Fighting their way through blinding smoke, their shaggy
coats at one time seared by a sudden burst of flame, the
maddened brutes forgot their prisoner, forgot everything
but their fear of the roaring flames. Even when they won
to the comparative safety of a courtyard they did not stop,
but ran on until they had swung open an outer gate and
rushed headlong from the vicinity of the castle.

Rhonda, almost equally terrified but retaining control of
her wits, took advantage of this opportunity to escape. Following the two gorillas, she came out upon the great ledge
upon which the castle stood. The rising flames now illuminated the scene, and she saw behind her a towering cliff,
seemingly unscalable. Below her lay the city, dark but for
a few flickering torches that spotted the blackness of the
night with their feeble rays.

To her right she saw the stairway leading from the castle
ledge to the city below—the only avenue of escape that she
could discern. If she could reach the city, with its winding,
narrow alleyways, she might make her way unseen across
the wall and out into the valley beyond.

The river would lead her down the valley to the brink of
the escarpment at the foot of which she knew that Orman
and West and Naomi were camped. She shuddered at the
thought of descending that sheer cliff, but she knew that she
would risk much more than this to escape the horrors of the
valley of diamonds.

Running quickly along the ledge to the head of the stairway, she started downward toward the dark city. She ran
swiftly, risking a fall in her anxiety to escape. Behind her rose
the roaring and the crackling of the flames gutting the castle
of God, rose the light of the fire casting her dancing shadow
grotesquely before her, illuminating the stairway; and then,
to her horror, a horde of gorillas rushing up to the doomed
building.

She stopped, but she could not go back. There was no
escape to the right nor to the left. Her only chance lay in

the possibility that they might ignore her in their excitement. Then the leaders saw her.

"The girl!" they cried. "The hairless one! Catch her! Take her to the king!"

Hairy hands seized her. They passed her back to those behind. "Take her to the king!" And again she was hustled and pushed on to others behind. "Take her to the king! Take her to the king!" And so, pulled and hauled and dragged, she was borne down to the city and to the palace of the king.

Once again she found herself with the shes of Henry's harem. They cuffed her and growled at her, for most of them did not wish her back. Catherine of Aragon was the most vindictive. She would have torn the girl to pieces had not Catherine Parr intervened.

"Leave her alone," she warned; "or Henry will have us all beaten, and some of us will lose our heads. All he needs is an excuse to get yours, Catherine," she told the old queen.

At last they ceased abusing her; and, crouching in a corner, she had an opportunity to think for the first time since she had followed Tarzan from the tower. She thought of the man who had risked his life to save hers. It seemed incredible that all of them had so misunderstood Stanley Obroski. Strength and courage seemed so much a part of him now that it was unbelievable that not one of them had ever discerned it. She saw him now through new eyes with a vision that revealed qualities such as women most admire in men and invoked a tenderness that brought a sob to her throat.

Where was he now? Had he escaped? Had they recaptured him? Was he a victim of the flames that she could see billowing from the windows of the great castle on the ledge? Had he died for her?

Suddenly she sat up very straight, her fists clenched until her nails bit into her flesh. A new truth had dawned upon her. This man whom yesterday she had considered with nothing but contempt had aroused within her bosom an emotion that she had never felt for any other man. Was it love? Did she love Stanley Obroski?

She shook her head as though to rid herself of an obsession. No, it could not be that. It must be gratitude and sorrow that she felt—nothing more. Yet the thought persisted. The memory of no other man impinged upon her thoughts in this moment of her extremity before, exhausted by fatigue and excitement, she finally sank into restless slumber.

And while she slept the castle on the ledge burned itself out, the magnificent funeral pyre of those who had been trapped within it.

28
Through Smoke and Flame

As the terrified horde fought for safety and leaped to death from the roof of the castle of God, the gorilla god himself scurried for a secret stairway that led to the courtyard of the castle.

Cranmer and some of the priests knew also of this stairway; and they, too, bolted for it. Several members of the gorilla guard, maddened by terror, followed them; and when they saw the entrance to the stairway fought to be the first to avail themselves of its offer of safety.

Through this fighting, screaming pack the gorilla god sought to force his way. He was weaker than his creatures, and they elbowed him aside. Screaming commands and curses which all ignored, he pawed and clawed in vain endeavor to reach the entrance to the stairs; but always they beat him back.

Suddenly terror and rage drove him mad. Foaming at the mouth, gibbering like a maniac, he threw himself upon the back of a great bull whose bulk barred his way. He beat the creature about the head and shoulders, but the terrified brute paid no attention to him until he sank his fangs deep in its neck; then with a frightful scream it turned upon him. With its mighty paws it tore him from his hold; then, lifting him above its head, the creature hurled him from it. The gorilla god fell heavily to the roof and lay still, stunned.

The crazed beasts at the stairway fought and tore at one another, jamming and wedging themselves into the entrance until they clogged it; then those that remained outside ran toward other stairways, but now it was too late. Smoke and flame roared from every turret and tower. They were trapped!

By ones and twos, with awful shrieks, they hurled themselves over the parapet, leaving the roof to the bodies of the gorilla god and his erstwhile captive.

The flames roared up through the narrow shafts of the towers, transforming them into giant torches, illuminating the face of the cliff towering above, shedding weird lights and shadows on the city and the valley. They ate through the roof at the north end of the castle, and the liberated gases shot smoke and flame high into the night. They gnawed through a great roof beam, and a section of the roof fell into the fiery furnace below showering the city with sparks. Slowly they crept toward the bodies of the ape-man and the gorilla god.

Before the castle, the Holy Stairway and the ledge were packed with the horde that had come up from the city to watch the holocaust. They were awed to silence. Somewhere in that grim pile was their god. They knew nothing of immortality, for he had not taught them that. They thought that their god was dead, and they were afraid. These were the lowly ones. The creatures of the king rejoiced; for they envisaged the power of the god descending upon the shoulders of their leader, conferring more power upon themselves. They were gorillas contaminated by the lusts and greed of men.

On the roof one of the bodies stirred. The eyes opened. It was a moment before the light of consciousness quickened them; then the man sat up. It was Tarzan. He leaped to his feet. All about him was the roaring and crackling of the flames. The heat was intense, almost unbearable.

He saw the body of the gorilla god lying near him. He saw it move. Then the creature sat up quickly and looked about. It saw Tarzan. It saw the flames licking and leaping on all sides, dancing the dance of death—its death.

Tarzan gave it but a single glance and walked away. That part of the roof closest to the cliff was freest of flames, and toward the parapet there he made his way.

The gorilla god followed him. "We are lost," he said. "Every avenue of escape is cut off."

The ape-man shrugged and looked over the edge of the parapet down the side of the castle wall. Twenty feet below was the roof of a section of the building that rose only one storey. It was too far to jump. Flames were coming from the windows on that side, flames and smoke, but not in the volumes that were pouring from the openings on the opposite side.

Tarzan tested the strength of one of the merlons of the battlemented parapet. It was strong. The stones were set in good mortar. He uncoiled his rope, and passed it about the merlon.

The gorilla god had followed him and was watching. "You are going to escape!" he cried. "Oh, save me too."

"So that you can kill and eat me later?" asked the ape-man.

"No, no! I will not harm you. For God's sake save me!"

"I thought you were God. Save yourself."

"You can't desert me. I'm an Englishman. Blood is thicker than water—you wouldn't see an Englishman die when you can save him!"

"I am an Englishman," replied the ape-man, "but you would have killed me and eaten me into the bargain."

"Forgive me that. I was mad to regain my human form, and you offered the only chance that I may ever have. Save me, and I will give you wealth beyond man's wildest dreams of avarice."

"I have all I need," replied Tarzan.

"You don't know what you are talking about. I can lead you to diamonds. Diamonds! Diamonds! You can scoop them up by the handful."

"I care nothing for your diamonds," replied the ape-man, "but I will save you on one condition."

"What is that?"

"That you help me save the girl, if she still lives, and get her out of this valley."

"I promise. But hurry—soon it will be too late."

Tarzan had looped the center of his rope about the merlon; the loose ends dangled a few feet above the roof below. He saw that the rope hung between windows where the flames could not reach it.

"I will go first," he said, "to be sure that you do not run away and forget your promise."

"You do not trust me!" exclaimed the gorilla god.

"Of course not—you are a man."

He lowered his body over the parapet, hung by one hand, and seized both strands of the rope in the other.

The gorilla god shuddered. "I could never do that," he cried. "I should fall. It is awful!" He covered his eyes with his hands.

"Climb over the parapet and get on my back, then,"

directed the ape-man. "Here, I will steady you." He reached up a powerful hand.

"Will the rope hold us both?"

"I don't know. Hurry, or I'll have to go without you. The heat is getting worse."

Trembling, the gorilla god climbed over the parapet; and, steadied and assisted by Tarzan, slid to the ape-man's back where he clung with a deathlike grip about the bronzed neck.

Slowly and carefully Tarzan descended. He had no doubt as to the strength of the rope on a straight pull, but feared that the rough edges of the merlon might cut it.

The heat was terrific. Flames leaped out of the openings on each side of them. Acrid, stifling smoke enveloped them. Where the descent at this point had seemed reasonably safe a moment before, it was now fraught with dangers that made the outcome of their venture appear more than doubtful. It was as though the fire demon had discovered their attempt to escape his clutches and had marshalled all his forces to defeat it and add them to his list of victims.

With grim persistence Tarzan continued his slow descent. The creature clinging to his back punctuated paroxysms of coughing and choking with piercing screams of terror. The ape-man kept his eyes closed and tried not to breathe in the thick smoke that enveloped them.

His lungs seemed upon the point of bursting when, to his relief, his feet touched solid footing. Instantly he threw himself upon his face and breathed. The rising smoke, ascending with the heat of flames, drew fresh air along the roof on which the two lay; and they filled their lungs with it.

Only for a moment did Tarzan lie thus; then he rolled over on his back and pulled rapidly upon one end of the rope until the other passed about the merlon above and fell to the roof beside him.

This lower roof on which they were was but ten feet above the level of the ground; and, using the rope again, it was only a matter of seconds before the two stood in comparative safety between the castle and the towering cliff.

"Come now," said the ape-man; "we will go around to the front of the castle and find out if the girl escaped."

"We shall have to be careful," cautioned the gorilla god. "This fire will have attracted a crowd from the city. I have many enemies in the palace of the king who would be glad to

capture us both. Then we should be killed and the girl lost—
if she is not already dead."

"What do you suggest, then?" Tarzan was suspicious. He
saw a trap, he saw duplicity in everything conceived by the
mind of man.

"The fire has not reached this low wing yet," explained
the other. "In it is the entrance to a shaft leading down to
the quarters of a faithful priest who dwells in a cave at the
foot of the cliff on a level with the city. If we can reach him
we shall be safe. He will hide us and do my bidding."

Tarzan scowled. He had the wild beast's aversion to entering an unfamiliar enclosure, but he had overheard enough
of the conversation between the gorilla god and Cranmer to
know that the former's statement was at least partially true
—his enemies in the palace might gladly embrace an opportunity to imprison or destroy him.

"Very well," he assented; "but I am going to tie this rope
around your neck so that you may not escape me, and remind you that I still have the knife with which I killed
several of your gorillas. I and the knife will be always near
you."

The gorilla god made no reply; but he submitted to being
secured, and then led the way into the building and to a
cleverly concealed trap opening into the top of a shaft descending into darkness.

Here a ladder led downward, and Tarzan let his companion
precede him into the Stygian blackness of the shaft. They
descended for a short distance to a horizontal corridor which
terminated at another vertical shaft. These shafts and cor-
ridors alternated until the gorilla god finally announced that
they had reached the bottom of the cliff.

Here they proceeded along a corridor until a heavy
wooden door blocked their progress. The gorilla god listened
intently for a moment, his ear close to the planking of the
door. Finally he raised the latch and pushed the door silently
ajar. Through the crack the ape-man saw a rough cave
lighted by a single smoky torch.

"He is not here," said the gorilla god as he pushed the door
open and entered. "He has probably gone with the others to
see the fire."

Tarzan looked about the interior. He saw a smoke black-
ened cave, the floor littered with dirty straw. Opposite the
doorway through which they had entered was another probably leading into the open. It was closed with a massive

wooden door. Near the door was a single small window.
Some sacks made of the skins of animals hung from pegs
driven into the walls. A large jar sitting on the floor held
water.

"We shall have to await his return," said the gorilla god.
"In the meantime let us eat."

He crossed to the bags hanging on the wall and examined
their contents, finding celery, bamboo tips, fruit, and nuts.
He selected what he wished and sat down on the floor. "Help
yourself," he invited with a wave of a hand toward the sacks.

"I have eaten," said Tarzan and sat down near the gorilla
god where he could watch both him and the doorway.

His companion ate in silence for a few minutes; then he
looked up at the ape-man. "You said that you did not want
diamonds." His tone was skeptical. "Then why did you come
here?"

"Not for diamonds."

The gorilla god chuckled. "My people killed some of your
party as they were about to enter the valley. On the body of
one of them was a map of this valley—the valley of diamonds.
Are you surprised that I assume that you came for the diamonds?"

"I knew nothing of the map. How could we have had a
map of this valley which, until we came, was absolutely
unknown to white men?"

"You had a map."

"But who could have made it?"

"I made it."

"You! How could we have a map that you made? Have
you returned to England since you first came here?"

"No—but I made that map."

"You came here because you hated men and to escape
them. It is not reasonable that you should have made a map
to invite men here, and if you did make it how did it get to
America or to England or wherever it was that these—my
people got it?" demanded Tarzan.

"I will tell you. I loved a girl. She was not interested in a
poor scientist with no financial future ahead of him. She
wanted wealth and luxuries. She wanted a rich husband.

"When I came to this valley and found the diamonds I
thought of her. I cannot say that I still loved her, but I
wanted her. I should have liked to be revenged upon her for
the suffering that she had caused me. I thought what a fine
revenge it would be to get her here and keep her here as

long as she lived. I would give her wealth—more wealth than any other creature in the world possessed; but she would be unable to buy anything with it." He chuckled as he recalled his plan.

"So I made the map, and I wrote her a letter. I told her what to do, where to land, and how to form her safari. Then I waited. I have been waiting for seventy-four years, but she has never come.

"I had gone to considerable effort to get the letter to her. It had been necessary for me to go a long way from the valley to find a friendly tribe of natives and employ one of them as a runner to take my letter to the coast. I never knew whether or not the letter reached the coast. The runner might have been killed. Many things might have happened. I often wondered what became of the map. Now it has come back to me—after seventy-four years." Again he chuckled. "And brought another girl—a very much prettier girl. Mine would be—let's see—ninety-four years old, a toothless old hag." He sighed. "But now I suppose that I shall not have either of them."

There was a sound at the outer door. Tarzan sprang to his feet. The door opened, and an old gorilla started to enter. At sight of the ape-man he bared his fangs and paused.

"It is all right, Father Tobin," said the gorilla god. "Come in and close the door."

"My Lord!" exclaimed the old gorilla as he closed the door behind him and threw himself upon his knees. "We thought that you had perished in the flames. Praises be to heaven that you have been spared to us."

"Blessing be upon you, my son," replied the gorilla god. "And now tell me what has happened in the city."

"The castle is destroyed."

"Yes, I knew that; but what of the king? Does he think me dead?"

"All think so; and, may curses descend upon him, Henry is pleased. They say that he will proclaim himself God."

"Do you know aught of the fate of the girl Wolsey rescued from Henry's clutches and brought to my castle? Did she die in the fire?" asked the gorilla god.

"She escaped, My Lord. I saw her."

"Where is she?" demanded Tarzan.

"The king's men recaptured her and took her to the palace."

"That will be the end of her," announced the gorilla god,

"for if Henry insists on marrying her, as he certainly will, Catherine of Aragon will tear her to pieces."

"We must get her away from him at once," said Tarzan.

The gorilla god shrugged. "I doubt if that can be done."

"You have said that some one did it before—Wolsey I think you called him."

"But Wolsey had a strong incentive."

"No stronger than the one you have," said the ape-man quietly, but he jerked a little on the rope about God's neck and fingered the hilt of his hunting knife.

"But how can I do it?" demanded the gorilla god. "Henry has many soldiers. The people think that I am dead, and now they will be more afraid of the king than ever."

"You have many faithful followers, haven't you?" inquired Tarzan.

"Yes."

"Then send this priest out to gather them. Tell them to meet outside this cave with whatever weapons they can obtain."

The priest was looking in astonishment from his god to the stranger who spoke to him with so little reverence and who held an end of the rope tied about the god's neck. With horror, he had even seen the creature jerk the rope.

"Go, Father Tobin," said the gorilla god, "and gather the faithful."

"And see that there is no treachery," snapped Tarzan. "I have your god's promise to help me save that girl. You see this rope about his neck? You see this knife at my side?"

The priest nodded.

"If you both do not do all within your power to help me your god dies." There was no mistaking the sincerity of that statement.

"Go, Father Tobin," said the gorilla god.

"And hurry," added Tarzan.

"I go, My Lord," cried the priest; "but I hate to leave you in the clutches of this creature."

"He will be safe enough if you do your part," Tarzan assured him.

The priest knelt again, crossed himself, and departed. As the door closed after him, Tarzan turned to his companion. "How is it," he asked, "that you have been able to transmit the power to speak and perhaps to reason to these brutes, yet they have not taken on any of the outward physical attributes of man?"

"That is due to no fault of mine," replied the gorilla god, "but rather to an instinct of the beasts themselves more powerful than their newly acquired reasoning faculties. Transmitting human germ cells from generation to generation, as they now do, it is not strange that there are often born to them children with the physical attributes of human beings. But in spite of all that I can do these sports have invariably been destroyed at birth.

"In the few cases where they have been spared they have developed into monsters that seem neither beast nor human —manlike creatures with all the worst qualities of man and beast. Some of these have either been driven out of the city or have escaped, and there is known to be a tribe of them living in caves on the far side of the valley.

"I know of two instances where the mutants were absolutely perfect in human form and figure but possessed the minds of gorillas; the majority, however, have the appearance of grotesque hybrids.

"Of these two, one was a very beautiful girl when last I saw her but with the temper of a savage lioness; the other was a young man with the carriage and the countenance of an aristocrat and the sweet amiability of a Jack the Ripper.

"And now, young man," continued the gorilla god, "when my followers have gathered here, what do you purpose doing?"

"Led by us," replied Tarzan, "they will storm the palace of the king and take the girl from him."

29
Death at Dawn

RHONDA TERRY awoke with a start. She heard shouting and growls and screams and roars that sounded very close indeed. She saw the shes of Henry's harem moving about restlessly. Some of them uttered low growls like nervous, half frightened beasts; but it was not these sounds that had awakened her—they came through the unglazed windows of the apartment, loud, menacing.

She rose and approached a window. Catherine of Aragon saw her and bared her fangs in a vicious snarl.

"It is she they want," growled the old queen.

From the window Rhonda saw in the light of torches a mass of hairy forms battling to the death. She gasped and pressed a hand to her heart, for among them she saw Stanley Obroski fighting his way toward an entrance to the palace.

At first it seemed to her that he was fighting alone against that horde of beasts, but presently she realized that many of them were his allies. She saw the gorilla god close to Obroski; she even saw the grass rope about the creature's neck. Now her only thought was of the safety of Obroski.

Vaguely she heard voices raised about her in anger; then she became conscious of the words of the old queen. "She has caused all this trouble," Catherine of Aragon was saying. "If she were dead we should have peace."

"Kill her, then," said Anne of Cleves.

"Kill her!" screamed Anne Boleyn.

The girl turned from the window to see the savage beasts advancing upon her—great hairy brutes that could tear her to pieces. The incongruity of their human speech and their bestial appearance seemed suddenly more shocking and monstrous than ever before.

One of them stepped forward from her side and stood in front of her, facing the others. It was Catherine Parr. "Leave her alone," she said. "It is not her fault that she is here."

"Kill them both! Kill Parr too!" screamed Catherine Howard.

The others took up the refrain. "Kill them both!" The Howard leaped upon the Parr; and with hideous growls the two sought each other's throat with great, yellow fangs. Then the others rushed upon Rhonda Terry.

There was no escape. They were between her and the door; the windows were barred. Her eyes searched vainly for something with which to beat them off, but there was nothing. She backed away from them, but all the time she knew that there was no hope.

Then the door was suddenly thrown open, and three great bulls stepped into the apartment. "His Majesty, the King!" cried one of them, and the shes quieted their tongues and fell away from Rhonda. Only the two battling on the floor did not hear.

The great bull gorilla that was Henry the Eighth rolled into the room. "Silence!" he bellowed, and crossing to the embattled pair he kicked and cuffed them until they desisted. "Where is the fair, hairless one?" he demanded, and then his eyes alighted upon Rhonda where she stood almost hidden by the great bulks of his wives.

"Come here!" he commanded. "God has come for you, but he'll never get you. You belong to me."

"Let him have her, Henry," cried Catherine of Aragon; "she has caused nothing but trouble."

"Silence, woman!" screamed the king. "Or you'll go to the Tower and the block."

He stepped forward and seized Rhonda, throwing her across one shoulder as though she had no weight whatever; then he crossed quickly to the door. "Stand in the corridor here, Suffolk and Howard, and, if God's men reach this floor, hold them off until I have time to get safely away."

"Let us go with you, Sire," begged one of them.

"No; remain here until you have news for me; then follow me to the north end of the valley, to the canyon where the east branch of the Thames rises." He turned then and hurried down the corridor.

At the far end he turned into a small room, crossed to a closet, and raised a trap door. "They'll never follow us here, my beauty," he said. "I got this idea from God, but he doesn't know that I made use of it."

Like a huge monkey he descended a pole that led downward into darkness, and after they reached the bottom Rhonda became aware that they were traversing a subterranean corridor. It was very long and very dark. The gorilla king moved slowly, feeling his way; but at last they came out into the open.

He had set Rhonda down upon the floor of the corridor, and she had been aware by the noises that she heard that he was moving some heavy object. Then she had felt the soft night air and had seen stars above them. A moment later they stood upon the bank of a river at the foot of a low cliff while Henry replaced a large, flat stone over the dark entrance to the tunnel they had just quitted.

Then commenced a trek of terror for Rhonda. Following the river, they hurried along through the night toward the upper end of the valley. The great brute no longer carried her but dragged her along by one wrist. He seemed nervous and fearful, occasionally stopping to sniff the air or listen. He moved almost silently, and once or twice he cautioned her to silence.

After a while they crossed the river toward the east where the water, though swift, was only up to their knees; then they continued in a northeasterly direction. There was no sound of pursuit, yet the gorilla's nervousness increased. Presently Rhonda guessed the reason for it—from the north came the deep throated roar of a lion.

The gorilla king growled deep in his chest and quickened his pace. A suggestion of dawn was tinging the eastern horizon. A cold mist enveloped the valley. Rhonda was very tired. Every muscle in her body ached and cried out for rest, but still her captor dragged her relentlessly onward.

Now the voice of the lion sounded again, shattering the silence of the night, making the earth tremble. It was much closer than before—it seemed very near. The gorilla broke into a lumbering run. Dawn was coming. Nearby objects became visible.

Rhonda saw a lion ahead of them and a little to their left. The gorilla king saw it too, and changed his direction toward the east and a fringe of trees that were visible now about a hundred yards ahead of them.

The lion was approaching them at an easy, swinging walk. Now he too changed his direction and broke into a trot with the evident intention of heading them off before they reached the trees.

Rhonda noticed how his flat belly swung from side to side to the motion of his gait. It is strange how such trivialities often impress one at critical moments of extreme danger. He looked lean and hungry. He was roaring almost continuously now as though he were attempting to lash himself into a rage. He commenced to gallop.

Now it became obvious that they could never reach the trees ahead of him. The gorilla paused, growling. Instantly the lion changed its course again and came straight for them. The gorilla hesitated; then he lifted the girl in his powerful paws and hurled her into the path of the lion, at the same time turning and running at full speed back in the direction from which they had come. His prize had become the offering which he hoped would save his life.

But he reckoned without sufficient knowledge of lion psychology. Rhonda fell face downward. She knew that the lion was only a few yards away and coming toward her, that she could not escape him; but she recalled her other experience with a lion, and so she lay very still. After she fell she did not move a muscle.

It is the running creature that attracts the beast of prey. You have seen that exemplified by your own dog, which is a descendant of beasts of prey. Whatever runs he must chase. He cannot help it. Provided it is running away from him he has to chase it because he is the helpless pawn of a natural law a million years older than the first dog.

If Henry the Eighth had ever known this he must have forgotten it; otherwise he would have made the girl run while he lay down and remained very quiet. But he did not, and the inevitable happened. The lion ignored the still figure of the girl and pursued the fleeing gorilla.

Rhonda felt the lion pass swiftly, close to her; then she raised her head and looked. The gorilla was moving much more swiftly than she had guessed possible but not swiftly enough. In a moment the lion would overhaul it. They would be some distance from Rhonda when this happened, and the lion would certainly be occupied for a few moments with the killing of its prey. It seemed incredible that the huge ape, armed as it was with powerful jaws and mighty fighting fangs, would not fight savagely for self-preservation.

The girl leaped to her feet, and without a backward glance raced for the trees. She had covered but a few yards when she heard terrific roars and growls and screams that told her that the lion had overtaken the gorilla and that the two beasts were already tearing at one another. As long as these sounds lasted she knew that her flight would not be noticed by the lion.

When, breathless, she reached the trees she stopped and looked back. The lion was dragging the gorilla down, the great jaws closed upon its head, there was a vicious shake; and the ape went limp. Thus died Henry the Eighth.

The carnivore did not even look back in her direction but immediately crouched upon the body of its kill and commenced to feed. He was very hungry.

The girl slipped silently into the wood. A few steps brought her to the bank of a river. It was the east fork of the Thames, the wood a fringe of trees on either side. Thinking to throw the lion off her trail should it decide to follow her, as well as to put the barrier of the river between them, she entered it and swam to the opposite shore.

Now, for the first time in many a long day, she was inspired by hope. She was free! Also, she knew where her friends were; and that by following the river down to the escarpment that formed the Omwamwi Falls she could find them. What dangers beset her path she did not know, but it seemed that they must be trivial by comparison with those she had already escaped. The trees that lined the river bank would give her concealment and protection, and before the day was over she would be at the escarpment. How she was to descend it she would leave until faced by the necessity.

She was tired, but she did not stop to rest—there could be no rest for her until she had found safety. Following the river, she moved southward. The sun had risen above the mountains that hemmed the valley on the east. Her body was grateful for the warmth that dispelled the cold night mists.

Presently the river turned in a great loop toward the east, and though she knew that following the meanderings of the river would greatly increase the distance that she must travel there was no alternative—she did not dare leave the comparative safety of the wood nor abandon this unfailing guide that would lead her surely to her destination.

On and on she plodded in what approximated a lethargy of fatigue, dragging one foot painfully after another. Her physical exhaustion was reflected in her reactions. They were dull and slow. Her senses were less acute. She either failed to hear unusual sounds or to interpret them as subjects worthy of careful investigation. It was this that brought disaster.

When she became aware of danger it was too late. A hideous creature, half man, half gorilla, dropped from a tree directly in her path. It had the face of a man, the ears and body of an ape.

The girl turned to run toward the river, thinking to plunge in and escape by swimming; but as she turned another fearsome thing dropped from the trees to confront her; then, growling and snarling, the two leaped forward and seized her. Each grasped her by an arm, and one pulled in one direction while the other pulled in the opposite. They screamed and gibbered at one another.

She thought that they must wrench her arms from their sockets. She had given up hope when a naked white man dropped from an overhanging branch. He carried a club in his hand, and with it he belabored first one and then the other of her assailants until they relinquished their holds upon her. But to her horror she saw that her rescuer gibbered and roared just as the others had.

Now the man seized her and stood snarling like a wild beast as a score of terrible beast-men swung from the trees and surrounded them. The man who held her was handsome and well formed; his skin was tanned to a rich bronze; a head of heavy blond hair fell about his shoulders like the mane of a lion.

The creatures that surrounded them were hybrids of all degrees of repulsiveness; yet he seemed one of them, for he made the same noises that they made. Also, it was evident that he had been in the trees with them. The others seemed to stand a little in awe of him or of his club; for, while they evidently wanted to come and lay hands upon the girl, they kept their distance, out of range of the man's weapon.

The man started to move away with his captive, to withdraw her from the circle surrounding them; then, above the scolding of the others, a savage scream sounded from the foliage overhead.

The man and the beasts glanced nervously aloft. Rhonda let her eyes follow the direction in which they were looking. Involuntarily she voiced a gasp of astonishment at what she beheld. Swinging downward toward them with the speed and agility of a monkey was a naked white girl, her golden hair streaming out behind her. From between her perfect lips issued the horrid screams of a beast.

As she touched the ground she ran toward them. Her face, even though reflecting savage rage, was beautiful; her youthful body was flawless in its perfection. But her disposition was evidently something else.

As she approached, the beasts surrounding Rhonda and the man edged away, making a path for her, though they growled and bared their teeth at her. She paid no attention to them, but came straight for Rhonda.

The man screamed at her, backing away; then he whirled Rhonda to a shoulder, turned, and bolted. Even burdened with the weight of his captive he ran with great speed. Behind him, raging and screaming, the beautiful she-devil pursued.

30
The Wild-girl

THE palace guard gave way before the multitude of faithful that battered at the doors of the king's house at the behest of their god. The god was pleased. He wished to punish Henry, but he had never before quite dared to assault the palace. Now he was victorious; and in victory one is often generous, especially to him who made victory possible.

Previously he had fully intended to break his promise to Tarzan and revenge himself for the affront that had been put upon his godhood, but now he was determined to set both the man and the girl free.

Tarzan cared nothing for the political aspects of the night's adventure. He thought only of Rhonda. "We must find the girl," he said to the gorilla god the moment that they had gained entrance to the palace. "Where could she be?"

"She is probably with the other women. Come with me— they are upstairs."

At the top of the stairs stood Howard and Suffolk to do the bidding of their king; but when they saw their god ascending toward them and the lower hall and the stairs behind him filled with his followers and recalled that the king had fled, they experienced a change of heart. They received God on bended knee and assured him that they had driven Henry out of the palace and were just on their way downstairs to fall tooth and nail upon God's enemies; and God knew that they lied, for it was he himself who had implanted the minds of men in their gorilla skulls.

"Where is the hairless she?" demanded the gorilla god.

"Henry took her with him," replied Suffolk.

"Where did he go?"

"I do not know. He ran to the end of the corridor and disappeared."

"Some one must know," snapped Tarzan.

"Perhaps Catherine of Aragon knows," suggested Howard.

"Where is she?" demanded the ape-man.

They led the way to the door of the harem. Suffolk swung the door open. "My Lord God!" he announced.

The shes, nervous and frightened, had been expecting to be dragged to their death by the mob. When they saw the gorilla god they fell on their faces before him.

"Have mercy, My Lord God!" cried Catherine of Aragon. "I am your faithful servant."

"Then tell me where Henry is," demanded the god.

"He fled with the hairless she," replied the old queen.

"Where?"

The rage of a jealous female showed Catherine of Aragon how to have her revenge. "Come with me," she said.

They followed her down the corridor to the room at the

end and into the closet there. Then she lifted the trap door.
"This shaft leads to a tunnel that runs under the city to the
bank of the river beyond the wall—he and that hairless thing
went this way."

The keen scent of the ape-man detected the delicate
aroma of the white girl. He knew that the king gorilla had
carried her into this dark hole. Perhaps they were down there
now, the king hiding from his enemies until it would be
safe for him to return; or perhaps there was a tunnel running
beyond the city as the old she said, and the gorilla had
carried his captive off to some fastness in the mountains surrounding the valley.

But in any event the ape-man must go on now alone—
he could trust none of the creatures about him to aid him in
the pursuit and capture of one of their own kind. He had
already removed his rope from around the neck of the gorilla
god; now it lay coiled across one shoulder; at his hip swung
his hunting knife. Tarzan of the Apes was prepared for any
emergency.

Without a word, he swung down the pole into the black
abyss below. The gorilla god breathed a sigh of relief when
he had departed.

Following the scent spoor of those he sought, Tarzan
traversed the tunnel that led from the bottom of the shaft to
the river bank. He pushed the great stone away from the
entrance and stepped out into the night. He stood erect, listening and sniffing the air. A scarcely perceptible air current
was moving up toward the head of the valley. It bore no
suspicion of the scent he had been following. All that this
indicated was that his quarry was not directly south of
him. The gorilla king might have gone to the east or the
west or the north; but the river flowed deep and swift on the
east, and only the north and west were left.

Tarzan bent close to the ground. Partly by scent, partly
by touch he found the trail leading toward the north; or,
more accurately, toward the northeast between the river and
the cliffs. He moved off upon it; but the necessity for stopping
often to verify the trail delayed him, so that he did not move
quite as rapidly as the beast he pursued.

He was delayed again at the crossing of the river, for he
passed the place at which the trail turned sharply to the right
into the stream. He had to retrace his steps, searching carefully until he found it again. Had the wind been right, had

the gorilla been moving directly upwind, Tarzan could have trailed him at a run.

The enforced delays caused no irritation or nervousness such as they would have in an ordinary man, for the patience of the hunting beast is infinite. Tarzan knew that eventually he would overhaul his quarry, and that while they were on the move the girl was comparatively safe.

Dawn broke as he crossed the river. Far ahead he heard the roaring of a hunting lion, and presently with it were mingled the snarls and screams of another beast—a gorilla. And the ape-man knew that Numa had attacked one of the great apes. He guessed that it was the gorilla king. But what of the girl? He heard no human voice mingling its screams with that of the anthropoid. He broke into a run.

Presently, from a little rise of rolling round, he saw Numa crouching upon his kill. It was light enough now for him to see that the lion was feeding upon the body of a gorilla. The girl was nowhere in sight.

Tarzan made a detour to avoid the feeding carnivore. He had no intention of risking an encounter with the king of beasts—an encounter that would certainly delay him and possibly end in death.

He passed at a considerable distance upwind from the lion; and when the beast caught his scent it did not rise from its kill.

Beyond the lion, near the edge of the wood, Tarzan picked up the trail of the girl again. He followed it across the second river. It turned south here, upwind; and now he was below her and could follow her scent spoor easily. At a trot he pressed on.

Now other scent spoor impinged upon his nostrils, mingling with those of the girl. They were strange scents—a mixture of mangani and tarmangani, of great ape and white man, of male and of female.

Tarzan increased his gait. That strange instinct that he shared with the other beasts of the forest warned him that danger lay ahead—danger for the girl and perhaps for himself. He moved swiftly and silently through the fringe of forest that bordered the river.

The strange scents became stronger in his nostrils. A babel of angry voices arose in the distance ahead. He was nearing them. He took to the trees now, to his native element; and he felt at once the sense of security and power that the trees always imparted to him. Here, as nowhere else quite in the same measure, was he indeed lord of the jungle.

Now he heard the angry, raging voice of a female. It was almost human, yet the beast notes predominated; and he could recognize words spoken in the language of the great apes. Tarzan was mystified.

He was almost upon them now, and a moment later he looked down upon a strange scene. There were a score of monstrous creatures—part human, part gorilla. And there was a naked white man just disappearing among the trees with the girl he sought across one shoulder. Pursuing them was a white girl with golden hair streaming behind her. She was as naked as the other beasts gibbering and screaming in her wake.

The man bearing Rhonda Terry ran swiftly, gaining upon the golden haired devil behind him. They both out-stripped the other creatures that had started in pursuit, and presently these desisted and gave up the chase.

Tarzan, swinging through the trees, gained slowly on the strange pair; and so engrossed were they in the business of escape and pursuit that they did not glance up and discover him.

Now the ape-man caught up with the running girl and passed her. Her burst of speed had taken toll of her strength, and she was slowing down. The man had gained on her, too; and now considerable distance separated them.

Through the trees ahead of him Tarzan saw a stretch of open ground, beyond which rose rocky cliffs; then the forest ended. Swinging down to earth, he continued the pursuit; but he had lost a little distance now, and though he started to gain gradually on the fleeing man, he realized that the other would reach the cliffs ahead of him. He could hear the pursuing girl panting a short distance behind him.

Since he had first seen the naked man and woman and the grotesque monsters that they had left behind in the forest, Tarzan had recalled the story that the gorilla god had told him of the mutants that had escaped destruction and formed a tribe upon this side of the valley. These, then, were the terrible fruits of the old biologist's profane experiment—children of the unnatural union of nature and science.

It was only the passing consciousness of a fact to which the ape-man now had no time to give thought. His every faculty was bent upon the effort of the moment—the over-taking of the man who carried Rhonda Terry. Tarzan marvelled at the man's speed burdened as he was by the weight of his captive.

The cliffs were only a short distance ahead of him now. At their base were piled a tumbled mass of fragments that had fallen from above during times past. The cliffs themselves presented a series of irregular, broken ledges; and their face was pitted with the mouths of innumerable caves.

As the man reached the rubble at the foot of the cliffs, he leaped from rock to rock like a human chamois; and after him came the ape-man, but slower; for he was unaccustomed to such terrain—and behind him, the savage she.

Clambering from ledge to ledge the creature bore Rhonda Terry aloft; and Tarzan followed, and the golden haired girl came after. Far up the cliff face the man pushed Rhonda roughly into a cave mouth and turned to face his pursuer.

Tarzan of the Apes turned abruptly to the right then and ran along a narrow ascending ledge with the intention of gaining the ledge upon which the other stood without having to ascend directly into the face of his antagonist. The man guessed his purpose and started along his own ledge to circumvent him. Below them the girl was clambering upward.

"Go back!" shouted the man in the language of the great apes. "Go back! I kill!"

"Rhonda!" called the ape-man.

The girl crawled from the cave out onto the ledge. "Stanley!" she cried in astonishment.

"Climb up the cliff," Tarzan directed. "You can follow the ledges up. I can keep him occupied until you get to the top. Then go south toward the lower end of the valley."

"I'll try," she replied and started to climb from ledge to ledge.

The girl ascending from below saw her and shouted to the man. "Kreeg-ah!" she screamed. "The she is escaping!"

Now the man turned away from Tarzan and started in pursuit of Rhonda; and the ape-man, instead of following directly after him, clambered to a higher ledge, moving diagonally in the direction of the American girl.

Rhonda, spurred on by terror, was climbing much more rapidly than she herself could have conceived possible. The narrow ledges, the precarious footing would have appalled her at any other time; but now she ignored all danger and thought only of reaching the summit of the cliff before the strange white man overtook her.

And so it was that by a combination of her speed and

Tarzan's strategy the ape-man was able to head off her pursuer before he overtook her.

When the man realized that he had been intercepted he
turned upon Tarzan with a savage, snarling growl, his handsome face transformed into that of a wild beast.

The ledge was narrow. It was obvious to Tarzan that the
two could not do battle upon it without falling; and while
at this point there was another ledge only a few feet below, it
could only momentarily stay their descent—while they
fought they must roll from ledge to ledge until one or both
of them were badly injured or killed.

A quick glance showed him that the wild-girl was ascending toward them. Below and beyond her appeared a
number of the grotesque hybrids that had again taken up the
chase. Even if the ape-man were the one to survive the duel,
all these creatures might easily be upon him before it was
concluded.

Reason dictated that he should attempt to avoid so useless
an encounter in which he would presumably lose his life
either in victory or defeat. These observations and deductions registered upon his brain with the speed of a camera
shutter flashing one exposure rapidly after another. Then the
decision was taken from him—the man-beast charged. With
a bestial roar he charged.

The girl, ascending, screamed savage encouragement; the
horrid mutants gibbered and shrieked. Above them all,
Rhonda turned at the savage sounds and looked down. With
parted lips, her hand pressed to her heart, she watched with
dismay and horror.

Crouching, Tarzan met the charge. The man-beast fought
without science but with great strength and feriocity. Whatever thin veneer of civilization his contacts with men had
imparted to the ape-man vanished now. Here was a beast
meeting a beast.

A low growl rumbled from the throat of the lord of the
jungle, snarling-muscles drew back his lip to expose strong,
white teeth, the primitive weapons of the first-man.

Like charging bulls they came together, and like mad
panthers each sought the other's throat. Locked in feral embrace they swayed a moment upon the ledge; then they
toppled over the brink.

At that moment Rhonda Terry surrendered the last vestige
of hope. She had ascended the cliff to a point beyond which
she could discover no foothold for further progress. The man

whom she believed to be Stanley Obroski, whose newly discovered valor had become the sole support of whatever hope of escape she might have entertained, was already as good as dead; for if the fall did not kill him the creatures swarming up the cliff toward him would. Yet self-pity was submerged in the grief she felt for the fate of the man. Her original feeling of contempt for him had changed to one of admiration, and this had grown into an emotion that she could scarcely have analysed herself. It was something stronger than friendship; perhaps it was love. She did not want to see him die; yet, fascinated, her eyes clung to the scene below.

But Tarzan had no mind to die now. In ferocity, in strength, he was equal to his antagonist; in courage and intellect, he was his superior. It was by his own intelligent effort that the two had so quickly plunged from the ledge to another a few feet below; and as he had directed the fall, so he directed the manner of their alighting. The man-beast was underneath; Tarzan was on top.

The former struck upon the back of his head, as Tarzan had intended that he should; and one of the ape-man's knees was at his stomach; so not only was he stunned into insensibility, but the wind was knocked out of him. He would not fight again for some considerable time.

Scarcely had they struck the lower ledge than Tarzan was upon his feet. He saw the monsters scrambling quickly toward him; he saw the wild-girl already reaching out to clutch him, and in the instant his plan was formed.

The girl was on the ledge below, reaching for one of his ankles to drag him down. He stooped quickly and seized her by the hair; then he swung her, shrieking and screaming, to his shoulder.

She kicked and scratched and tried to bite him; but he held her until he had carried her to a higher ledge; then he threw her down and made his rope fast about her body. She fought viciously, but her strength was no match for that of the ape-man.

The creatures scaling the cliff were almost upon them by the time that Tarzan had made the rope secure; then he ran nimbly upward from ledge to ledge dragging the girl after him; and in this way he was out of her reach, and she could not hinder him.

The highest ledge, that from which Rhonda watched wide-eyed the changing scenes of the drama being enacted below her, was quite the widest of all. Opening on to it was the mouth of a cave. Above it the cliff rose, unscalable, to the summit.

To this ledge Tarzan dragged the now strangely silent wild-girl; and here he and Rhonda were cornered, their backs against a wall, with no avenue of escape in any direction.

The girl clambered the last few feet to the ledge; and when she stood erect, facing Tarzan, she no longer fought. The savage snarl had left her face. She smiled into the eyes of the ape-man, and she was very beautiful; but the man's attention was now upon the snarling pack, the leaders of which were mounting rapidly toward this last ledge.

"Go back," shouted Tarzan, "or I kill your she!"

This was the plan that he had conceived to hold them off, using the girl as a hostage. It was a good plan; but, like many another good plan, it failed to function properly.

"They will not stop," said the girl. "They do not care if you kill me. You have taken me. I belong to you. They will kill us all and eat us—if they can. Throw rocks down on them; drive them back; then I will show you how we can get away from them."

Following her own advice, she picked up a bit of loose rock and hurled it at the nearest of the creatures. It struck him on the head, and he tumbled backward to a lower ledge. The girl laughed and screamed taunts and insults at her former companions.

Tarzan, realizing the efficacy of this mode of defense, gathered fragments of rock and threw them at the approaching monsters; then Rhonda joined in the barrage, and the three rained down a hail of missiles that drove their enemies to the shelter of the caves below.

"They won't eat us for a while," laughed the girl.

"You eat human flesh?" asked Tarzan.

"Not Malb'yat nor I," she replied; "but they do—they eat anything."

"Who is Malb'yat?"

"My he—you fought with him and took me from him. Now I am yours. I will fight for you. No one else shall have you!" She turned upon Rhonda with a snarl, and would have attacked her had not Tarzan seized her.

"Leave her alone," he warned.

"You shall have no other she but me," said the wild-girl.

"She is not mine," explained the ape-man; "you must not harm her."

The girl continued to scowl at Rhonda, but she quit her

efforts to reach her. "I shall watch," she said. "What is her name,"

"Rhonda."

"And what is yours?" she demanded.

"You may call me Stanley," said Tarzan. He was amused, but not at all disconcerted, by the strange turn events had taken. He realized that their only chance of escape might be through this strange, beautiful, little savage, and he could not afford to antagonize her.

"Stanley," she repeated, stumbling a little over the strange word. "My name is Balza."

Tarzan thought that it fitted her well, for in the language of the great apes it meant golden girl. Ape names are always descriptive. His own meant white skin. Malb'yat was yellow head.

Balza stooped quickly and picked up a rock which she hurled at a head that had been cautiously poked from a cave mouth below them. She scored another hit and laughed gaily.

"We will keep them away until night," she said; "then we will go. They will not follow us at night. They are afraid of the dark. If we went now they would follow us, and there are so many of them that we should all be killed."

The girl interested Tarzan. Remembering what the gorilla god had told him of these mutants, he had assumed that her perfect human body was dominated by the brain of a gorilla; but he had not failed to note that she had repeated the name he had given her—something no gorilla could have done.

"Do you speak English?" he asked in that language.

She looked at him in surprise. "Yes," she replied; "but I didn't imagine that you did."

"Where did you learn it?" he asked.

"In London—before they drove me out."

"Why did they drive you out?"

"Because I was not like them. My mother kept me hidden for years, but at last they found me out. They would have killed me had I remained."

"And Malb'yat is like you?"

"No, Malb'yat is like the others. He cannot learn a single English word. I like you much better. I hope that you killed Malb'yat."

"I didn't, though," said the ape-man. "I see him moving on the ledge down there where he has been lying."

The girl looked; then she picked up a rock and flung it at

the unfortunate Malb'yat. It missed him, and he crawled to shelter. "If he gets me back he'll beat me," she remarked.

"I should think he'd kill you," said Tarzan.

"No—there is no one else like me. The others are ugly— I am beautiful. No, he will never kill me, but the shes would all like to." She laughed gaily. "I suppose this one would like to kill me." She nodded toward Rhonda.

The American girl had been a surprised and interested listener to that part of the conversation that had been carried on in English, but she had not spoken.

"I do not want to kill you," she said. "There is no reason why we should not be friends."

Balza looked at her in surprise; then she studied her carefully.

"Is she speaking the truth?" she asked Tarzan.

The ape-man nodded. "Yes."

"Then we are friends," said Balza to Rhonda. Her decisions in matters of love, friendship, or murder were equally impulsive.

For hours the three kept vigil upon the ledge, but only occasionally was it necessary to remind the monsters below them to keep their distance.

31
Diamonds!

AT LAST the long day drew to a close. All were hungry and thirsty. All were anxious to leave the hard, uncomfortable ledge where they had been exposed to the hot African sun since morning.

Tarzan and Rhonda had been entertained and amused by the savage little wild-girl. She was wholly unspoiled and without inhibitions of any nature. She said or did whatever she wished to say or do with a total lack of self-consciousness that was disarming and, often, not a little embarrassing.

As the sun was dropping behind the western hills across the valley, she rose to her feet. "Come," she said; "we can go now. They will not follow, for it will soon be night."

She led the way into the interior of the cave that opened upon the ledge. The cave was narrow but quite straight. The girl led them to the back of the cave to the bottom of a natural chimney formed by a cleft in the rocky hill. The twilight sky was visible above them, the light revealing the rough surface of the interior of the chimney to its top a few yards up.

Tarzan took in the situation at a glance. He saw that by bracing their backs against one side of the chimney, their feet against the other, they could work themselves to the top; but he also realized that the rough surface would scratch and tear the flesh of the girls' backs.

"I'll go first," he said. "Wait here, and I'll drop a rope for you. It's strange, Balza, that your people didn't come to the cliff top and get us from above—they could have come down this chimney and taken us by surprise."

"They are too stupid," replied the girl. "They have brains enough only to follow us; they would never think of going around us and heading us off."

"Which is fortunate for us and some of them," remarked the ape-man as he started the ascent of the chimney.

Reaching the top, he lowered his rope and raised the two girls easily to his side, where they found themselves in a small, bowl-shaped gully the floor of which was covered with rough, crystallized pebbles that gave back the light of the dying day, transforming the gully into a well of soft luminance.

The moment that her eyes fell upon the scene, Rhonda voiced an exclamation of surprised incredulity. "Diamonds!" she gasped. "The valley of diamonds!"

She stooped and gathered some of the precious stones in her hands. Balza looked at her in surprise; the gems meant nothing to her. Tarzan, more sophisticated, gathered several of the larger specimens.

"May I take some with me?" asked Rhonda.

"Why not?" inquired the ape-man. "Take what you can carry comfortably."

"We shall all be rich!" exclaimed the American girl. "We can bring the whole company here and take truck loads of these stones back with us—why there must be tons of them here!"

"And then do you know what will happen?" asked Tarzan.

"Yes," she replied. "I shall have a villa on the Riviera, a town house in Beverly Hills, a hundred and fifty thousand dollar cottage at Malibu, a place at Palm Beach, a penthouse in New York, a——"

"You will have no more than you have always had," the ape-man interrupted, "for if you took all these diamonds back to civilization the market would be glutted; and diamonds would be as cheap as glass. If you are wise, you will take just a few for yourself and your friends; and then tell nobody how they may reach the valley of diamonds."

Rhonda pondered this for a moment. "You are right," she admitted. "From this moment, as far as I am concerned, there is no valley of diamonds."

During the brief twilight Balza guided them to a trail that led down into the valley some distance below the cave dwellings of the tribe of mutants, and all during the night they moved southward toward the escarpment and Omwamwi Falls.

The way was new to all of them, for Balza had never been far south of the cave village; and this, combined with the darkness, retarded them, so that it was almost dawn when they reached the escarpment.

For much of the way Tarzan carried Rhonda who was almost exhausted by all that she had passed through, and only thus were they able to progress at all. But Balza was tireless, moving silently in the footsteps of her man, as she now considered Tarzan. She did not speak, for experience and instinct both had trained her to the necessity for stealth if one would pass through savage nights alive. Every sense must be alert, concentrated upon the business of self-preservation. But who may know what passed in that savage little brain as the beautiful creature followed her new lord and master out into a strange world?

In the early dawn the scene from the top of the escarpment looked weird and forbidding to Rhonda Terry. The base was mist-hidden. Only the roar of the falls, rising sepulchral, like the voices of ghostly Titans from the tomb, belied the suggestion of bottomless depth. She seemed to be gazing down into another world, a world she would never reach alive.

Strong in her memory was that other experience when the giant gorilla had carried her up this dizzy height. She knew that she could never descend it safely alone. She knew that Stanley Obroski could not carry her down. She had learned that he could do many things with the possibility of which none might ever have credited him a few weeks before, but here was something that no man might do. She even doubted his ability to descend alone.

Even as these thoughts passed quickly through her mind the man swung her across one broad shoulder and started the descent. Rhonda gasped, but she clenched her teeth and made no outcry. Seemingly with all the strength of the bull gorilla and with far greater agility he swung down into the terrifying abyss, finding foothold and handhold with unerring accuracy; and after him came Balza, the wild-girl, as sure of herself as any monkey.

And at last the impossible was achieved—the three stood safely at the foot of the escarpment. The sun had risen, and before it the mist was disappearing. New hope rose in the breast of the American girl, and new strength animated her body.

"Let me down, Stanley," she said. "I am sure I can walk all right now. I feel stronger."

He lowered her to the ground. "It is not a great way to the camp where I left Orman and the others," he said.

Rhonda glanced at Balza and cleared her throat. "Of course we're all from Hollywood," she said, "but don't you think we ought to rig some sort of skirt for Balza before we take her into camp?"

Tarzan laughed. "Poor Balza," he said; "she will have to eat of the apple soon enough now that she is coming into contact with civilized man. Let her keep her naturalness and her purity of mind as long as she may."

"But I was thinking of her," remonstrated Rhonda.

"She won't be embarrassed," Tarzan assured her. "A skirt would probably embarrass her far more."

Rhonda shrugged. "O.K." she said. "And Tom and Bill forgot how to blush years ago, anyway."

They had proceeded but a short distance down the river when Tarzan stopped and pointed. "There is where they were camped," he said, "but they are gone."

"What could have happened to them? Weren't they going to wait for you?"

The ape-man stood listening and sniffing the air. "They are farther down the river," he announced presently, "and they are not alone—there are many with them."

They continued on for over a mile when they suddenly came in sight of a large camp. There were many tents and motor trucks.

"The safari!" exclaimed Rhonda. "Pat got through!"

As they approached the camp some one saw them and commenced to shout; then there was a stampede to meet

them. Everyone kissed Rhonda, and Naomi Madison kissed
Tarzan; whereat, with a growl, Balza leaped for her. The ape-
man caught the wild-girl around the waist and held her, while
Naomi shrank back, terrified.

"Hands off Stanley," warned Rhonda with a laugh. "The
young lady has annexed him."

Tarzan took Balza by the shoulders and wheeled her about
until she faced him. "These are my people," he said. "Their
ways are not as your ways. If you quarrel with them I
shall send you away. These shes are your friends."

Every one was staring at Balza with open admiration,
Orman with the eye of a director discovering a type, Pat
O'Grady with the eye of an assistant director—which is
something else again.

"Balza," continued the ape-man, "go with these shes. Do
as they tell you. They will cover your beautiful body with
uncomfortable clothing, but you will have to wear it. In a
month you will be smoking cigarettes and drinking high balls;
then you will be civilized. Now you are only a barbarian.
Go with them and be unhappy."

Every one laughed except Balza. She did not know what
it was all about; but her god had spoken, and she obeyed.
She went with Rhonda and Naomi to their tent.

Tarzan talked with Orman, Bill West, and O'Grady. They
all thought that he was Stanley Obroski, and he did not attempt to undeceive them. They told him that Bill West had
spent half the previous night trying to scale the escarpment.
He had ascended far enough to see the camp fires of the
safari and the headlights of some of the trucks; then, forced
to abandon his attempt to reach the summit, he had returned
and led the others to the main camp.

Orman was now enthusiastic to go ahead with the picture.
He had his star back again, his leading woman, and prac-
tically all the other important members of his cast. He de-
cided to play the heavy himself and cast Pat O'Grady in
Major White's part, and he had already created a part for
Balza. "She'll knock 'em cold," he prophesied.

32

Good-bye, Africa!

FOR two weeks Orman shot scene after scene against the gorgeous background of the splendid river and the magnificent falls. Tarzan departed for two days and returned with a tribe of friendly natives to replace those that had deserted. He led the cameramen to lions, to elephants, to every form of wild life that the district afforded; and all marvelled at the knowledge, the power, and the courage of Stanley Obroski.

Then came a sad blow. A runner arrived bringing a cablegram to Orman. It was from the studio; and it ordered him to return at once to Hollywood, bringing the company and equipment with him.

Every one except Orman was delighted. "Hollywood!" exclaimed Naomi Madison. "Oh, Stanley, just think of it! Aren't you crazy to get to Hollywood?"

"Perhaps that's the right word," he mused.

The company danced and sang like children watching the school house burn, and Tarzan watched them and wondered. He wondered what this Hollywood was like that it held such an appeal to these men and women. He thought that some day he might go and see for himself.

Over broken trails the return journey was made with ease and speed. Tarzan accompanied the safari through the Bansuto country, assuring them that they would have no trouble. "I arranged that with Rungula before I left his village," he explained.

Then he left them, saying that he was going on ahead to Jinja. He hastened to the village of Mpugu, where he had left Obroski. Mpugu met him with a long face. "White bwana die seven days ago," announced the chief. "We take his body to Jinja so that the white men know that we did not kill him."

Tarzan whistled. It was too bad, but there was nothing to do about it. He had done the best that he could for Obroski.

Two days later the lord of the jungle and Jad-bal-ja, the

Golden Lion, stood on a low eminence and watched the long caravan of trucks wind toward Jinja.

In command of the rear guard walked Pat O'Grady. At his side was Balza. Each had an arm about the other, and Balza puffed on a cigarette.

33

Hello, Hollywood!

A YEAR had passed.

A tall, bronzed man alighted from The Chief in the railroad station at Los Angeles. The easy, majestic grace of his carriage; his tread, at once silent and bold; his flowing muscles; the dignity of his mien; all suggested the leonine, as though he were, indeed, a personification of Numa, the lion.

A great throng of people crowded about the train. A cordon of good natured policemen held them back, keeping an aisle clear for the alighting passengers and for the great celebrity that all awaited with such eagerness.

Cameras clicked and whirred for local papers, for news syndicates, for news reels; eager reporters, special correspondents, and sob-sisters pressed forward.

At last the crowd glimpsed the celebrity, and a great roar of welcome billowed into the microphones strategically placed by Freeman Lang.

A slip of a girl with green hair had alighted from The Chief; her publicity agent preceded her, while directly behind her were her three secretaries, who were followed by a maid leading a gorilla.

Instantly he was engulfed by the reporters. Freeman forced his way to her side. "Won't you say just a word to all your friends of the air?" he asked, taking her by the arm. "Right over here, please, dear."

She stepped to the microphone. "Hello, everybody! I wish you were all here. It's simply mahvellous. I'm so happy to be back in Hollywood."

Freeman Lang took the microphone. "Ladies and gentlemen," he announced, "you have just heard the voice of the most beautiful and most popular little lady in motion pictures today. You should see the crowds down here at the station to welcome her back to Hollywood. I've seen lots of these home-comings, but honestly, folks, I never saw anything like this before—all Los Angeles has turned out to greet B.O.'s beautiful star—the glorious Balza."

There was a suspicion of a smile in the eyes of the bronzed stranger as he succeeded at last in making his way through the crowd to the street, where he hailed a taxi and asked to be driven to a hotel in Hollywood.

As he was registering at The Roosevelt, a young man leaning against the desk covertly noted his entry, John Clayton, London; and as Clayton followed the bell boy toward the elevator, the young man watched him, noting the tall figure, the broad shoulders, and the free, yet cat-like stride.

From the windows of his room Clayton looked down upon Hollywood Boulevard, upon the interminable cars gliding noiselessly east and west. He caught glimpses of tiny trees and little patches of lawn where the encroachment of shops had not obliterated them, and he sighed.

He saw many people riding in cars or walking on the cement sidewalks and the suggestion of innumerable people in the crowded, close-built shops and residences; and he felt more alone than he ever had before in all his life.

The confining walls of the hotel room oppressed him; and he took the elevator to the lobby, thinking to go into the hills that he had seen billowing so close, to the north.

In the lobby a young man accosted him. "Aren't you Mr. Clayton?" he asked.

Clayton eyed the stranger closely for a moment before he replied. "Yes, but I do not know you."

"You have probably forgotten, but I met you in London." Clayton shook his head. "I never forget."

The young man shrugged and smiled. "Pardon me, but nevertheless I recognized you. Here on business?" He was unembarrassed and unabashed.

"Merely to see Hollywood," replied Clayton. "I have heard so much about it that I wished to see it."

"Got a lot of friends here, I suppose."

"No one knows me here."

"Perhaps I can be of service to you," suggested the young man. "I am an old timer here—been here two years. Nothing to do—glad to show you around. My name is Reece."

Clayton considered for a moment. He had come to see Hollywood. A guide might be helpful. Why not this young man as well as some one else? "It is kind of you," he said.

"Well, then, how about a little lunch? I suppose you would like to see some of the motion picture celebrities—they all do."

"Naturally!" admitted Clayton. "They are the most interesting denizens of Hollywood."

"Very well! We'll go to the Brown Derby. You'll see a lot of them there."

As they alighted from a taxi in front of the Brown Derby, Clayton saw a crowd of people lined up on each side of the entrance. It reminded him of the crowds he had seen at the station welcoming the famous Balza.

"They must be expecting a very important personage," he said to Reece.

"Oh, these boobs are here every day," replied the young man.

The Brown Derby was crowded—well groomed men, beautifully gowned girls. There was something odd in the apparel, the ornaments, or the hair dressing of each, as though each was trying to out-do the others in attracting attention to himself. There was a great deal of chattering and calling back and forth between tables: "How ah you?" "How mahvellous you look!" "How ah you?" "See you at the Chinese tonight?" "How ah you?"

Reece pointed out the celebrities to Clayton. One or two of the names were familiar to the stranger, but they all looked so much alike and talked so much alike, and said nothing when they did talk, that Clayton was soon bored. He was glad when the meal was over. He paid the check, and they went out.

"Doing anything this evening?" asked Reece.

"I have nothing planned."

"Suppose we go to the première of Balza's latest picture, Soft Shoulders, at the Chinese. I have a ticket; and I know a fellow who can get you one, but it will probably cost you twenty-five smackers." He eyed Clayton questioningly.

"Is it something that I ought to see if I am to see Hollywood?"

"Absolutely!"

* * *

A glare of lights illuminated the front of Grauman's Chinese Theater and the sky above, twenty thousand people milled and pushed and elbowed in Hollywood Boulevard, filling the street from building line to building line, a solid mass of humanity blocking all traffic. Policemen shouldered and sweated. Street cars were at a standstill. Clayton and Reece walked from The Roosevelt through the surging crowd.

As they approached the theater Clayton heard loud speakers broadcasting the arrival of celebrities who had left their cars two or three blocks away and forced their way through the mob to the forecourt of the theater.

The forecourt of the theater was jammed with spectators and autograph seekers. Several of the former had brought chairs; many had been sitting or standing there since morning that they might be assured of choice vantage spots from which to view the great ones of filmdom's capital.

As Clayton entered the forecourt, the voice of Freeman Lang was filling the boulevard from the loud speakers. "The celebrities are coming thick and fast now. Naomi Madison is just getting out of her car—and there's her new husband with her, the Prince Mudini. And here comes the sweetest little girl, just coming into the forecourt now. It's Balza herself! I'll try to get her to say something to you. Oh, Sweetheart, come over here. My, how gorgeous you're looking tonight. Won't you say just a word to all your friends of the air? Right over here, please, dear."

A dozen autograph pests were poking pencils and books toward Balza, but she quieted them with her most seductive smile and approached the microphone.

"Hello, everybody!" she lisped. "I wish you were all here. It's simply mahvellous. I'm so happy to be back in Hollywood."

Clayton smiled enigmatically, the crowd in the street roared its applause, and Freeman turned to greet the next celebrity. "And here comes—well, he can't get through the crowd. Honestly, folks, this crowd is simply tremendous. We've officiated at a lot of premières, but we've never seen anything like this. The police can't hold 'em back. They're crowding right up here on top of the microphone. Yes, here he comes! Hello, there, Jimmie! Right over here. The folks want to hear from you. This is Jimmie Stone, second assistant production manager of the B.O. Studio, whose super feature, Soft Shoulders, is being premièred here tonight in Grauman's Chinese Theater."

"Hello, efferybody. I wish you was all here. It's simply marvellous. Hello, Momma!"

"Let's go inside," suggested Clayton.

* * *

"Well, Clayton, how did you like the picture?" asked Reece.

"The acrobats in the prologue were splendid," replied the Englishman.

Reece looked a little crestfallen. Presently he brightened. "I'll tell you what we'll do," he announced. "I'll get hold of a couple more fellows and we'll go to a party."

"At this time of night?"

"Oh, it's early. There's Billy Brouke now. Hi, there, Billy! Say, I want you to meet Mr. Clayton, an old friend of mine from London. Mr. Clayton, this is Billy Brouke. How about a little party, Billy?"

"O.K. by me! We'll go in my car; it's parked around the corner."

On a side street near Franklin they climbed into a flashy roadster. Brouke drove west a few blocks on Franklin and then turned up a narrow street that wound into the hills.

Clayton was troubled. "Perhaps your friends may not be pleased if you bring a stranger," he suggested.

Reece laughed. "Don't worry," he admonished; "they'll be as glad to see you as they will be to see us."

That made Brouke laugh, too. "I'll say they will," he commented.

Presently they came to the end of the street. "Hell!" muttered Brouke and turned the car around. He turned into another street and followed that for a few blocks; then he turned back toward Franklin.

"Forgotten where your friends live?" asked Clayton.

On a side street in an otherwise quiet neighborhood they sighted a brilliantly lighted house in front of which several cars were parked; laughter and the sounds of radio music were coming from an open window.

"This looks like the place," said Reece.

"It is," said Brouke with a grin, and drew up at the curb.

A Filipino opened the door in answer to their ring. Reece brushed in past him, and the others followed. A man and a girl were sitting on the stairs leading to the upper floor. They were attempting to kiss one another ardently without spilling the contents of the cocktail glasses they held. They succeeded in kissing one another, paying no attention to the newcomers.

To the right of the reception hall was a large living room in which several couples were dancing to the radio music; others were sprawled about on chairs and divans; all were drinking. There was a great deal of laughter.

"The party's getting good," commented Brouke, as he led the way into the living room. "Hello, everybody!" he cried. "Where's the drinks? Come on, boys!" and he started for the back of the house, doing a little dance step on the way.

A middle-aged man, greying at the temples, rose from a divan and approached Reece. There was a puzzled expression on his face. "I don't believe—" he started, but Brouke interrupted him.

"It's all right, old man!" he exclaimed. "Sorry to be late. Shake hands with Mr. Reece and Mr. Clayton of London. How about a little drink?" and without waiting for an answer he headed for the kitchen. Reece and the host followed him, but Clayton hesitated. He had failed to note any exuberant enthusiasm in the attitude of the greying man whom he assumed to be the master of the house.

A tall blond, swaying a little, approached him. "Haven't I met you somewhere before, Mr.—ah——"

"Clayton," he came to her rescue.

"How about a little dance?" she demanded. "My boy friend," she confided, as they swung into the rhythm of the music, "passed out, and they had to put him to bed."

She talked incessantly, but Clayton managed to ask her if she knew Rhonda Terry.

"Know Rhonda Terry! I should say I do. She's in Samoa now starring in her husband's new picture."

"Her husband! Is she married?"

"Yes, she's married to Tom Orman, the director. Do you know her?"

"I met her once," replied Clayton.

"She was all broken up over Stanley Obroski's death, but she finally snapped out of it and married Tom. Obroski sure made a name for himself in Africa. Say, that bunch is still talking about the way he killed lions and gorillas with one hand tied behind him."

Clayton smiled politely.

After the dance she drew him over to a sofa on which two men were sitting. "Abe," she said to one of the men, "here's a find for you. This is Mr. Potkin, Mr. Clayton, Abe Potkin, you know; and this is Mr. Puant, Dan Puant, the famous scenarist."

"We've been watching Mr. Clayton," replied Potkin.

"You'd better grab him," advised the girl; "you'll never find a better Tarzan."

"He isn't exactly the type, but he might answer; I've been noticing him," said Potkin. "What do you think, Dan?"

"He's not my idea of Tarzan, but he might do."

"Of course his face doesn't look like Tarzan; but he's big, and that's what I want," replied Potkin.

"He hasn't a name; nobody ever heard of him, and you said you wanted a big name," argued Puant.

"We'll use that platinum blond, Era Dessent, opposite him; she's got a lot of sex appeal and a big name."

"I got an idea!" exclaimed Puant. "I'll write the story around Dessent and some good looking juvenile, bring in another fem with 'It' and a heavy with a big name; and we can use Clayton in long shots with apes for atmosphere."

"That's a swell idea, Dan; get in a lot of sex stuff and a triangle and a ballroom or cabaret scene—a big one with a jazz orchestra. What we want is something different."

"That ought to fix it so that we can use this fellow," said Puant, "for it won't make much difference who takes the part of Tarzan."

"How about it, Mr. Clayton?" inquired Potkin with an ingratiating smile.

At this juncture Reece and Brouke romped in from the kitchen, each with a bottle. The host was following, expostulating.

"Have a drink, everybody!" cried Brouke. "The party's goin' stale."

They passed about the room filling up glasses with neat bourbon or gin; sometimes they mixed them. They paused occasionally to take a drink themselves. Finally they disappeared into the hallway looking for other empty glasses.

"Well," demanded Potkin, after the interruption had passed, "how about it?"

Clayton eyed him questioningly. "How about what?"

"I'm going to make a jungle picture," explained Potkin. "I got a contract for a Tarzan picture, and I want a Tarzan. I'll make a test of you tomorrow morning."

"You think I might fill the rôle of Tarzan of the Apes?" inquired Clayton, as a faint smile touched his lips.

"You ain't just what I want, but you might do. You see, Mr. Puant, here, can write a swell Tarzan story even if we ain't got no Tarzan at all. And, say! it will make you. You ought almost to pay me for such a chance. But I tell you what I do; I like you, Mr. Clayton; I give you fifty dollars a week, and look at all the publicity you get that it don't cost you nothing. You be over at the studio in the morning; and I make a test of you, eh?"

Clayton stood up. "I'll think it over," he said and started across the room.

A good-looking young woman came running in from the reception hall. Brouke was pursuing her. "Leave me alone, you cad!" she cried.

The greying host was close behind Brouke. "Leave my wife alone," he shouted, "and get out of here!"

Brouke gave the man a push that sent him staggering back against a chair, over which he fell in a heap next to the wall; then he seized the woman, lifted her in his arms, and ran out into the hall.

Clayton looked on in amazement. He turned and saw the girl, Maya, at his elbow. "Your friend is getting a little rough," she said.

"He is not my friend," replied Clayton. "I just met him this evening. He invited me to come to this party that is being given by a friend of his."

The girl laughed. "Friend of his!" she mimicked. "Joe never saw any of you guys before. You—" she looked at him closely—"you don't mean to say you didn't know you were crashing a party in a stranger's house!"

Clayton looked bewildered. "They were not friends of these people?" he demanded. "Why didn't they order us out? Why didn't they call the police?"

"And have the police find a kitchen full of booze? Quit your kidding, Big Boy."

A woman's scream was wafted down from the upper floor. The host was staggering to his feet. "My God, my wife!" he cried.

Clayton sprang into the hall and leaped up the stairs. He heard cries coming from behind a closed door; it was locked; he put his shoulder to it, and it flew open with a crash.

Inside the room a woman was struggling in the clutches of the drunken Brouke. Clayton seized the man by the scruff of the neck and tore him away. Brouke voiced a scream of pain

and rage; then he turned upon Clayton, but he was helpless in the giant grip of those mighty muscles.

A police siren wailed in the distance. That seemed to
sober Brouke. "Drop me, you damn fool," he cried; "here
come the police!"

Clayton carried the struggling man to the head of the
stairs and pitched him down; then he turned back to the
room where the woman lay on the floor where she had fallen.
He raised her to her feet.

"Are you hurt?" he asked.

"No, just frightened. He was trying to make me tell him
where I kept my jewels."

The police siren sounded again, much closer now. "You
better get out. Joe's awful sore. He'll have all three of you
arrested."

Clayton glanced toward an open window, near which the
branches of a great oak shone in the light from the street
lamps in front of the house. He placed a foot upon the sill
and leaped into the darkness. The woman screamed.

*　　*　　*

In the morning Clayton found Reece waiting for him in
the lobby of the hotel. "Great little party, eh, what?" demanded the young man.

"I thought you would be in jail," said Clayton.

"Not a chance. Billy Brouke has a courtesy card from one
of the big shots. Say, I see you're going to work for Abe Potkin, doing Tarzan."

"Who told you that?"

"It's in Louella Parsons' column in the *Examiner*."

"I'm not."

"You're wise. But I'll tell you a good bet, if you are thinking of getting into the movies. Prominent Pictures is casting
a new Tarzan picture, and——"

A bell boy approached them. "Telephone call for you, Mr.
Clayton," he said.

Clayton stepped to the booth and picked up the receiver.
"This is Clayton," he said.

"This is the casting office of Prominent Pictures. Can
you come right over for an interview?"

"I'll think about it," replied Clayton, and hung up.

"That was Prominent Pictures calling me," he said as he

rejoined Reece. "They want me to come over for an interview."

"You'd better go; if you get in with Prominent, you're made."

"It might be interesting."

"Think you could do Tarzan?"

"I might."

"Dangerous part. I wouldn't want any of it in mine."

"I think I'll go over." He turned toward the street.

"Say, old man," said Reece, "could you let me have ten until Saturday?"

*　　*　　*

The casting director sized Clayton up. "You look all right to me; I'll take you up to Mr. Goldeen; he's production manager. Had any experience?"

"As Tarzan?"

The casting director laughed. "I mean in pictures."

"No."

"Well, you might be all right at that. You don't have to be a Barrymore to play Tarzan. Come on, we'll go up to Mr. Goldeen's office."

They had to wait a few minutes in the outer office, and then a secretary ushered them in.

"Hello, Ben!" the casting director greeted Goldeen. "I think I've got just the man for you. This is Mr. Clayton, Mr. Goldeen."

"For what?"

"For Tarzan."

"Oh, m-m-m."

Goldeen's eyes surveyed Clayton critically for an instant; then the production manager made a gesture with his palm as though waving them away. He shook his head. "Not the type," he snapped. "Not the type, at all."

As Clayton followed the casting director from the room the shadow of a smile touched his lips.

"I'll tell you what," said the casting director; "there may be a minor part in it for you; I'll keep you in mind. If anything turns up, I'll give you a ring. Good-bye!"

*　　*　　*

Later in the day as Clayton was looking through an afternoon paper he saw a banner spread across the top of the theatrical page: CYRIL WAYNE TO DO TARZAN. FAMOUS ADAGIO DANCER SIGNED BY PROMINENT PICTURES FOR STELLAR RÔLE IN FORTHCOMING PRODUCTION.

*   *   *

A week passed. Clayton was preparing to leave California and return home. The telephone in his room rang. It was the casting director at Prominent Pictures. "Got a bit for you in the Tarzan picture," he announced. "Be at the studio at seven-thirty tomorrow morning."

Clayton thought a moment. "All right," he said; "seven-thirty."

He felt that it might be an interesting experience that would round out his stay in Hollywood.

*   *   *

"Say, you," shouted the assistant director, "what's *your* name?"

"Clayton."

"Oh, you're the guy that takes the part of the white hunter that Tarzan rescues from the lion."

Cyril Wayne, garbed in a loin cloth, his body covered with brown make-up, was eyeing Clayton and whispering to the director, who now also turned and looked.

"Geeze!" exclaimed the director. "He'll steal the picture. What dumb-egg ever cast him?"

"Can't you fake it?" asked Wayne.

"Sure, just a flash of him. We won't show his face at all. Let's get busy and rehearse the scene. Here, you, come over here. What's your name?"

"Clayton."

"Listen, Clayton. You're supposed to be comin' straight toward the camera through this jungle in the first shot. You're scared stiff; you keep lookin' behind you. You're about all in, too; you stagger like you was about ready to fall down. You see, you're lost in the jungle. There's a lion stalkin' you. We'll cut the lion shots in. Then in the last scene the lion is right behind you—and the lion's really in this scene with you, but you needn't be scared; he won't hurt you. He's perfectly tame and gentle. You scream. You draw your knife. Your knees shake. Tarzan hears you and comes swinging through the trees. Say, is that double here that's goin' to swing through the trees for Cyril?" he interrupted himself to address his assistant. Assured that the double was on the set, he continued, "The lion charges; Tarzan swings down between you and the lion. We get a close up of you there; keep your back to the camera. Then Tarzan leaps on the lion and kills it. Say, Eddie, has that lion tamer that's doublin' for Cyril in the kill got his make-up on even? He looked lousy in the rushes yesterday."

"Everything's all O.K., Chief," replied the assistant.

"All ready then—everybody!" yelled the director. "Get in there, Clayton, and remember there's a lion behind you and you're scared stiff."

The rehearsal was satisfactory and the first shots pleased the director; then came the big scene in which Wayne and Clayton and the lion appeared. The lion was large and handsome. Clayton admired him. The trainer cautioned them all that if anything went wrong they were to stand perfectly still, and under no circumstances was any one to touch Leo.

The cameras were grinding; Clayton staggered and half fell. He looked fearfully behind him and uttered a scream of terror. Cyril Wayne dropped from the branch of a low tree just as the lion emerged from the jungle behind Clayton. And then something went wrong.

The lion voiced an ugly roar and crouched. Wayne, sensing danger and losing his head, bolted past Clayton; the lion charged. Leo would have passed Clayton, who had remained perfectly still, and pursued the fleeing Wayne; but then something else happened.

Clayton, realizing more than any of the others the danger that menaced the actor, sprang for the beast and leaped upon its back. A powerful arm encircled the lion's neck. The beast wheeled and struck at the man-thing clinging to it, but the terrible talons missed their mark. Clayton locked his legs beneath the sunken belly of the carnivore. The lion threw itself to the ground and lashed about in a frenzy of rage.

With his hideous growls mingled equally bestial growls from the throat of the man. The lion regained its feet and reared upon its hind legs. The knife that they had given Clayton flashed in the air. Once, twice, three times it was driven deep into the side of the frenzied beast; then Leo slumped to the ground, shuddered convulsively and lay still.

Clayton leaped erect; he placed one foot upon his kill

and raised his face to the heavens; then he checked himself and that same slow smile touched his lips.

An excited man rushed onto the set. It was Benny Goldeen, the production manager.

"My God!" he cried. "You've killed our best lion. He was worth ten thousand dollars if he was worth a cent. You're fired!"

*　*　*

The clerk at The Roosevelt looked up. "Leaving us, Mr. Clayton?" he asked politely. "I hope you have enjoyed Hollywood."

"Very much indeed," replied Clayton; "but I wonder if you could give me some information?"

"Certainly; what is it?"

"What is the shortest route to Africa?"